PAST PRAISE FOR CLAIRE MATTURRO'S LILLY CLEARY SERIES OF LEGAL MYSTERIES:

"Funny, sharp, savvy, both as to the courtroom and the human condition...This new kid on Grisham's block is one to watch." —*Kirkus Reviews*

"Witty, intelligent novel of suspense. It's chick lit meets Perry Mason in this lively novel full of quirky characters and a dash of romance." —*Publishers Weekly*

"As she did in her debut novel, *Skinny-dipping*, Matturro devises a unique and complex plot with a lot of high energy juice. She is a welcome addition to the growing list of notable crime writing novelists inspired by the beauty and insanity of Florida." —*Miami Herald.*

"Matturro has a wicked sense of comedic timing." — *Boston Globe*

"A smart legal mystery." —*New York Times*

"Claire Matturro is very much worth reading." —*Cleveland Plain Dealer*

"Off the wall humor...The dialogue is sharp and the suspense sharper." —*Ft. Lauderdale Sun-Sentinel.*

"Matturro has a fresh voice and lively style (think Janet Evanovich meets John Grisham), and as a former appellate attorney and member of the writing faculty at Florida State University College of Law, she's certainly qualified to write about the law." —*Library Journal*

"Matturro proves that multilayered mysteries don't have to be put solely in the hard-boiled category." —*Charleston Gazette*

Matturro is "crafty and talented." —*Romantic Times Mystery Reviews*.

TROUBLE IN TALLAHASSEE

Trouble Cat Mysteries # 3

CLAIRE MATTURRO

KaliOka Press

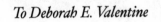

To Deborah E. Valentine

CHAPTER ONE

The ignominy of it all. Catnapped. By some idiot out of Miami with a craving for a green-eyed black cat but wholly lacking the human kindness to go to a shelter and rescue one. No, this cretin had to sweep me up and toss me into a pillow case and tie a knot, snortling as he did. He had been visiting a neighbor of my biped, Tammy Lynn, and claimed to be charmed by me. Of course, most people are quite smitten with me. After all, I'm a fine, sleek cat with an elegant tail, and even for a cat I have a high degree of intelligence and exceptional detective skills inherited from Familiar, my father.

Exceptional intelligence notwithstanding, I've been seized by this rude, loud person. I refuse to let the shame of it distress me. After all, even Sherlock Holmes and Agent 007 occasionally found themselves captives of imbeciles. The trick now is to extricate myself as soon as possible, and maybe teach this cretin biped a lesson.

As the miscreant speeds down the interstate, playing a raucous rap station on his radio, I set about putting my teeth and claws to work. All I need is a tiny rip in the pillow case to start with—ahh, that was easy enough to accomplish with my sharp teeth. The cheap polyester

*fabric gives way quickly enough. In no time at all, I have what I need:
a space large enough for me to crawl through.*

*Poking my nose out first, I inhale. Thankfully, my catnapper is
running the air conditioning full blast as it is September, which in the
South is very much still summer.*

And that damn pillow case is airless and hot.

*Now the trick is to wait until the best time to escape the truck.
After all, my catnapper has to stop sometime. In the meantime, I decide
to nap, dreaming of my home in Wetumpka, Alabama and my beloved
Tammy Lynn. I drift off, but wake when I feel the gears shifting and
the truck slowing down. The next thing I know this wonky hominoid
is exiting the interstate. I poke my head over the back of the seat and
look around. Traffic whizzes by; horns honk. Neither a tree nor a house
is in sight. I hunker down and wait for some place with green lawns
and kind-looking bipeds to make my bid for freedom.*

*After a few more minutes, the lazy sod cruises through a sweet,
green neighborhood. A sign with bold print framed by ivy-covered
columns proclaims Killearn Estates, Tallahassee, Florida. As I pop my
head further up to look around better, I appreciate the streets lined
with giant live oaks dripping with gray Spanish moss and the well-
kept brick homes. A good place to make my escape.*

*This wanker is too busy gobbling a candy bar to pay me any mind.
In the cup holder beside him, an opened highboy of beer sits, sweating
condensation. I slink forward for a broad view out of the front
window. A four-way stop is coming up, with a lovely berm and lake to
the left of the driver's seat.*

*The idiot opens the window and tosses out the candy wrapper.
Litterbug, I want to hiss, but keep my own counsel on his tawdry
habits. I leap, with my claws out, deliberately knocking over the beer
can and splashing beer over him and the seat. With as ugly and vicious
a sound as I can make, I yowl as I jump on his chest, digging my sharp
nails through his thin T-shirt and drawing blood. He yelps and*

screams, then slaps at me with both hands, losing control of the steering wheel and spinning into the berm.

The highboy can rolls under the brake pedal, splashing beer as it tumbles. With a jolt and a walloping noise, the truck slams into a sign post and abruptly stops. My catnapper moans and rubs his head before he unhooks his seatbelt. Given the slow speed of the truck, he's probably not really hurt. Already I spy a biped on the sidewalk punching in numbers on his cell phone, no doubt 9-1-1. This nutter catnapper will have some explaining to do to the law enforcement officers who will soon be on their way, especially as both he and the vehicle now reek of beer.

Quite satisfied with myself, I retract my claws and soar through the open window and take off running. No need to look back.

What I need now is water, and, oh, maybe a filet of salmon. Seeking something cool and wet to drink and a bit of a nosh, I spot a lovely, petite young lady with red hair—just like Tammy's— outside a small brick house watering a butterfly garden. She looks to be in her early thirties, she's trim, and her face is heart shaped with full lips and her big eyes are vivid amber. She's talking on a smartphone as she arches water over the flowers.

"I'll do it, Delphine, I promise. Yes, tonight, yes, I will. I'll get it done." Her voice is loud, but not rudely so, earnest with a touch of angst, but not desperate. She says her goodbyes and slips the phone into a wide pocket in her billowy shorts.

Experience has taught me to be careful approaching bipeds who are holding watering hoses. I sneak closer but keep out of sight, all the while eyeing the water pooling on leaves. Just as my thirst nearly compels me to lick the leaves, the redhead sprays a stream of water into a blue tiled birdbath and turns the water off at the spigot.

The front door bangs open and another woman, taller and younger than the redhead, steps out. She has wild curling black hair and wears a long, flowered skirt and black tank top accented with beads and big gold hoop earrings. A retro-hippie style. It's a look not just anyone can pull off, but on her it works. Yet she almost ruins it by smacking gum.

"Yo, Abby, are you really going back to the office, or should we open that bottle of wine?" Hippie Girl laughs.

I like her at once. I bet she'll cook me a filet of salmon if I purr nicely. Slinking out from the bush where I'm hiding, ready to claim these two bipeds, I catch a shadow and flicker of movement at the far edge of the house—definitely dodgy, as if someone is ducking around the corner to hide.

The red-haired woman—Abby— hasn't noticed, nor has Hippie Girl. I don't bother trying to alert the young women to the intruder. They don't know me, as Tammy would say, from Adam's house cat, so how could they understand any warning I might give them? Instead, I dash around the corner to see what I can see.

"Oh, a kitty," Abby sings out as I zip by, but I keep going until I can study the backyard. After prowling among the many bushes and trees, I spot no one, but catch a spicy scent of perfume or aftershave. Something like patchouli mixed with a light flowery sweetness.

I stroll back to the front in time to hear Abby calling the other woman by the name Layla. I purr, thinking how well that name fits her.

"I absolutely have to finish that brief for Delphine's pre-trial hearing." Abby wipes her hands off and heads back toward the front door.

Layla smacks her gum, her forehead creased by a slight frown, as she tags along. "Okay, okay, I'll go back with you. I'll do the research and you write. We can sneak in the back door so nobody will bother us."

"You don't have to do that," Abby says.

"Come on, you took me in while they're fixing my apartment from the fire. I owe you."

My ears perk up. Layla's apartment has been damaged in a fire? I creep forward to study her, checking her for any burns or wounds. I'm *close enough to smell the minty tang of her gum, but keep low under the scrubs so she doesn't see me.*

"You don't owe me. Having you here will be fun," Abby says. But I hear a question mark in her statement—she's not sure. Maybe the two women are not close friends? And I'm sensing something else. Someone was spying on them.

Instead of dashing into the house, I drink lavishly from the bird bath—glad to see Abby keeps it clean—and then jump into the open window of a Honda parked in the driveway.

Wherever this office is, I'm going with them. I have a feeling they're going to need me. Call it a sixth sense if you will. But I know to heed it when I feel something is amiss.

CHAPTER TWO

*A*bby clenched her jaw as Layla sped down Thomasville Road in her sparkling new Honda Civic. An empty diet soda bottle rolled out from under the seat and across Abby's foot as Layla took the entrance ramp to the Capital Circle flyover far too fast. Abby wished she'd driven her own vehicle, but Layla's car had been blocking her Prius and it had been easier to just let Layla drive. Abby swore not to make that mistake again.

She sighed. It was going to be a long night and fussing with her temporary roommate wouldn't help anything. But Abby couldn't help it, she had to say it. "Maybe you should go...slower."

"Yeah, well, we've almost there. I want to get this done. Maybe if we can get home before midnight, we can still crack open that bottle of wine."

Abby wished that her client hadn't gifted her with that bottle of first growth Bordeaux Chateaux after she'd won a trial for him. Frankly, she'd rather have had the hundred bucks the wine had cost him. Even after four years of work at Phillip

Draper's law firm, she still had outstanding student loans from her three years at Florida State University College of Law, plus the mortgage on her little brick house. Sometimes she wondered if the legal ladder of success was really worth it. Maybe ambition was a curse. She could have stayed a librarian and not gone back to law school. Her days at FSU's main campus library had been pleasant—and she hadn't had to work eighty-hour weeks like she did now.

Layla said something else about the wine, words Abby barely processed.

"You're not even supposed to drink wine," Abby said, pulling herself out of her mope.

"Uh, why is it I'm not supposed to drink wine?" Layla asked, giving the Honda the gas as she pulled onto Park Avenue near downtown Tallahassee.

"You know, the diabetes." Abby hadn't known a damn thing about diabetes—she'd always been healthy as a horse as the saying went—until Layla moved in yesterday with her blood sugar monitors, insulin, and a host of pills and eating regiments. As Layla had packed the cheese drawer in the refrigerator full of insulin, all neatly kept in a plastic box with a blue lid, she explained that she was type one. Born that way. The genetic curse of a grandfather who had died young from the disease.

"Yeah, well, I won't drink the whole bottle or anything." Layla turned sharply into an alley that ran behind the law firm and parked the Honda.

Abby scanned the alley, looking up and down slowly, but she didn't see anyone lurking. Then she turned around to the back seat to grab her laptop and saw a black cat sitting on top of the orange and pink paisley backpack Layla used as a purse, medicine chest, and portable filing cabinet. The cat meowed as if saying hello as he stepped daintily onto Layla's matching paisley laptop case.

"Oh, Kitty, how'd you get in here?" Abby reached out a hand toward the animal. "I bet you're the one I saw in the front yard earlier." The cat reached its head up to her fingers and sniffed. Abby scratched under his chin and the animal purred. "Aren't you a beauty?"

Layla turned around and offered the cat her hand too. "No collar, but doesn't look abandoned. Too shiny and well-fed looking."

"Bet it's from the neighborhood and just jumped into your open window exploring. You know how cats are. Curious." Abby was thinking that she'd mentioned to Layla that she should roll her windows up and lock her doors, but Layla said the car would get too hot. Of course, Abby had also mentioned Layla should hang her clothes up and stop spitting her gum out into the potted plants in her house. Oh well, at least she wasn't dropping the used gum into Abby's aquarium of neon tetras and black mollies.

The cat rubbed his head against first Abby's and then Layla's hands. "Marking us, I see," Layla said. "I bet this one's going to be trouble."

When Layla said "trouble," the cat purred several decibels louder and hopped into the front seat and head-butted Layla's shoulder. "Yes, sir, trouble," Layla said. As Layla repeated "trouble," the cat licked her chin, his purring louder still. Layla reached over and picked him up, putting the animal in her lap. "I think his name might be Trouble," she said. The cat stretched up, putting its two front paws on her shoulders, one on either side of her head, and bobbed his head.

"I swear he's nodding yes at me," Layla said. "Trouble, isn't it?" The cat licked her on the chin again, making her laugh. "That's what we'll call you, Trouble."

"Well, don't get attached, okay? We'll have to find his owner. Put up posters, a photo on Craigslist." Abby felt a strange jab of jealousy that the cat seemed to like Layla better. But just then, as if the animal had read her mind, he leapt from Layla's lap into Abby's, rubbing against her blouse and purring.

"Ah, so you're my buddy too, are you?" Abby ran her fingers down his sleek coat. No evidence of wounds or ticks or fleas. She decided he was definitely not a stray.

Layla cranked up the windows. "Don't want him dashing out in this alley."

"Oh, he's such a pretty kitty, so shiny." Abby rubbed her nose across the cat's face lightly, and wondered why she'd never gotten a cat. Her fish were great. She loved having an aquarium, but none of those tetras or mollies had ever purred against her like this cat was doing. "Aren't you the softest, sweetest thing?"

"Now who's getting attached?" Layla laughed. "Okay, I'll go in and get some milk from the kitchen for him and we can decide whether we need to take him back to your house or not." She studied the cat for a long moment. "Hold on to him when I open the door—we don't want him running away downtown." Abby hugged the cat closer to her as Layla grabbed her backpack and opened the Honda door and hopped out. As Layla hurried away, Abby bent her head down to the animal and rubbed her cheek along his soft fur, not paying any attention to Layla at all. "Trouble," she crooned. The cat purred against her cheek again. Maybe she wouldn't hurry to put up those found-cat posters.

Suddenly the cat—Trouble—tensed in her arms.

Layla's scream reverberated through the alley.

Abby jerked her head up just in time to see a dark figure in a hoodie grab Layla's backpack and put something shiny against her neck.

"Oh, no!" Abby screamed.

The man in the hoodie had what looked to be a knife at Layla's throat.

CHAPTER THREE

*V*ictor sat glumly at his desk in his small rental house in Tallahassee and slammed shut his gift and estate tax textbook. That stuff didn't make a lick of sense.

What the hell was he doing in law school anyway? He missed being in the Navy. Those had been good years and he'd gotten his college degree and valuable experiences. Before he'd resigned his commission, he'd been useful, he'd had adventures, and, most importantly, he'd served his country well.

Victor ran his fingers through his sandy-colored hair. Maybe he should have fought to stay in the Navy. But there was no going back now.

He had just turned thirty-five and considered himself in his prime. Maybe he could join a police department. Or get a job working construction. Better yet, become an electrician or plumber. They made good money and were highly useful individuals.

Anything but more law school.

Victor stood and paced to the refrigerator. Too early for beer, too late for supper.

Finally, he threw himself down on the floor and did thirty sit-ups. After that, he felt a little better. Almost clear-headed enough to tackle the gift and estate tax textbook again. He opened the book, read a page, slammed it shut.

He needed Layla. No question about it. He'd never have gotten through that truly hideous income tax class without her careful tutoring. She was the smartest damn student in the whole law school.

But he hated to ask for help from her again. Especially since she was officially mad at him. Furious in fact. And all he'd been trying to do was save her from a serious heartbreak and a bad reputation. Okay, maybe he used stronger words than that. Better to let her calm down some before he called her.

He did twenty jumping jacks and was glad he had a small rental house so he didn't have to worry about a downstairs neighbor yelling about the thumping.

Breathing hard, he opened the textbook again.

This time he didn't even make it through a single page.

Victor snatched up his phone and called Layla. They could just damn well get over being mad at each other.

The call went straight to voice mail.

"Layla, call me. Please." He snapped his old flip phone shut, glancing for a moment at the scratches on the plastic cover. The rep at Verizon had made fun of him over it. "Man, get with it, get a smartphone," the sales guy had said. But Victor had cut him off quick. The flip phone still worked and he didn't have to worry about the battery exploding. Besides, he didn't want to be addicted to a smartphone.

He slid the phone into his pocket and ambled over to his desk—a solid wood piece he'd gotten cheap off Craigslist—and opened a drawer. He pulled out a file with Layla's name on it and flipped it open. For a long time, he sat and stared at the single photograph inside the file. Layla, laughing, as she pressed tightly against Phillip Draper, her boss. He had his arm around her waist and he was holding her close. The look on both of their faces was very telling.

Layla was in over her head, and with a married man. All Victor wanted to do was help her escape from that relationship with a minimum of damage. But he didn't know if she'd let him.

Ever since that day he'd sat down next to Layla in the orientation for new students, she'd been his best friend in law school. Nothing more than friends though, as he wasn't her type romantically. Truth was, she wasn't his either—too flamboyant. But he loved her like a friend and wanted to do whatever he could for her.

But helping Layla was tricky, not just because of her independent streak, but because she was so mad she wasn't speaking to him. Maybe that was his fault.

Once more he studied the photograph before sliding it back into the file. It wasn't just the damn photo. He hadn't forgotten that phone call. They'd been studying and her cell rang. As soon as Layla looked at the caller ID, she'd asked Victor to give her some privacy, which he did. But he'd managed to hear some of the conversation from the other room—something about keeping a secret and a reference to oil and gas exploration. The one thing he'd heard clearly was Layla saying she wouldn't hide "them" at her apartment. Maybe she'd sensed Victor was listening because she'd lowered her voice after that. He caught a muted reference to hiding "them" at "your" house, or the law firm—at least that's what he thought she'd said.

Later, when she'd left the room, he'd checked her cell

phone. The call came from the Drapers' home phone. Phillip's house.

Mulling that conversation over in his mind now, he began to fear that Layla might be into something deeper than just an inappropriate relationship with her boss. Yet he didn't get the sense that Layla was hiding something from Phillip, but was concealing something Philip knew about and wanted kept private.

Victor jumped up and grabbed his car keys. "I have to talk to her," he said to the empty room.

CHAPTER FOUR

I'm trapped in Abby's car as Layla screams and Abby punches in 9-1-1 on her cell phone. The attacker wrestles the backpack off Layla and drops it to the ground as he continues thrusting what looks to be a knife at her throat. With things in shambles, there's no time for 9-1-1.

I jump on the horn, sounding an alarm. The attacker swings around and looks at the car. In the Honda's headlights, his red-rimmed eyes and three-day beard look like something out of a knackered bum's mug shot.

I spot Layla's key ring where she dropped it on the driver's side seat and I pounce, my paw finding the panic button. I don't know if it will scare off the assailant or not, but until Abby opens the door for me, I can't do much else. A split second later, a loud audacious noise screams in my sensitive ears, the panic button at work. Despite the horrid sound, the assailant still holds Layla, even as she struggles against him.

I jump up to the window, my paws scratching at the glass. Let me out, I try to telepathically communicate to Abby.

Abby is ignoring me as she rifles through stuff in the glove compartment. I swing my head back and forth, looking from Layla to

Abby, then back again. The assailant says something. I can't hear the words, but I see his mouth moving. The panic button continues to shriek. Abby pulls out a tire pressure gauge as if it could be used as a weapon.

The empty bottle, I scream at her, but she doesn't understand. I jump to the floor and roll the bottle toward her.

At once Abby picks it up, and still holding the tire gauge, she jumps out of the car. In one swift move, she pulls back her arm and throws the bottle at the assailant and points the tire gauge at him. She holds it in both hands like a gun, screaming, "I'll shoot, I will."

The bottle bounces off the assailant's shoulder and he jerks from the hit. Layla jams her heel down hard on his foot. Not the toes, but the instep. Good girl, she's obviously taken some self-defense courses. I launch myself out of the open door and land, claws out, on the attacker's barely exposed face under the hoodie. I catch a whiff of body odor, stale and offensive.

As I mark the attacker's face with my sharp claws, he yells out and drops the shiny thing he held. It hits the concrete with a little ding. Without pausing in my own attack, I glance down for a split-second to realize it's only a plastic knife. The assailant knocks at me with frantic hands until I drop to the ground. Free of my claws, he runs out of the alley. The panic button continues to scream, and somebody slams open the back door of the office and shouts, "Shut that damn thing off."

"Help us," Abby calls back.

I take off after the fleeing marauder, eager for an even better look at this malefactor with his pathetic plastic knife. But as I race around the corner of the alley out onto the street with the assailant a few yards in front, a crowd comes out from a building between me and the running felon. Not even one of them gives chase to the assailant, though they do manage to block me in my pursuit.

The assailant is lost to me. There's nothing else I can do. I dart back to Abby and Layla. The young man who came out the rear door of the building is ranting into a cell phone and Abby is holding Layla in her arms. Neither of them is crying, and I purr, "Good girls."

"He wanted my backpack, that's all," Layla says as she pulls away from Abby. "Just a mugger. Don't be so melodramatic."

"He wanted to kill you," Abby says. "I saw the knife."

"You saw a plastic knife." Layla suddenly laughs. "This whole thing was like a dumb high school skit, really. Him with his dinky plastic and you with the tire gauge. Nobody with a real weapon."

"This isn't funny. Stop laughing. He wanted to kill you."

"If he'd wanted to kill me, he'd have killed me." Layla says it with a certain sense of finality, as if she no longer wishes to talk about it.

I must admit, she has a point.

A police car drives into the alley, lights flashing but no siren, and a young officer steps out. Everyone talks at once, even the chap from inside the office, who didn't see a thing but seems to believe his opinion is as valid as if he had. Abby calls him Emmett in a tone that suggests they are not going to be exchanging Christmas cards. I give Emmett a hard look—he's chubby, dark-haired, dressed in white shirt and gray canvas pants and wears thick glasses. He strikes me as one of those all-mouth-no-trousers types, and I turn back to Abby and Layla.

After making sure no one is hurt, the police officer rattles off the obvious questions. Layla insists that her attacker was looking for drugs or money to get drugs and it was nothing personal.

Everybody's attention soon focuses on a Mercedes sport car that speeds into the alley. A lean, elegant man steps out, his thick black hair streaked with silver. Definitely toff and stylish even in his casual clothes, the man looks like someone off a movie poster.

"Layla, are you hurt?" As he speaks, the man moves toward Layla, his hands lifting and opening as if offering to hold her.

She turns and run into his arms.

"Who's that?" the police officer asks.

Exactly what I am wondering too.

"*That's Phillip Draper, the named partner in the law firm.*" *Abby glances back at Layla, then turns her attention to the officer. "Emmett here called him.*"

Emmett pushes forward, offering his hand to the police officer. "Emmett Winchester Layton, sir. Third-year law student, working late. Totally devoted to this law firm and these young ladies. Glad to be of service. I felt a senior partner needed to be apprised of the situation."

The cop shakes Emmett's hand but then ignores him.

Abby continues as if Emmett had never spoken. "Layla is Mr. Draper's law clerk and assistant and they work together closely."

I scamper up on a trash can for a better look at Layla and Mr. Draper.

Very closely, it would seem.

CHAPTER FIVE

"*W*ell, at least the cop was cute," Layla said.

"How can you possibly joke?" Abby was driving Layla's car at a considerably safer speed than Layla had earlier, and they were nearly back to her house.

"Oh, come on, lighten up. The guy only had a plastic knife. I mean, his breath was more of a deadly weapon. And I wasn't joking. The cop was cute." Layla twisted a loop of her black wavy hair around a finger. "And, unless I can't read the signs anymore, he was interested in you. Even flirty."

Yes, the cop had been flirty. But Abby hadn't felt even the slightest inclination to flirt back. Besides, they'd met at a mugging—how could that be a good start to anything romantic?

Thinking about bad ways to meet men made Abby remember how she'd met Jason, the man who officially broke her heart. She'd met him at a funeral. That should have told her something. After a hot, intense, six months with late night whisperings about moving in together, she'd caught him cheating. And he'd had the nerve to defend himself by blaming her.

She still remembered how crushed—almost suicidal—she'd felt after he'd rationalized his actions by saying she was boring and dull and played it safe all the time, while he needed excitement and passion.

If Jason hadn't been bad enough, there was that huge crush she'd had on her law professor, Miguel Angel Castillo. Or that date with the tax attorney who explained in exquisitely painful details the tax regulations pertaining to her 401(k). Or that highly placed government official that Delphine set her up with—the man might have headed an important state agency, but he'd put on so much self-tanning lotion that he looked like a sweet potato and he kept touching her inappropriately. Or—

Layla's voice cut through Abby's bitter memories. "No offense, but you live like a nun." Layla held Trouble in her lap as the car crept around a turn. "You work all day, go home and tend your little garden and your potted plants and that aquarium, then you work some more and go to sleep."

"That's not fair. I do other stuff too." But Abby's mood sank lower. First the mugging, not even getting started on Delphine's trial brief, reliving Jason's taunting, and now Layla was needling her.

The cat—Trouble—stretched over toward her and rubbed his face against her hand as she slowed the car nearly to a stop at the round-about on Killearny Way. He purred, and Abby suddenly felt like the cat understood how she felt.

"Okay, what other stuff do you do exactly?" Layla stared at Abby.

As Abby glanced over to Layla, Trouble reached up and tapped Layla on her jaw with his paw. He was telling her to shut up!

Suddenly Abby knew she wasn't going to put that lost-cat notice on Craigslist, any more than she was going to post notices around the neighborhood. She wanted to keep this fellow. If she wasn't fated to have a great love, she could have a great cat.

"Yo, you listening to me, or what?" Layla sounded snappish. "What other stuff do you do?"

"I cook, I exercise...I ..." Abby floundered to a sputtering stop. Jogging and going to the gym and sautéing cod or salmon with broccoli hardly counted as a life.

"Oh, come on, you don't even eat ice cream." Layla sounded vaguely disgusted.

"And you can eat it. I can't." But at that last, a little note of pity sounded in her voice.

"I'm sorry," Abby said. "Let's not fight. You take your insulin or whatever you need to do when we get home and we'll drink that wine. It'll help you relax after what you went through. And tomorrow I'll stop and get some sugar-free ice cream for you."

They pulled into Abby's street and neither of them spoke. Abby thought back for a moment to the harrowing scene in the alley and how brave Layla had been. Trouble purred and head-butted her hand softly as if to remind her that she'd been brave too, though no one could have really thought the tire gauge was a gun. But Trouble himself had been the bravest of all. That stunt with the panic button was awesome. Abby wondered if it was accidental or somehow the cat had known what he was doing. And Trouble's full-fledged attack on the mugger made the assailant drop everything and run.

Yes, this cat was something special.

The policeman had finally agreed that the mugger was just a mugger. Not a stalker or a rapist or a serial murderer. The raggedy clothes, the plea for drugs or money to buy drugs, the back alley and the fact Layla said the man smelled like someone who hadn't bathed in days. It all fit—just a sad, pitiful homeless substance abuser looking for drugs, cash, or something to sell.

And Mr. Draper coming all the way back from his house to see about Layla, how sweet was that?

Abby rounded the curve on her home street and put on her blinker to turn into her driveway even though no other car was on the road. But as the Honda's lights swept the area, she saw a strange pickup parked at the far edge of her wide driveway. There was room for Layla's Honda to fit beside it, but Abby parked on the street and checked to see if the automatic locks had indeed secured the doors.

"It's all right." Layla sounded tired. "It's just Victor from law school."

While Abby had never met Victor, she'd heard Layla arguing with him on the phone. Abby assumed Layla and Victor had one of those turbulent, hot romances where fighting was part of the passion—that would seem to fit Layla's personality. But now Abby was worn out and didn't want to be caught up in a scene. "What's he doing here?"

"Who knows?" Layla glared at the pickup. "Since getting out of the Navy, Victor marches to his own drummer, if you know what I mean."

No, Abby didn't know what Layla meant. She didn't unlock the car doors and she didn't switch off the lights. Instead, she watched as a man stepped out of the pickup. In the high beams, she could tell he was maybe five-ten or so and had sandy-colored hair, worn longer than convention or current style. As he walked toward the Honda, she took in the drape of his T-shirt against a flat stomach and muscled arms.

She stared in appreciation. Layla definitely had good taste in men.

When he got to the car, he drummed his fingers on Layla's window, but Layla turned her face to the front and didn't open her door or power down the window.

Victor walked over to Abby's window and tapped on the glass.

Abby stared up into his square jaw, saw the one dimple on his cheek near his full lips, and she thought of Robert Redford in *The Way We Were*. Not a movie for her generation, but she, her mom, and grandmom had watched it so often on the DVD player when she was growing up she could recite parts of the dialogue.

Layla assured her again that the man was totally harmless, so Abby powered down her window. When she noticed the furrowed forehead and the squint lines around his blue eyes, Abby was certain that things had not come too easily in this man's life.

"Hello," he said. "My name is Victor Rutledge. I'm Layla's friend." He paused, glancing past Abby to Layla. "At least I hope I still am."

Beside Abby, Layla crossed her arms tightly across her chest and stared forward. Trouble arched up and purred.

Abby thought the best thing she could do was leave them alone and let them work out this lover's quarrel. She pushed the car door open, said a firm goodnight to the man, and hurried toward her front door.

CHAPTER SIX

*V*ictor eased into Abby's house, keenly aware no one had invited him inside and no one seemed to want him there except maybe the cat. But Layla had been attacked and he wanted to be sure she was all right. And maybe he'd like to try to make a better impression on the redhead.

As he pushed an irritating lock of his shaggy hair out of his face, he gazed around the house. Might as well take a good look since no one was talking to him. The redhead and Layla had marched into the kitchen, where they were busy warming up some left-over baked cod for the cat.

Neat, clean, and well-organized. That was his initial impression of the house, though as he walked further into the living room, he reassessed. It was like a jungle. Potted plants everywhere, some on the floor, some on stands, some hanging from brackets on the wall. Interesting groupings of flowering scrubs and tropical-looking things in one corner with what he assumed was a grow light pointed at them. Then he saw the aquarium.

"Wow." Victor said it aloud, though no one was listening. The aquarium was twenty-five gallons and filled with brightly colored neon tetras, dashing about in their seemingly frantic way, well balanced by a few calm black mollies. The water was sparkling, and a high-tech pump hummed on the side. Snails, aquatic plants, a couple of bottom feeding catfish—a perfectly balanced and healthy aquarium. He should know. He had one too. Only smaller. After all those years in the Navy, where a potted Christmas cactus was about all he could handle as he moved about, he'd been hungry for a tank of fish, a cat, and a dog. So far, he had an aquarium.

The redhead came out of the kitchen and gave him a curious look.

"I'm sorry I barged in, but I want to be sure Layla is really okay." He brushed his hair back again and admired her shiny red mane. Thick, shoulder-length, kind of a chestnutty red. "I'm Victor," he added, though he'd already said that.

"Abby," she said.

"I love the fish. I've got a tank too. Someday I'd like to try a saltwater aquarium."

"Oh, me too. I've been studying about it for years." Abby's voice lifted and there was no mistaking her sudden enthusiasm. "I want sea horses. Did you know the male raises the young and—"

"Okay, so you two are bonding over fish. Trouble the cat is gorging on fish, and I'm ready to take a shower and go count fish to see if I can sleep." Layla stood in the doorway between the kitchen and the living room, casting her gaze back and forth between Victor, Abby, and the aquarium.

Victor refrained from mentioning one counted sheep to encourage sleep. If Layla wanted to count fish, or toads, or whatever, that was fine with him.

"Layla," Victor said, his voice soft and mellow. "I've—"

"I'm not—"

The cat sauntered out of the kitchen, licking his mouth, and let out a plaintive meow. They all stared at him. He scampered to the door and scratched on it.

"Litter box," Abby said. "I don't have one."

"Let him outside," Layla said.

"What if he runs away?" Abby knelt and petted the cat.

Victor glanced at the clock on Abby's mantel. After nine, but the Publix on Thomasville Road would still be open. "Give me half an hour, I'll be back with a litter box."

Nobody objected and he hurried to his car.

As he drove to the store, he thought about Abby. What a lovely young woman. He couldn't help but be attracted to her slim, petite figure and her big eyes. But besides being cute, she obviously had a green thumb and a nurturing spirit. And taking in both a stray cat and a temporarily homeless Layla—that told Victor that Abby was generous and kind-hearted.

Even so, he might as well forget her. He was so damn busy studying and trying to stay afloat in law school, there was no way he had time to date. Besides, his forced resignation from the Navy was sure to come up. He didn't want to face accusations and rejection, especially from a woman who seemed so fundamentally decent and sweet.

As he hurried into the store, thoughts of Abby drifted to his concern for Layla. Her kitchen caught fire—even though she wasn't home at the time and the landlord had the fire out before too much damage. She was mugged—though it appeared to be a random act and nothing personal.

Was it just a run of bad luck? Or was there more to it?

Maybe she was mixed up in something worse than he'd first suspected.

Or maybe she really had left a greasy skillet on a hot stove like the fire inspector claimed. Maybe it was just coincidence a homeless person grabbed her backpack at the law firm.

But as he picked up a large bag of cat litter and a litter pan, he couldn't shake the growing unease he felt.

CHAPTER SEVEN

*A*bby glared at a pile of affidavits scattered on the rosewood table in front of her in the plush conference room at the law office, and pulled her jacket closed. Outside, the September sun might be sending the temperatures soaring, but in the conference room, the air conditioning kept the room just shy of freezing.

She glanced at the teak-framed clock on the wall. The court reporter, her client, and the opposing attorney should be there any moment. She didn't feel at all ready for taking a deposition, especially with only a couple of hours of sleep. What with the mugging and the new cat, her mind had whirled with anxiety most of the night.

Not just anxiety either. To make matters worse, she'd kept thinking of Victor, his shaggy hair, that dimple, and how helpful he'd been. She kept reminding herself that he was Layla's boyfriend, even if they were fighting at the moment. But she couldn't deny the tingly feelings she had when she thought of him. Even now, a flush of warmth swept over her as she sat in the cold conference room.

It had been a long time—a very long time—since any man had awakened such arousal in her.

And, damn it all, he was somebody else's boyfriend. More precisely, he was her temporary roommate's lover, which made it all worse somehow.

The conference room door opened and she shifted toward the sound. Instead of her client, Miguel Angel Castillo and Phillip Draper stepped into the conference room, with its silk wallpaper, lush plants, and fresh flowers. She was semi-hidden by a large peace lily in a brass pot, a thriving plant she'd been nurturing for years. Mr. Draper and Professor Castillo paused just inside the door and stood chatting about FSU football.

She hadn't seen Professor Castillo since he'd been one of her professors at Florida State's law school. Funny, she'd just been thinking about him last night and that ridiculous infatuation she'd had, like a teenage girl with her first crush.

She peeked around the giant peace lily for a better look at Miguel. Still gorgeous. He was the classic tall, dark, and handsome, with an oval face framed by jet-black hair, and lots of it. His tortoise-shell glasses framed nearly black eyes and rested on a straight nose. But it was his mouth that really made his face so captivating—full lips with a natural hint of color and a thicker lower lip that gave him a hint of a pout. On a less masculine man, his lips would have been feminine. But on him, they were sensual.

The man had simply radiated sexual allure back in Abby's law school days. But if Miguel had ever even remotely noticed Abby back then, he'd managed to hide the evidence. Of course, during that era of her life, Abby had been dumpy.

Dumpy, hell, she'd been fat. Okay, not fat...but definitely plump.

Miguel, whether he knew it or not, had spurred her into a

total make-over—or rather her crush on him had. A diet. A gym membership. Regular trips to a top beauty salon where the stylist had convinced her that redheads, not blondes, had more fun. Her natural chestnut hair took on some red and gold highlights that glimmered. Unfortunately, her metamorphosis had taken place after she graduated and Miguel never saw the new her.

"Why don't I explain a bit of my problem with the seminar?" Miguel's deep voice broke in on Abby's reverie of her improvements since law school. "And gather your ideas for ways to cure them." He paused, smiling at Mr. Draper. "And when we have all of that worked out, maybe this weekend you and your beautiful wife can join me at my place on the lake."

Uh, oh, it was time to stand up. Abby rattled some papers to alert them of her presence. She put on a smile she hoped looked natural.

"Ah, Miss Coleridge," Mr. Draper said. "We didn't see you there."

She stepped toward the men, doing her best to reflect gracious good manners and not look like she was fall-down fatigued. "Good morning." She nodded toward Mr. Draper, then turned to Professor Castillo, and held out her hand. "Abby Coleridge, Professor Castillo. So pleased to see you again."

The professor took her hand, holding her gaze with his dark eyes. Slowly he smiled, curving his full lips to show straight, white teeth. Abby didn't see a flicker of recognition on his face, but maybe that was just as well.

"Miss Coleridge, how delightful." He gave her hand a little squeeze before he let it go.

"Please, do call me Abby. I was your student in Legal Ethics and American Jurisprudence. Wonderful classes, both of

them." Actually, the classes had been dull as soggy cornflakes
and Miguel had been an uninspired teacher—though his looks
had held her attention even when his boring lectures hadn't.

Mr. Draper cleared his throat. Abby and the professor both
turned to him.

"Miguel and I were just about to discuss a joint-teaching
venture at the law school. And this conference room is quite
comfortable." Mr. Draper's tone of voice suggested that Abby
should offer to vacate the conference room.

Abby thought quickly. She knew Mr. Draper was an adjunct
professor at the law school, teaching seminars on oil and gas
issues, but she couldn't imagine what he and Miguel could co-
teach, or why. But the important thing at the moment was her
upcoming deposition. She could gather up her notes and move.
It was, after all, Mr. Draper's office building and law firm.
Surely one of the other conference rooms was free, especially
this early in the morning.

Before Abby said anything, Miguel spoke. "Phillip, she's
already spread out some documents and obviously needs this
room. Let's you and I retire to your office and let Abby
continue her work here."

Mr. Draper narrowed his eyes at Abby for a split second.
"Fine. My office is not quite so comfortable, but I'm sure we'll
make do."

What did he mean, his office wasn't comfortable? She had
lived in apartments that were smaller than his corner suite. But
regardless of what she thought, Abby nodded. "I do have a
deposition scheduled and my client should be here any
moment." She refrained from mentioning she'd reserved the
room a month in advance.

"Well, then, it's settled. We'll leave you to it." Miguel
smiled again, with that same slow curve of his lips as he stared

into her eyes. "So very lovely to see you again, Abby," he added. "I do remember you from my first year of teaching, with your captivating red hair right there in the front of the class room."

Abby's smile suddenly felt glued on. She hadn't been a redhead in his classes, and she'd never have sat near the front unless someone made her do so upon the threat of expulsion. "I really appreciated your lectures on how the first Supreme Court justices shaped American history," she said. That was as untrue as his comment, so they were even. What she'd really enjoyed was his book, *A Thesis on Early American Jurisprudence: A Study of the First U. S. Supreme Court*. Most people who read such books considered it brilliant, and she still had a signed copy.

"Shall we then?" Miguel led Mr. Draper out of the conference room.

Once the two men were truly gone, Abby sat down hard on her chair. Miguel had flirted with her and yet, despite her law-school crush on the man, his attentions meant nothing to her now. She wondered if her eighty-hour work weeks had killed any hope of passion.

But as she turned back to her legal documents, she thought of Victor.

No, she wasn't entirely dead to those kinds of feelings.

She just had them for the wrong man.

CHAPTER EIGHT

$\mathcal{A}$bby wanted to put her head down on her desk and nap on her pile of mail and unanswered phone messages. But the steady hum of caffeine and anxiety in her veins wouldn't let her, nor would the demands of the rest of the morning. At least her deposition was done and she could soon start on Delphine's trial brief, which she'd failed to finish last night due to the mugging.

As if summoned by Abby's very thought of her, Delphine knocked and entered the office in one smooth, quick move. "Heads up." Delphine put a steaming cup of coffee on Abby's desk.

Abby lifted her eyes from the stack of unanswered phone messages and looked at Delphine. The woman was fifty, but looked thirty, and worked nonstop. As the firm's first African-American partner, perhaps Delphine felt she had something to prove. But surely she'd done so by now, Abby thought. After all, Delphine had won the largest single judgment of any jury trial in the history of Draper's law firm.

"Sip it slowly," Delphine said. "My own personal beans, honey-processed Brazilian."

Abby looked at the steaming cup. Though she had never heard of honey-processed, she knew it would be excellent. But dare she drink more coffee?

She also knew if Delphine was bringing her coffee, the woman wanted something. But rejecting the offering wouldn't make Delphine go away, so Abby reached for the cup. She sipped. "Delicious."

As Abby drank, she became conscious that Delphine was studying her a bit too closely. She ran her hand over her red hair, smoothing it down, and tugged at her blouse. Maybe she had dressed in a bit of a hurry—but she'd only just gotten to sleep when the alarm had gone off that morning.

"You might need to go home at lunch and change. Something very sharp and professional." Delphine narrowed her eyes as she continued to stare at Abby. "I know, wear that blue seersucker suit, the one with the belted, peplum jacket. Very becoming. Shows off that tiny waist of yours and yet very professional."

Yes, one of Abby's favorite suits, but one she reserved for special occasions or court appearances.

"We're having important visitors today, potential clients of the utmost prestige and I want everyone to look their best. And to behave." Delphine smiled at Abby. "But you always behave."

Abby smiled back, but guardedly. The other shoe hadn't dropped yet and she didn't sip anymore coffee.

"But Layla, damn it." Delphine sighed, long and slow. "We need to keep her out of the office all afternoon."

Abby frowned. Delphine hadn't even asked about Layla's health after she'd been attacked. She admired Delphine, but sometimes the woman's focus could be too ambitious and single-minded.

"I'll have Phillip call her and tell her to take the afternoon off." Delphine nodded, as if pleased with herself. "He'll just have to do without her today, whatever it is she does for him." Delphine's voice held a trace of snideness.

Abby had also wondered exactly what Layla did for Mr. Draper since he appeared to be more rainmaker and glad-hander than lawyer. But what did she know about them, really? Abby rarely had contact with Mr. Draper as she worked exclusively with Delphine, and she preferred to keep it that way.

"What's the name of that law clerk in the library who always sticks his head in where it's not wanted?" Delphine frowned and tilted her head in the general direction of the firm's library.

"Ah, you must mean Emmett." Abby knew Emmett was intelligent, ambitious, and served as an associate editor of the law review. But he hadn't learned that a law clerk's role was to be seen and not heard.

"Yes, him." Delphine grinned. "Smart boy, but we can't let him loose among our visitors or he'll be spewing forth his resume."

"And his family lineage," Abby said.

"All the way back to Jamestown," Delphine and Abby said in concert.

The two women laughed. Abby felt a bit mean about it, but Emmett had trapped them all with his family tree more than once and it had become a standing joke.

"You know, he's actually quite competent when he calms downs. He just wants to be an associate here too badly after he graduates in June." Delphine shook her head. "Sorry to say we're only hiring one associate after graduation and Layla's got a lock on it."

"Really? Layla?" Abby watched Delphine and hoped for more information.

"Don't look at me. I wouldn't hire her to take out the garbage, but Phillip's already promised her a position." Delphine raised a finger to her lips. "But you didn't hear that from me."

Delphine headed for the door, turning back to add, "I'll send Emmett to the courthouse to look something up after lunch and get him out of the way. Oh, and email me a copy of that trial brief in progress." With that, Delphine left Abby's office, closing the door behind her.

Abby took a long gulp of the coffee. Once more, she couldn't help but think Delphine should have asked how Layla was doing. After all, the young woman had been mugged. But Delphine seemed too caught up with the potential new clients to worry about that.

Ambition before compassion, Abby thought. Was that the law firm rule?

Or just Delphine's?

CHAPTER NINE

*V*ictor pulled up his sturdy combat boots and hopped into his pickup. Classes were over for the day, thank goodness. He hated law school. All that sitting still inside a room with no windows was against his basic nature. Of late, this was troubling him. What if he hated being a lawyer as much as he despised his classes? He'd started law school full of drive and energy. He wanted to redeem himself and was motivated by a different sense of purpose than he'd had in the Navy. Look how badly the Navy had turned out. So maybe it was all right this time to shoot for the money and prestige?

Stop moping. Focus on Layla, he told himself. None of that endless introspection about law school mattered at the moment. His best friend Layla might be mad at him because he'd cautioned her against a relationship with a married man, but she was still his best friend. And she was in trouble.

He was coming to the bitter conclusion that the mugging was just too much of a coincidence on the heels of the fire in her apartment. Those acts had to be connected with the phone call he'd overheard. Whatever those items were that Layla said she'd hide might have put her in harm's way. She said she wouldn't hide "them" at her apartment, which left a lot of other options. But Phillip's house was a definite possibility given what Victor'd heard, or at least what he thought he'd heard. He needed to find or figure out what the secret was before she got in worse trouble, and he figured he might as well start at Phillip's house.

Hopefully, what he was about to do would ultimately help Layla.

If it didn't get him arrested.

Victor wore an old work jumpsuit that had belonged to his dad. He drove his older model pickup, but the piece de resistance was his Dad's old plumber's license and giant tool box. He was going to present himself at Phillip Draper's house, claim that he had been called to check on a leaky toilet in the upstairs back bathroom, and hope that he'd get a chance to snoop. From the many online newspaper articles on Phillip's socialite wife, Jennifer Draper, Victor had learned she went to some kind of Junior League meeting on Wednesday afternoon. This being Wednesday, he figured he had a clear shot at dealing just with the housekeeper.

He'd found a photo spread of the Draper house in an *Architectural Digest* article that gave him a good idea of the floor plan. The back bath on the second floor might give him the best chance at an undisturbed study of Mr. Draper's den. Humming an old George Jones song his father had favored, Victor carefully tucked his hair up under a baseball cap, snapped down his Dad's old aviator sunglasses on his face, and hoped this counted as some kind of disguise.

Twenty minutes later, he eased his truck around the curved driveway of the Draper mansion on Live Oak Plantation Road and turned the engine off.

An older woman in a crisp white uniform and an apron opened the door to his knock. "May I help you?"

"Gordon Rutledge, plumber. Someone called about a toilet that keeps running in the bathroom on the second floor." Victor glanced at a work order he'd written up himself. "Says it's the guest bath near the den."

"May I see that?"

He handed the work order over to the woman, noticing as he did that she frowned.

She scrutinized it closely before she looked up, studying him as carefully as she had the work order.

He had the sudden feeling this was a bad idea.

"Mr. Draper ordered this?" She waved the paper in the air. "Yes."

The woman looked at the work order again. Finally she stood back. "Wipe your feet."

Victor knew a good deal about toilets and plumbing in general from all those summers in high school he'd been forced to work for his father. So he wasn't flustered at all when the housekeeper in her crisp whites followed him upstairs and stood watch. He could fake her out easily. "Probably just needs a new ballcock." He glanced up at the woman and smiled.

She sniffed as if he had said something dirty to her.

"Or maybe the flapper," he added quickly.

"Nobody told me there was any problem. And it's certainly not running now." The woman glowered as if this oversight was Victor's fault, which of course it was in a backhanded kind of way.

From off somewhere in the house, a phone rang. The woman frowned. "I better get that." She gave him a quick once over and said she'd be right back.

Victor smiled at her retreating footsteps. It hadn't been that hard to convince his handball partner to call the house and pretend to be doing a follow-up interview for the *Tallahassee Magazine* on the Drapers' culinary tastes.

As soon as she was gone, Victor peered out in the hallway, looking around. He didn't see or hear anyone. As quietly as he could, he tiptoed into the den, where *Architectural Digest* had said Mr. Draper liked to retire to his "man cave" and work in the evenings. Layla had once let it slip that she and Mr. Draper worked in his den when Mrs. Draper was out. When he'd raised his eyebrows at that, she snapped that it was much quieter at their house than at the law firm.

The den was immaculate. Victor didn't have a clue where to start looking, or what exactly he might be looking for in the room. The phrase "needle in a haystack" came to mind and he started to just leave.

But leaving wouldn't help Layla.

He studied Phillip's den for another moment before he tiptoed over to a filing cabinet. He pulled open a drawer, pleased that it wasn't locked. He flipped through the files, but the documents all related to the house. Repressing a sigh, he closed the drawer, and opened the next one, only to find it was full of newspaper and magazine clippings of Philip and his wife.

Victor shut the drawer and rifled through some papers on top of the desk and in the top drawer. Finished with the desk, he glanced around the room, before scouring through the credenza and finding nothing of interest in it or the heavy barrister's bookcase. Frustrated, he cocked his head, listening for the housekeeper's voice or her footsteps. Not hearing a thing, he stepped out of the room and listened as he stood at the head of the stairs. He heard a low murmur and caught the word "organic" and "asparagus." Grinning, he made up his mind to intentionally lose the next handball game to pay the guy back for faking this interview. Then he crept down the hall to a guest bedroom.

A second later, he stepped into an oddly plain room and began to feel under the mattress. Nothing. The chest of drawers and night stand were empty. Out in the driveway, a car drove up, and someone honked. Victor peered out the window and saw the housekeeper hurry outside. Mrs. Draper—Jennifer —was getting out of the car with an armload and the housekeeper struggled to take all the packages.

Damn. So much for Jennifer Draper's afternoon meeting. Victor cursed himself for taking a big risk for nothing and hurried back to the bathroom, lifted the top off the tank, and tinkered with the chain and flapper until the toilet definitely would be running improperly. As he placed the top back, he spotted something taped under the tank. He felt it with his fingers. Small, wrapped in plastic. With his fingernails, he pried it off and dropped it in the pocket of his overalls.

Time enough to look at it when he was safely out of the house.

Below him, he could hear women talking.

Now might be a very good time to leave.

Victor abandoned the toilet, which was filling with water improperly, and slipped down the stairs and out the back door.

He made himself wait until he was two blocks away before he pulled over and unwrapped the package he'd pulled off the toilet tank.

Inside he found a flash drive. In the telltale bright pink that Layla favored for her flash drives.

He spun out on the road, gave the pickup the gas, and sped back to his house, eager to read whatever it was on the flash drive that was worth somebody hiding it.

CHAPTER TEN

y the time Abby returned to the law offices after lunch, she was panting from the heat and the hurrying. Coming in from the parking lot, she was grateful for the rush of air conditioning that hit her face as soon as she stepped inside the steady hum of technology, tension, and talking that filled the office.

As Abby dashed down the long hallway, she spied Mr. Draper and Delphine with their heads together just outside her office door, whispering like co-conspirators. Mr. Draper looked up and caught Abby's eye. He waved her to join him and Delphine, and Abby picked up her pace. As soon as she paused in front of them, Delphine smiled her big teeth-baring grin and Abby felt the trap door about to spring.

"Lovely," Delphine said, nodding at Abby's change of clothes.

"Very professional looking," Mr. Draper said, though he barely glanced at her.

"Thank you, Mr. Draper." Abby tried not to blush, which of course made her blush more.

"Don't you think it's about time you call me Phillip?"

Abby blushed deeper. No, she didn't think it was time to call him Phillip. She preferred addressing him as Mr. Draper as if that formality might protect her against the vagaries of named partners and their demands.

"Yes, Phillip." Abby could count on one hand the meaningful conversations she'd had with him as from day one she'd been assigned to work with Delphine.

"Well, then, good, let's get ready for our guests." Delphine fiddled with her jacket and patted at her short-cropped hair. "They should be coming in any moment now."

Abby still didn't know who was coming to the office. But if Delphine was nervous, they had to be big. Just as Abby opened her mouth to ask, Layla came bounding down the hallway. Delphine positively hissed.

Even Philip inhaled a bit too sharply, but then, after a heartbeat, he began to smile.

Abby couldn't take her eyes off Layla. Gone were the beads, the long, flowered skirts, the giant hoop earrings, and the whole wild Boho look. Layla's curly hair was coiffed in something like a French Twist, and she was wearing a smooth, pale peach suit that set off her dark complexion beautifully. She was stunning. And she looked every bit as professional as Delphine.

"Didn't I reaffirm Phillip's communication and tell you—" Delphine started to say.

"To stay the hell away," Layla finished.

This time it was Abby who sucked in air so fast she made a gasping noise. Layla had been told to stay away. Yet here she was, disobeying a direct order from Phillip and Delphine both.

Layla turned to Phillip. "You won't ever need to be ashamed of me."

Abby cut her eyes back and forth between Delphine, who was steaming mad, and Phillip, who beamed at Layla with pride in his eyes.

What the hell is going on? But Abby didn't have a chance to ponder the situation. Their gracious office manager ambled down the hallway with Pam Bondi, Florida's attorney general, on one side and the governor, Mr. Dread Shaw, on the other side. Everyone was chatting at once.

Abby wiped her hands nervously on her skirt. She'd lived in the state capital since her undergraduate days at Florida State University, but she'd never shaken hands with a governor. She suspected she was about to get the chance. But as she lifted her gaze to take the man in, the first thing she thought was that he looked like a giant Q-tip. She bit the inside of her lip to stifle a giggle.

Of course, the office manager introduced Pam Bondi to Philip first, and then the usual polite exchanges between Delphine, Philip, Gov. Shaw, and Ms. Bondi flew over Abby's head. She glanced once at Layla and saw she was standing still with unusual poise. And she wasn't chewing gum.

"And, Ms. Bondi and Governor, may I introduce two of our most promising associates." Philip's voice had a lift, as if he were a proud parent. "Miss Abigail Coleridge, who has been with us four years and won a national moot court tournament in law school. She's one of our appellate experts, though we use her in trial work also."

Actually, during her law school days, even the thought of moot court competition had scared Abby to stuttering. Yet she knew to keep her mouth shut about Phillip's misrepresentation. She stepped forward and took each politician's hand in turn, murmuring how pleased and honored she was to meet them.

Philip turned to Layla. "And our youngest associate, Layla Freemont, is the editor of the FSU's law review. She's rapidly becoming an expert on oil and gas exploration and leases, which will be of great assistance to us if you decide to retain our firm."

Layla shook hands, repeating as if scripted nearly the same words Abby had said. Beside her, Abby could hear Delphine utter a soft sigh as of relief.

But then Layla winked at the governor. "I'm not really an associate just yet as I'm a third-year law student, but I will be an associate as soon as I pass my bar exam."

Abby couldn't believe Layla would wink at the governor. Or correct a partner. No one ever corrected a partner.

Delphine reached out and snatched Layla's hand. "I need Miss Freemont's assistance, right now, on a legal emergency. I'll rejoin you in just a moment." Delphine tugged on Layla's arm until finally Layla took a step, then another, and followed Delphine down the hallway.

"Abby," Phillip said, "might you join us in showing our guests around?"

With a sinking feeling, Abby realized she was not going to get Delphine's trial brief done this afternoon either. Instead, she was going to have her first formal foray into seducing new clients to join the firm—the rainmaking for which Phillip Draper was famous.

CHAPTER ELEVEN

"Stop throwing your used gum in my potted plants." Abby was so tired she yelled at Layla. Whatever had possessed her to invite Layla into her home while the contractor repaired Layla's own apartment? The young woman had only been there two days, and already Abby's house and life jumbled with messes.

Trouble gave Abby an intense stare and made a guttural sound, half-hiss, half purr.

Great. Even the cat was fussing at her now. Abby glared back at Trouble, keeping her eyes off Layla, but already she felt guilty about snapping.

"Okay, it wasn't my best day either, but I'm not taking it out on you, am I?" Layla was curled up on the couch in Abby's living room, her feet bare. Trouble sat Buddha-like next to her. Layla had taken down her hair and it curled about her face in such wild profusion that she looked rather exotic.

"I'm sorry, really. I'm just so worn out and I still have to finish that damn trial brief and this afternoon I realized I need to get some frigging old cases—too old for computerized research—and I'm going to have to go to the law school library to dig through all that ancient stuff in the basement, and all I want to do is eat a bite and go to bed." Abby didn't like to raise her voice, and she certainly didn't like to whine. But somehow she'd just done both in the space of two minutes. "And the library closes to the public in a couple of hours and I don't know if I can make it there in time to finish —"

"Inhale, exhale." Layla swung her legs off the couch and stood up. "I have an access card—all of us on the law review do. I'll lend it to you so you can get into the library's basement and stay as long as you want." She paused, looking at Abby, with a tentative look on her face. "I'll go with you if you need me to help."

Abby sighed. Layla didn't appear too eager to actually go with her to the library, but she was great at research and would make the job go much faster.

Yet, as Layla had just said, it hadn't been her best day either.

Abby should let Layla off the hook and just borrow her library access card and go. But the thought of all that work—all by herself in the basement of the law school—felt overwhelming at the moment. "Okay, yes, I'd like your help."

Layla nodded, for once not talking. She chewed on her gum with renewed vigor.

"Well, if we're going, let's get ready and go," Abby said, hoping Layla would show a little more enthusiasm. After all, Layla had volunteered, hadn't she?

"All right, but let me check my blood sugar and grab a quick shower."

"Quick, okay? I'll fix some supper." Abby could zap some frozen fish and broccoli while Layla showered and dressed.

As Abby opened the fridge, she spotted Layla's insulin in

its plastic container with the blue lid, and she sighed. Here she was, irritated at Layla, when she should be more patient and compassionate. After all, the young woman had a serious medical condition that required constant monitoring.

After promising to herself to be nicer to Layla, Abby grabbed two pieces of fish for the microwave and dropped some broccoli in the steamer. Trouble rubbed against her and purred in high octaves. "Okay, three pieces, Trouble."

The doorbell chimed. Abby hit the start button on the microwave and went to the door. She peered out the peephole and jerked backed, sucking in air.

Jennifer Draper, Philip's socialite wife, whose photos appeared regularly in the *Tallahassee Magazine* and the *Tallahassee Democrat*, was standing on Abby's front stoop. Jennifer was so eternally calm she never even broke a sweat at that awful outdoor Fourth of July firm picnic they'd had in the one hundred-degree heat. Frankly, the woman scared the wits out of Abby.

Abby peeked again in case stress and fatigue were making her hallucinate. Nope, no mistaking that smooth, peaches-and-cream complexion and the perfect blond pageboy and the linen sheath dress that didn't have a wrinkle on it.

Abby opened the door, pasting a smile on her face as she did. "Oh, hello, Mrs. Draper."

Jennifer didn't speak. She didn't smile. She didn't offer her hand to Abby. She didn't explain a thing. The woman whose name was practically synonymous with Southern Hospitality and graciousness just stared.

"Uh, hello." Abby repeated it as Trouble eased up beside her, brushing his fur against her bare leg. "Would you...er, ... like to come in?"

"Is my husband's law clerk, Layla, here? I understand she's

been staying with you?" Jennifer's words were slow and oddly spaced.

"Ah, yes, I mean she's staying here. But she's in the shower. And we're getting ready to go to the law school...I mean to the library. The law school library. To the basement. Old cases and old books. We've got this huge project. You know, work, work, work." Abby made herself shut up. Under the best of circumstances, Jennifer Draper made her nervous, but this was not the best of circumstances. And when ultra- nervous, sometimes Abby babbled.

"It's important that I speak with her. Might I come in and wait?"

Abby nodded, standing back to let Jennifer inside, yet wondering why in the world Phillip's wife needed to speak with Layla. Because of the attack behind the law firm maybe? A sorry-you-were-mugged-visit? She was dying to ask, but instead offered Jennifer tea, water, or coffee.

"No, thank you. I'll just wait." Jennifer idled in the entryway, though she glanced into the living room.

"Please, come in and have a seat." Abby practically bit her own tongue to keep from jabbering.

The microwave dinged.

Jennifer took a seat in the living room, and Abby excused herself. As she stepped into the doorway between the kitchen and the living room, Abby caught a glimpse of Layla hurrying out of the bathroom, a cloud of stream following her. She was dressed in a bathrobe with a wild pattern of golds and reds, and she saw Jennifer almost at once and hurried down the hallway toward her.

In the living room, Layla gave Jennifer a curt nod, which didn't appear at all friendly. Layla sat down on the couch next to Jennifer and their heads bent together as they whispered.

No matter how hard Abby tried to hear what they said, she couldn't.

Layla looked up at Abby, who was standing in the doorway and obviously spying, and shook her head. Embarrassed at being caught eavesdropping so blatantly, Abby stepped into the kitchen and popped open the microwave. A moment later, the front door opened and closed, Jennifer was gone, and Layla dashed away into her borrowed bedroom.

Looking down at Trouble as he kept step with her, Abby asked him, "Could this day get any weirder?"

Trouble vocalized a noise that sounded suspiciously like the word "yes."

CHAPTER TWELVE

*I*t would have definitely been better if those two women had taken me with them to the law school library. They were going alone into a basement at night. A bit off the trolley if you ask me. Have they never seen a slasher movie?

But they didn't take me, so I have to content myself with having a proper snoop around the house without any interference.

Boring is my immediate assessment of Abby's things after my meticulous exploration, especially all those papers in her den. But I must laud her for her neatness. And for her thriving jungle of potted plants. As for the aquarium, I'm not sure why she so obviously adores it. I watch the fish swim in circles and fail to see the point of it at all. The fish are far too small to be bothered with, not a decent meal if one caught and ate the whole lot of them.

Dull as dishwater, that fish tank.

Well organized that young lady might be, but her house certainly suggests a humdrum life. Yet all my instincts tell me that her safe, boring life is about to change.

Actually, it has already changed. I'm here now. And having Layla as a flat mate is akin to opening a private Pandora's Box in the guest room.

So thinking, I paw open the door to Layla's room and traipse inside. Definitely a shamble. These two women are a modern day Odd Couple. Probably good the arrangement is temporary.

Putting aside my criticism of Layla's housekeeping, I nose around the top of the dresser she appears to be using for a desk and a waste-basket both. The first thing that hits my nose is the scent of mint gum as random packs and wrappers are scattered across the dresser. Sugarless, I'm glad to see, given her diabetes.

On the corner of the dresser, she's piled several textbooks. I doubt any of them will shed light on why someone mugged her. Or why the senior partner's wife was dropping by for a tete-a-tete and acting just a tiny bit stoned if you ask me. Though the books themselves are of little independent interest, I sniff them carefully in case I pick up any scent clues. And I peer carefully at the pages to be sure no secret notes are shoved inside any of the books.

I spot no notes and learn nothing useful from the books. Next I concentrate on a smaller, separate piece of soft-sided canvas luggage, something like Tammy Lynn's gym bag except Layla's has a psychedelic design in garish reds, oranges and pinks that makes me dizzy if I stare at it too long. Tammy Lynn has far better taste, I might add, and thinking such, for a moment I am homesick for my biped and our home in Wetumpka.

Regardless of the design, the bag is well made and probably expensive. As Layla appears to be using it for a suitcase, I paw through the mess of things thrown in there. I see two gaudy pink flash drives in a plastic bag, a blood glucose monitor, a handful of alcohol wipes, a few folded five-dollar bills, some random notepaper with tiny, neat writing all about a law review article—I yawn twice while looking at these. Definitely not my cup of tea.

I am a lot more interested when I spot several changes of bras and *panties—Victoria's Secret and very sexy I might add. But what's really interesting is how Layla has hidden a small silk jewelry bag inside the padding of a push-up bra. I pull the bag out to the bed where I can study it better. Using a combination of teeth, claws, and determination, I get the damn thing unsnapped and opened. Inside, I paw out one delicate gold earring in the shape of a teardrop with a pearl in the center. There is only the one earring.*

As I look closer, I see the earring is quite posh in a way Layla's other jewelry is not. This makes me more curious. Carefully, I roll it over with my paw. On the back, I spot an engraving that spells out the word "love." Ah, a gift perhaps from a sweetheart. Maybe that's why it is so different than Layla's other earrings. Or perhaps it isn't hers at all. But I have other things to scrutinize, so I poke the earring back where it belongs and move on.

I crawl under the bed and find an additional hoard of gum wrappers and some discarded clothes. I start to back out, but then I catch a distinct whiff of something quite familiar.

What wafts up at me is that same spicy, yet flowery scent I caught my first night here when I ran after the shadow into the back yard. A woman's perfume? Or a man's aftershave? Bipeds are so peculiar in their tastes I can't say which it is. But I am certain that it is the scent I smelled the night I ran after the intruder in Abby's backyard.

Had what I'd picked up in the yard been a fragrance Layla had left?

Or had the person who'd left the scent been somehow prowling though Layla's dirty clothes?

VICTOR SAT AT his desk in his small rental house and checked his cell phone for possibly the tenth time in ten minutes. No missed calls, no messages. Layla had not returned his calls all day, and now it was night. He needed to talk to her about that damn flash drive. Maybe it had nothing to do with Layla. After all, Phillip Draper was a lawyer, he was heavily involved with the oil and gas industry, taught a seminar on the subject at the law school, wrote articles about the topic, and represented a corporation that was perpetually trying to get permits to drill for oil off the coast at Panama City Beach. Phillip could have taped the flash drive to the back of the toilet tank.

No, that didn't make sense. First off, Layla was the only person he knew who used bright pink flash drives. Further, Phillip no doubt had a secure safe somewhere in his office and house. Why hide something in a bathroom, especially something that looked surprisingly like a first and second draft of a law review article about offshore oil drilling? He'd read the two versions of the same article three times on the pink flash drive, noting some differences between the two drafts. Then he'd studied them again. He couldn't find anything that would drive someone to mug Layla and try to burn down her apartment.

Nope, all there was on that flash drive was technical stuff, heavily laced with citations to laws and obscure documents, with a discussion of endless government regulations—exactly the kind of stuff Layla excelled at finding, deciphering, and writing about. No doubt given her father's oil business in Houston, she'd been studying oil exploration and drilling issues since long before she entered law school. But the stuff in the articles made the back of his neck tense with frustration and disgust. Couldn't those oil and gas people just leave the Gulf of Mexico alone? Hadn't they done enough harm to the Gulf already?

Victor had to find Layla, that was all there was to it. He'd make her explain what the materials on the flash drive meant. He also had to study his estate and gift tax reading assignment, and finish it tonight.

Wearily, he grabbed his textbook and a notebook, threw them into his backpack and headed out. He'd talk to Layla, then head to the law library to study.

Victor gunned his small Ford Ranger pickup, a vintage model for sure, but churning along just fine year after year, and headed over to Abby's house. When he saw Layla's Honda in the driveway, he parked, and knocked on the door. The cat poked his head through the curtain on the front window and meowed at him. Victor tapped the glass and spoke to the cat, wishing he could get inside to pet it and toss it a few treats.

Obviously, neither Layla nor Abby were home—or if they were, they weren't opening the door for him.

Victor jumped back into his truck and headed to the law school. Maybe he'd find Layla in her law review office, where she sometimes worked late at night. He desperately wanted to ask her if she had hidden the flash drive on the back of Phillip Draper's toilet, and, if so, why.

CHAPTER THIRTEEN

*A*bby steered her Prius with concentration as she merged into the never-ending traffic on the Fly-Over that led downtown to the law school. She was dying to ask Layla what she and Jennifer had discussed, but Layla's expression didn't invite questions. Abby, raised to be polite, didn't ask.

They drove in silence, Abby with her hands at nine and three o'clock on the steering wheel and Layla twirling her hair and looking out the window. Turning down Pensacola Street, Abby was glad to see that this late at night she could snag a parking spot right in front of the school.

They crawled out of the Prius and walked toward the law school. Suddenly Layla spun around, facing Abby, and grabbed her arm as if to stop her. Abby jerked to a halt.

"What?" Abby blurted it out, stunned by Layla's aggression.

"Don't tell anyone." Layla snapped it out like an order. But, perhaps recognizing how she sounded, she gave Abby a half-way smile. "I mean, please. Promise me you won't mention Jennifer's visit to anyone."

Abby nodded, not sure how to reply.

"I mean, not anyone." Layla looked pleadingly into Abby's eyes. "This is something just between Jennifer and me, all right? It doesn't have a thing to do with the law firm. Private stuff that needs to stay private."

Abby nodded again.

"Promise me. Say it out loud. That you will not mention to anyone, no matter what, that Jennifer came over tonight." Layla's fingers dug into Abby's arm.

"All right. Yes. I promise." Abby pulled her arm from Layla's grip and started to accuse Layla of being melodramatic. But what good would that do? Layla was dramatic and flashy. That was her style.

"Say it. You promise not to tell anyone no matter what that Jennifer visited me at your house."

"Oh, for heaven's sake." Abby blurted it out, sorry now that she'd agreed to Layla going with her to the law library. Nonetheless, she dutifully repeated, "I promise not to tell anyone, no matter what, that Jennifer visited you at my house."

"Good. Let's go inside and get this damn brief done for Delphine." Layla said Delphine's name like a cuss word. "I want to get home as soon as we can."

A moment later, Layla slid her access card through a side door so they could cruise right in. They hurried up a flight of stairs, but at the top, Abby paused and turned to the wide doors that led to the student lounge. "Let's grab some bottled tea before we head downstairs."

Layla nodded as they trudged down the hallway. When they stepped into the student lounge, Abby was startled to see Miguel with Phillip, their heads bent over a pile of papers.

"Miguel," Layla said under her breath. "And Phillip?" Despite the puzzled tone in Layla's voice, she fluffed her wild hair with her finger tips and turned toward them. Miguel spotted them and waved. Phillip looked up, his face a blank mask.

A moment later, the two men gathered up their papers and moved toward them. Layla put on a smile so big her molars showed.

Phillip nodded. "Abby, Layla, I'm surprised to see you two here."

As if to make up for Phillip's curt greeting, Miguel beamed. His voice was enthusiastic as he said, "Ladies, how wonderful to see you both. Layla, my brightest student, and Abby, delightful to meet again so soon."

Abby felt a blush spreading up her face. Layla stood beside her, watching Miguel and Phillip, her big smile still in place.

"Well," Phillip said, glancing at his Rolex, "it's getting late. Jennifer will be waiting for me. If you will excuse me, I'll bid everyone a good night."

They said their goodbyes and watched Phillip leaving the lounge. As he disappeared out the door, Miguel turned back to Layla and Abby, his expression both quizzical and pleased.

"What brings you two to the law school so late?" Miguel glanced at Abby, before casting his eyes back on Layla.

"What brings *you* to the law school so late?" Layla's voice had gone low and throaty, and she tilted her head toward Miguel and eased a step closer.

She's flirting with him, Abby thought as a wave of indignation on Victor's behalf hit her.

Miguel laughed. "Seminar night. Phillip was my guest speaker. We were just going over some student feedback. Now, your turn. What's so important that you're here this late?"

Abby glanced over his head to the wall clock. Only a little

after 9:30. Not *that* late. Not for law students and young associates. She looked back at Miguel and said,

"Trial brief. Due tomorrow."

"We won't be here very long. Just a quick in and out." Layla grinned at Miguel when she said that. "I'm just here to help speed it up."

Abby wondered where Layla got the idea this would be a quick job, but smiled too. Everybody was smiling, so why not?

"Layla does excellent research." Miguel winked at Layla. "I can vouch for her talents and persistence. She's even digging into the ancient stacks at the Library of Congress on a project for me."

Layla made a strange noise at the back of her throat. To Abby, Layla sounded as if she were trying to purr. Next she'll be rubbing against him, Abby thought, once more resentful on Victor's behalf.

To cover up her indignation, Abby spoke quickly. "I'm sure she'll be a big help to both of us." Abby felt like a third wheel and was eager to get out from between Layla and Miguel. She could feel the sparks vibrating between them.

Layla flipped her hair back, and the bangle bracelets on her arm chimed as she gave Miguel a quick look, something either cautious or coy which Abby couldn't quite read.

"Speaking of which, if you two could excuse me for just a moment. I need to pick up something in my law review office. Don't go away." With that, Layla stepped back toward the hallway, dragging her backpack and laptop with her.

Abby glanced at Miguel, puzzled by Layla's abrupt leaving and wondering what to say to Miguel.

"Has Phillip really got you working this late? I'll have to speak to him." Miguel leaned close to Abby, his eyes focused deeply on her own.

Nervous from the attention, Abby blurted out, "No, it's Delphine that has us working late. We'll be in the basement since I need some really old Florida case law and we were just going to get a boost of green tea before we start."

"I'd be glad to have you and Layla come with me to the faculty lounge." Miguel eased closer to Abby. "I'll brew you a fresh hot cup of coffee, hot chocolate, or tea. Perhaps some chai tea? We've got a complete selection, far better than the student lounge vending machines."

Abby hesitated, not wanting to waste the time or get trapped again between Layla and Miguel as they traded pheromones. "We better not. We really need to get this brief done." Abby smiled up at Miguel, making her keenly aware of how tall he was.

"Very well." He gave her a brief smile, but looked over her shoulder as if waiting for Layla.

Abby glanced toward the doorway. Where was Layla anyway? When she looked back at Miguel, he glanced at Abby.

"So, Professor," she blurted out, "what's up with you these days? How're your seminar plans with Phillip coming?"

"Excellent. He's a gem to work with. But I imagine you know that."

Abby nodded, her eagerness to get to work and her fatigue colliding. She didn't even have the energy to trade small talk.

"Has Layla told you I'm up for tenure this year? That's one reason I'm designing the seminar for Phillip and me. To show the committee I'm totally dedicated to this school and my students. And we'll be opening it to a few disadvantaged undergrad students free of charge to show my commitment to public service."

"How wonderful for you."

"Not so wonderful. It's very rigorous. The school really

puts a professor through the wringer before granting tenure. But you know about that, right?" Miguel gave her an inquiring look.

Of course, she knew about the tenure process. A professor had to meet certain strict criteria, including publication of original research in a well-respected law review or having one's manuscript published as a book. The old "publish or perish" rule was especially brutal for law professors. If Miguel did not have the appropriate publications, he simply would not get tenure, no matter how many extra seminars he taught.

Thinking about "publish or perish," Abby wondered if Miguel had written another book. "Do you have a new book? I still have your first one, even read it again last year." She actually had reread Miguel's history of how the early United States Supreme Court had shaped America's future, and still found the tidbits of personal information on the court justices fascinating.

"No, no new book yet, but I'm working on one. Layla is helping me with the research."

"Really?" Abby wondered why Layla hadn't mentioned anything about working with Miguel.

As if on cue, Layla hurried into the lounge and headed toward them. Abby waved at her, then felt foolish for waving.

"We better skip the tea and hurry," Layla said, as she stepped up to Abby. "Victor and Emmett are meeting us downstairs in a moment."

Puzzled, Abby turned to look at Layla, her mouth opened to ask why in the world Emmett and Victor would be meeting them. But Miguel spoke before she got the question out.

"No, come on, let me show off the faculty lounge and fix you two a cup of something to drink. Your boyfriends will wait for you."

Abby's tone was all but snippy when she exclaimed, "Emmett's not my boyfriend." She was embarrassed anyone might even think that.

"You've met Victor," Layla said, staring right at Miguel as if daring him to deny it.

"Oh, yes, your military man. The former Navy police officer, right?"

Layla smiled in a way that confirmed Abby's belief that Layla and Victor were very much an item. At the thought that they'd obviously made up, Abby felt strangely disappointed. But more than that, she puzzled over this flirtation if Miguel knew Layla had a boyfriend. Maybe the challenge was part of the fun for him? But thinking back to the way he'd been with her at the law firm, Abby decided it was just Miguel's way to flirt.

Which didn't explain Layla's hair flipping and throaty answers.

"We really need to go meet them." This time Layla sounded all business.

Glad to get to work, Abby didn't argue.

"Good night, then, ladies," Miguel said, smiling once more at Layla in that slow, sensual way. He began to drift off, but turned once to look back at them.

Layla hurried toward the basement stairs, but Abby stopped at the drink machine that had been their original goal. She dug out some dollar bills and pushed them in, selecting a bottle of sweet green mango tea for herself and a bottle of unsweetened green tea with mint for Layla.

Juggling her purse, the bottled teas, and her laptop, Abby hurried after Layla.

As they made their way down the stairs to the basement

floor of the library, Abby asked, "So, you're helping Miguel with research on his book?"

"Yeah." Layla swiped her access card and they stepped inside the basement room of the library where old case law and old legal books were kept. All the lights were blazing and the room was frigid with full-tilt air conditioning, yet a diffused musty smell still floated in the air.

Abby stared at Layla, conscious again that Layla didn't mind asking Abby the most personal questions, but she didn't ever seem inclined to share much information about herself. "Yeah?" Abby repeated. "That's all you've got to say about it?"

"Yeah."

"What about Victor and Emmett? You didn't really invite them to come help us, did you?"

"Yes, actually, I did. Emmett, anyway. He's delighted in that nerdy way of his. I need to call Victor now."

Abby wasn't sure the "more the merrier" was a good plan on legal research, especially when Emmett was involved. It looked like Victor and Layla had made up though, and no doubt that was the real reason Layla had invited the men— Emmett to help with the research and Victor to visit with Layla.

Abby sighed, dreading Emmett's hovering and unable to shake her lingering disappointment over Layla and Victor getting back together.

CHAPTER FOURTEEN

The outer door to the suite of law review offices was unlocked and Victor stepped inside. He didn't see anyone, but headed straight for Layla's office. Maybe she wasn't over being mad at him. But, damn it all, she was in some kind of trouble. If she wasn't in her office where he could ask her about the flash drive he'd found taped to the Drapers' toilet tank, he might just snoop a bit and see if he spotted anything that matched with the materials on the flash drive.

Victor jiggled Layla's door. Naturally it was locked. The lights were out and it didn't make any kind of sense that she'd be sitting inside in the dark. He looked around. Nobody anywhere in sight. He switched off his cell phone. It wouldn't do to have it ring while he was breaking, entering, and snooping. Once the cell phone was off, he tried the door again, shaking the knob with a bit more force. Then he bent down and scrutinized the locking mechanism on the door.

The intricacies of plumbing weren't the only thing his father had pressed Victor to learn. The man might have been a jerk with a ruthless attitude toward most things, but he was an ace mechanic, a fearless high-rise window cleaner, a competent roofer, and a jack-leg locksmith. He'd taught these skills to Victor, insisting as he did that his son would always know how to make a living.

Victor laughed, wondering if his dad ever used his skills to break in. Manipulating the thin, narrow blade on his pocket knife, Victor worked the cheap lock opened in less than a minute. It wasn't the first time he felt grateful to his father for all the how-to-do lessons over the rough years of his youth. He ought to mention to Layla that the door didn't provide any real security.

Fortunately, enough light from the hallway and the high office window filtered in that he could see his way around. Victor booted up the PC on Layla's desk. While it was going through its gyrations, he flipped through a few loose papers on her desk. Quickly bored with them, he looked through her drawer and spotted a library access card. There were also collections of other access cards labeled law review, which he assumed might be keys to the law review offices. But right now, it was the library access card that held his interest. He could slide the card through the scanner on any of the locked rooms or basement and get inside—one of the perks Layla particularly enjoyed. Victor was tempted, but he'd never been a thief.

Yet, if Layla was in the library, she might well be in the basement. Something about all those old books down there fascinated her of late. He slipped the access card into his shirt pocket, promising himself he'd bring it back tomorrow. Then as an afterthought, he also pocketed one of the access cards labeled law review. If he didn't need it to find Layla tonight, he'd return it. He sat down in her chair, planning to scan through her various folders on her computer, looking for something that might be the "secret" he'd heard her mention.

The computer demanded a password.

He leaned back in his chair to think. Layla wouldn't be so simple-minded as to use just a catchy word. No names of dead pets or old boyfriends for her. No, she'd have a complicated string of symbols, letters, and numbers. There was no use trying to guess; he'd just get locked out after the third failed try and she'd know somebody had tried to access her files.

He felt under the keyboard to see if there was any paper that might have the password. Finding nothing, he stood up, eyeing things in her office, then yanked open the filing cabinet.

Victor had his nose buried in a file labeled offshore oil drilling when the door banged open. He spun around just as Emmett yelled out, "What the hell are you doing here?"

Lifting the file out of the cabinet as easy and smooth as if he were not stealing something, Victor smiled sheepishly. "You startled me."

"I beg your pardon." Emmett's sarcastic tone was obvious. "But I repeat. What are you doing in here? You are not on law review."

Victor recognized Emmett as they were both third-year law students. He also knew that Emmett worked at the Draper law firm in the afternoons and that Layla thought he was an overly ambitious buffoon. But none of that solved the immediate problem.

"Picking up something for Layla." Victor held up the file as if to show it to Emmett. Everyone knew Layla and Victor were friends, so he hoped the lie would be believable.

"Well, okay." Emmett stepped up to Victor and eyed the file, squinting as if to read the label.

Victor gave Emmett a quick grin and darted for the door.

"Hey, why's her PC on?" Emmett yelled after him. "Did you turn it on? And where's your key? Show me your key."

Victor kept going.

CHAPTER FIFTEEN

*a*bby headed toward a study carrel in a corner, put down her laptop and her two bottles of green tea and pulled out the chair. It was going to be a long night.

Layla punched in a number on her cell phone and sighed when she got voice mail. "Yo, Victor. It's me. Abby and I are in the law school library basement and need your help. Come find us as soon as you can. Give me a call on your cell when you get here, and I'll let you in the door." Layla disconnected the call and glanced at Abby. "He'll be here soon. He's as reliable as Lassie."

The Layla-Victor relationship puzzled Abby, but lots of couples were on-again, off-again. She wondered if he flirted around like Layla did. Still, she had to accept it: Victor and Layla were an item, however dysfunctional their relationship might be. And Abby didn't steal other women's boyfriends.

Layla plopped her backpack and laptop on a table near the carrel. She dug through a pocket and pulled out a stick of gum. Abby sighed as she watched Layla stuff the gum in her mouth. Smacking on the gum, Layla booted up the laptop. A second later, she sat down in a chair and hunched over it as if trying to cover up whatever she was typing.

Abby frankly didn't care if Layla was writing smutty emails to Victor or what, so long as she didn't take long doing it and got to work soon.

Ah, Victor. Abby couldn't help but think about him yet again. Was he already on his way here to see Layla?

Work, Abby told herself. Stop daydreaming about somebody else's boyfriend.

Abby opened her laptop, pulled up the incomplete trial brief and her notes, and reviewed them quickly. With any luck at all, she could whip through the first part and be ready to finish once Layla brought her the case law she needed. After rubbing her eyes, she opened her bottled tea and took a sip, looked at the calorie content, and made a vow to do two extra workouts tomorrow.

At the carrel next to her, Layla kept typing like a maniac. Abby tried to pretend she wasn't sneaking covert glances at Layla's screen. With a sideways glance at Abby, Layla slammed the laptop shut and stood up. "Just law review stuff. Don't worry, I'm all yours now."

Abby shoved a list of cases over toward Layla. "These are the main ones I need, really old stuff about dower rights and the rule against perpetuities."

"Okay. Keep an eye on my stuff, while I go dig them up." Layla wandered off, chewing gum as she went.

Half an hour or so into the typing, Abby needed to pee. She didn't want to shout out for Layla to come guard their piles of stuff, yet she knew unprotected laptops were a frequent target of library thieves. She crossed her legs and tried to think about dower rights instead of all the coffee and tea she'd drunk that day.

No, there was no getting around it. She needed to pee. She stood and looked down the nearest corridors between book cases and didn't see a soul. Cocking her head like a curious cat, she listened. Nothing. Where were Victor and Emmett? Where was Layla anyway?

If nobody was in the basement but them, nobody would steal their stuff, and she couldn't wait. Knowing how fanatical Layla was over her laptop and backpack, Abby put them on the floor under the carrel and piled a stack of books and magazines from the library over them. Satisfied she'd hidden them well enough, Abby sprinted to the bathroom. Done, she hurried back, relieved to see the laptops were right where she left them. Ditto Layla's precious backpack.

Hoping for a boost, Abby reached for her tea, and took a long swallow. Odd, she didn't remember it having such a bitter aftertaste. Bitter or not, she took another gulp, licked her lips against the astringent taste of the stuff, dug out her laptop, and started typing again.

A moment later, she heard the steady padding of someone walking toward her and she looked up. Emmett approached, his face perky, yet determined. Suddenly she couldn't stand the thought of Emmett chattering, buttering her up, and showing off. She wanted to get rid of him, and soon.

"So glad Layla invited me to help." Emmett's voice practically chirped. "I am a skilled researcher and have an ardent interest in dower and the rule against perpetuities issues." He grinned as if he'd made a joke. In a way, he had. Nobody had an "ardent" interest in dower and the rule against perpetuities.

Once more, Abby wondered why in the world Layla had invited Emmett to join them. All Abby could think of was that Layla wanted Emmett to do the research so she could make up —and make out—with Victor.

Emmett loomed over her, grinning. Abby wanted to shoo him away more than ever, but out of politeness, she struggled for a nice way of moving him along. "Layla said she'd invited you to help, but we've really got this under control. I'm sorry if you made the trip for nothing. Really. But thank you. I'll be sure to tell Delphine how eager you are to help on this case."

"I doubt you'll be getting much help from Layla. She's up in the computer room, playing on Facebook."

Abby didn't believe for a moment that Layla was on Facebook, but she didn't want to argue with Emmett. "I'll talk to you in the morning. Anything we don't get done tonight, you can help with tomorrow. And, yes, I'll be sure to tell Delphine you helped." Abby renewed her determination to finish the brief tonight so she wouldn't have to deal with Emmett in the morning.

Emmett left and Abby went back to work. She kept listening for Layla or anyone else. Finally, Layla came back with her arms full of ancient-looking books. Abby was seriously yawning and moaned when she saw the stack Layla held. This stuff was boring. It was late. The library was quiet. A nap would have been nearly as blissful as a big bowl of ice cream.

"Yo, wake up, Sleeping Beauty." Layla dropped the books with a loud thwack on the table.

"Quiet. It's a library."

"And it's pushing midnight and nobody is here except you and me and the Ghost of Christmas Past." But Layla yawned too. "Where the hell are Victor and Emmett?"

"Emmett came and I just couldn't deal with him, so I sent him away. He's such a toad."

Layla glared at Abby.

"I'm tired, and you know what a pest he is." Abby wasn't sure why she had to defend herself to Layla, but Layla's expression seemed to demand an explanation. "I just couldn't stand the thought of him prattling about."

Layla hesitated a moment. "Oh, well, Victor'll come soon enough." She popped some gum, her face scrunched up like she was thinking hard. Then she shrugged. "I put bookmarks where the cases are in the books. Didn't want to haul ass up the stairs to the copy machines."

Trying to fight her sleepiness, Abby opened one of the books. She had to grin.

Layla had marked the right place in the thick book with a gum wrapper.

"I'm going to try Victor again." Layla stretched. "First some fresh gum."

Abby sighed as Layla pulled out her backpack from where Abby had covered it up, and dug around inside. She offered Abby a stick of mint gum. "Sugarfree."

"No, thanks." Abby found gum somewhat disgusting.

"Keep an eye on things, okay?" As she spoke, Layla piled some magazines back over her backpack as if to keep it hidden.

"Yeah, I'll be sure to keep your backpack safe from the Ghost of Christmas Past."

Abby laughed, more to try to wake herself up than because anything struck her as funny.

She watched Layla walk off, blinked twice, and then caught Layla dropping her wad of gum into an umbrella stand by the elevator door.

Oh, well, at least it wasn't a potted plant. Abby started reading the first case. But slowly and completely against her will, her eyes began to shut.

CHAPTER SIXTEEN

*V*ictor searched the main library for Layla. After satisfying himself she wasn't there, he tried the law review access key to the library basement. The card worked like a charm and he cruised right down the stairs. He knew the scanner recorded the ID on the card, but since it would just show law review, no one would know he was in the basement after it was officially closed for the night.

He spotted Abby right off, with her head down on her laptop, eyes closed, and making little kitten-like snores. No wonder she'd dozed off, he thought, looking at the pile of books and magazines beside the study carrel. She'd obviously been working hard that night.

She was so cute that he just stood there, studying her. Her face rested on an opened book, its pages yellowed and contrasting with her creamy skin. He wanted to lean down and kiss her, but he knew better than to surprise her like that. Still, a slow smile crept onto his face. Just watching her sleep made him feel happy.

He eased around to her other side to be sure her pile of

books wasn't going to trip her. As he did, the overhead light caught the shine in her hair, emphasizing its reddish color in a way that nearly hypnotized him.

Finally, Victor shook himself out of the strange trance he'd fallen into while staring at Abby's sleeping form. He wondered if he should wake her up. Then he wondered if Layla was with her, and he nosed around the carrel. He didn't see Layla's paisley laptop case or her backpack, just that large pile of books and magazines piled on the floor beside Abby, so he doubted Layla was in the library with Abby after all. Still he figured he'd better look around anyway.

Leaving Abby, he searched high and low in the basement of the library, finding no one but the napping Abby. He camped outside the women's bathroom for a bit, but drew the line at ducking inside to look. After a while, he was satisfied Layla was not in the bathroom or the basement.

Easing back over to Abby, he found her still sleeping, her breathing deep and relaxed. Once more he debated waking her up, but she looked so peaceful. In the end, he'd decided the thing to do was just to stay near her, keeping a close and protective eye on her and her laptop. That way, he'd be there when she woke up.

He settled into the nearest study carrel and started reading *Estate and Gift Tax in a Nutshell*. Immediately, he was bored. He stood up, stretched, and leaned over Abby's carrel. She was still sleeping, and he decided once again to leave her be. But she had two bottles of green tea in the carrel. One was empty. He didn't figure the little bit of caffeine in the other bottle would do him much good, but drinking it meant he could postpone reading more estate tax, if only for a moment. He didn't think she'd mind if he drank it. He took the bottle and sipped, frowning at the bitter aftertaste. He walked around, finished the tea, put the bottle on his carrel so he could recycle it, and picked up the cursed estate tax book.

He fought off the yawns and the sleep as long as he could, but something stronger than his own will power won. Inside an hour, he was fast asleep without ever turning his cell phone back on or checking his voice mail.

ABBY'S LANDLINE RINGS, jarring me from a perfectly peaceful catnap on top of the couch. I lift my ears, waiting to see if the answer machine picks up a message. I glance at the clock, 1:05 at night, very late for a call. And shouldn't Layla and Abby be home by now?

Whoever the caller is, he or she doesn't leave a voice mail.

Despite a rising sense of worry for Layla and Abby, I pad quietly toward the kitchen, nosh a bit on the dried cat food Abby left for me, and contemplate whether further snooping serves any particular purpose. Just as I'm heading back toward Layla's temporary room, I hear somebody at the back door that leads into the kitchen. It's not like Abby to come in that door, so I'm immediately on alert. Keeping my head low, I run toward the sound. Pressed against the door, I hear the unmistakable sounds of scratching and prying—as if some beastly person is trying to break into Abby's house.

For the briefest second, I debate. Should I let the bugger get in and attack him or her? Or knock the phone off the hook and hit 9-1-1? But the burglar might be armed and my claws, ferocious as they are, are no match for a gun. And 9-1-1 would take too long—even if the radio operator understood a cat's call for help.

The tinkering sounds get louder.

With my keen cat reasoning, I realize that whoever just called was probably checking to see if anyone was at home. So perhaps the safest way to protect Abby's house is to convince the wanker trying to break in that someone is home after all.

I hop up on the kitchen counter and butt the switch. Light floods the kitchen. For good measure, I run across the counter to the other side and butt the switch for the backyard flood lights. Then I push the curtains back and poke my nose against the window pane. All I can make out is the quickly disappearing figure of someone wearing a hoodie and heading toward a large, dark car. I can't even tell if the figure is male or female.

In the exercise of extreme cat caution, I decide to leave the flood lights on.

In fact, maybe I'll just turn all the lights in the house on as I pace, room to room, worrying quite seriously now about Abby and Layla.

VICTOR WAS STILL deep in the Land of Nod when a scream roused him. He shook himself awake, and immediately checked on Abby, who was struggling to wake up, but appeared to be fine. At any rate, it wasn't Abby who had cried out.

"Did you hear a scream?" Victor asked.

"I...I don't know. Something...but what are you doing here?"

Someone screamed again. Victor spun around and raced toward the sound. Behind him, he heard Abby hurrying after him.

He crashed into a mop bucket right before he saw a maintenance woman standing in the doorway of the women's bathroom. She was shaking and crying, punching in numbers on a cell phone. Victor pushed past her just as Abby ran up.

"Stay back." He put out a hand to stop Abby. But she gave him a sharp look and tried to barrel past him. "Let me go first." Instinctively he reached for where his weapon would have been if he had still been on patrol in the Navy.

He shoved into the women's bathroom, every one of his

senses on alert. A large pool of blood spread over the floor and splatters dripped down tiled walls. On the lavatory counter, a note stained with red curled in a puddle of water. Above the note, someone had scrawled "ransom" on the mirror in what appeared to be blood.

"Layla," Abby cried out as she pushed in behind Victor. "Oh, God, no."

Victor handed her his cell phone. "Go back outside and call 9-1-1. Let me search the stalls."

Abby took the phone, a horrified look on her face. He pushed past her and flung open the first stall door. Nothing. Frantically, Victor looked in each stall, but neither Layla nor anyone else was anywhere to be seen. He hurried back to Abby, who was still pressed against the wall, though she fiddled with his phone.

"Ransom? Someone kidnapped her?" Abby's speech sounded thick. "I can't make the phone work."

Victor snatched his cell from Abby, only to realize it was still turned off. He turned it on, and punched in 9-1-1.

"She's diabetic," Abby said. "She can't go without her meds. She'll die."

Victor tried to close his ears to Abby's worried words as he reported a possible kidnapping with violence.

After he agreed to stay on the line until police officers arrived, he stared up at Abby, who was shaken, but functioning. She rushed to the woman with the bucket and the cell phone and began to question her.

Victor's gaze shifted to the bathroom floor. All that blood was a bad sign. Layla might already be dead. He knew better than to touch the stained note on the lavatory, but he suspected it might be a ransom note given the word scribbled above it.

Yet, with all that blood, he had to doubt Layla could have survived. The ransom note must just be a ruse to confuse the cops.

He turned to Abby as she moved back next to him. A few tears pooled in her eyes. He had to struggle to keep his own emotions in check.

Someone had murdered Layla.

CHAPTER SEVENTEEN

*a*bby rested against Victor, grateful for the strength and comfort he offered. They were crowded together on the floor as the first law enforcement officer on the scene had ordered them not to touch any furniture. The law school's associate dean stood nearby as if guarding them. Abby pressed against Victor and he threw his arm around her, pulling her closer. They hadn't said more than a few words in the twenty minutes or so since the associate dean had assumed watch over them, except when Victor assured her things would be all right.

But it wasn't going to be all right. How could it be? Layla had disappeared, there was enough blood in that bathroom for a scene in the worst slasher movie, and some horrid, cruel, dangerous person had scrawled "ransom" in blood above a note left behind on the sink.

Who would want to kidnap Layla anyway? No, that ransom thing had to be some kind of subterfuge. But for what purpose? Abby couldn't figure out why in the world somebody would pretend to kidnap someone they had just murdered. And why haul the body off if it was murder?

No, she calmly reasoned, Layla was still alive. She had to be, all that blood notwithstanding.

As they waited for whatever was coming next, Abby thought more about the possible kidnapping angle. Layla's many outfits had not come cheaply. That Boho style she wore didn't sell big in Tallahassee and her clothes had New York City boutique labels. She drove a brand-new Honda Civic. True, she lived in a small garage apartment in the back of her landlord's house, but her laptop was top of the line, and her jewelry was real gold. Abby knew because she'd tried some of it on at Layla's invitation. Same with a couple of the long skirts, which had looked ridiculous on Abby's petite frame.

"Is Layla rich?" Abby broke the silence as she lifted her head to look into Victor's blue eyes. The associate dean stepped closer as if to hear more perfectly what was said.

"Her parents are. I can't say she was ashamed of it, but she didn't like to...you know, flaunt it." Victor shifted his body a bit, then relaxed his arm around Abby. "She was...damn it, she *is*...determined to make it on her own." He paused as if debating whether to say more.

"What?"

"Layla and her parents aren't close. They...well, she had money from the family business, but not much contact with her mom or dad. I mean, she *has* money from them, but not much else."

Abby shivered at Victor's use of the past tense, even if he had quickly corrected himself. Layla couldn't be dead. She just couldn't be.

"Her dad is some CEO in this big oil company out in

Houston," Victor added. "It's a company her grandfather started."

"She never mentioned her folks to me, not once." But Abby realized boyfriends knew things temporary roommates didn't. "So, Layla's from oil money."

"Yes. That's one reason she was so keen to work with Phillip and his oil and gas clients." Again, Victor paused, cocking his head toward the listening dean and lowering his voice. "I think she was trying to get her dad's attention— maybe his approval—by working on that oil and gas stuff. She really hated the idea of drilling for oil in the Gulf of Mexico, but that's what Phillip and her father were working on."

Someone over by the bathroom shouted out "careful" and Abby straightened up to look over that way. More and more law enforcement officials were pouring in and their voices bounced around the library's basement.

An older man with thinning gray hair, but straight posture and a flat stomach despite his obvious age, hurried over to Abby and Victor. He wore a sloppy gray suit and no tie, with a plainly visible gun under his jacket. "Detective Joe Rizzo," he said. A younger man wearing a similar suit and expression hurried up behind him. "This is my partner, Lucas Kelly."

Victor stood up, pulling Abby with him. When he offered the older man his hand, Abby studied the look in the detective's eyes. Not good.

"Layla's diabetic. You have to find her. Now." Abby hated the hysterical tone of her voice. "And all that blood, she must be seriously wounded."

"Yes, you mentioned the diabetes." Rizzo eyed her carefully.

Abby didn't remember speaking with this man before, but

when the younger detective motioned her to another corner of the library, she stiffened. In all of her three decades of life, she'd never been questioned by a police detective, never even had a parking ticket or been stopped by a traffic cop. She didn't even handle criminal cases. Those were left to others at the law firm.

Abby hesitated. Maybe she should refuse to talk to the detective. She could call Delphine to come to the library and act as her attorney. But, no, that would make her look guilty—and it might slow down the search for Layla. And after all, Abby was an attorney too. Even if she didn't practice criminal law, she knew she had a right to refuse to answer.

"If you'll come with me, now," the younger detective asked.

Abby nodded, ready to follow the officer. But Victor took her hand and gripped it as if he didn't want her to go.

Was she about to be arrested? A tingle of apprehension began to travel up Abby's whole body, landing in her stomach. She felt ill. She squeezed Victor's hands, seeking some kind of comfort.

"I won't bite." Detective Kelly gave her a warm, friendly smile as he broke Abby and Victor apart and led her away. "And please, call me Lucas. May I call you Abby?"

She nodded.

Abby only had to tell the truth. She'd done nothing wrong. She and Victor were not in any kind of trouble. But as Abby turned back for a nervous glance at Victor, his expression suggested he might be thinking otherwise.

"How about we sit here and chat?" Lucas pulled out a chair for Abby.

She waited for him to tell her she had a right to remain silent. Instead, he asked, "Why were you down here?"

Abby nervously babbled out a tumble of words and told Lucas the whole story. Start to finish, pretty much without any pause, she included the mugging at the law firm and Emmett's visit to the basement.

Lucas nodded, his body leaning in close to Abby's as if listening intently to every word. But he didn't take any notes.

"May I get you a cup of water? Or something else to drink?" he asked.

Abby shook her head, though her mouth was dry. She just wanted to get this over with as quickly as possible.

"All right, then. Let's start over. Who knew you and Layla Freemont would be here tonight in the library basement?" Lucas pulled out a notebook and a pen.

Abby blurted out, "My boss Delphine, you know, at the law firm. Delphine Summers. Plus Phillip Draper, he saw us here. And, um...well Miguel, that is Professor Miguel Angel Castillo. I told you about Emmett, the firm's law clerk, being here to help with the research, and then—" She stopped as Lucas scribbled in his notebook. She realized she was making a list of suspects. But why would any of these people want to hurt Layla?

Lucas stopped writing and looked up, his eyes narrowed with concentration as he studied her face. "Go on. Who else?"

Sitting quietly, Abby looked down at her hands, folded primly in her lap. "Well, practically everyone at the law firm."

Abby kept hearing Layla pressing her to promise not to tell anyone "no matter what" that Jennifer had been at their house talking with Layla. But did "no matter what" include being murdered, or cut and kidnapped?

Lucas kept staring at her as if he could read her mind.

Abby licked her lips and shrugged. "Like I told you.

Everyone at the law firm knew we'd be here. And, I suppose…"
she hesitated. Would emphasizing that their spouses might
know alert Lucas without breaking her promise to Layla?

"Yes?" Lucas leaned closer to Abby, his gaze penetrating.

"All of the lawyers would have known, and their wives too."

"Wives?" Lucas's voice had a note of surprise. "Why do you
say wives?"

"Well, you know, wives. They'd know what their husbands
knew." She struggled not to avert her eyes from Lucas's.

"All right, so what you're telling me is that it was no secret
and a lot of people knew you two would be spending the night
in the law library basement." Lucas sounded disgusted.

Abby nodded.

"Fine then, go back to why Miss Freemont was staying with
you? Then bring me up to date to this evening."

It took Abby a nervous few minutes to repeat the story
about the fire in Layla's kitchen, the mugging, and all the rest
of it. Lucas squiggled in his notebook the whole time. She
began to sweat.

"Okay, now, let's get back to who knew Layla would be here
in the library basement with you tonight?" Lucas glared at her,
a certain menace in his eyes that she hadn't seen before. "That
is, besides you, the whole law firm, that professor, the law
clerk, and Mr. Victor Rutledge."

"Are we suspects?" Abby hated the squeak in her voice.

"Any reason you should be suspects?"

Abby shut her mouth, pressing her lips together. She had
already said too much.

Lucas stretched, shook his hand like his wrist was sore, and
focused on Abby once more. "Now, explain to me exactly why
you and Miss Freemont were in the basement of the library
tonight?"

By the time they were done going over everything, not once, not twice but several times, Abby was faint with hunger and thirst and the queasy feeling in her stomach was worse. "Are we done yet?"

"Yep, done for now. I've got your contact info and you have mine." Lucas stood up and folded his notebook shut. "You should go back upstairs to the main library."

Abby popped out of her chair so quickly she was dizzy, but shook it off and hurried toward the stairway to the main floor of the library. She wondered how Victor had fared with Rizzo as she climbed the stairs.

When she opened the door and stepped into the main entrance of the law library, Delphine rushed up and took Abby in her arms and hugged her. "Oh, my poor dear," she whispered. Over Delphine's shoulder, Abby saw Phillip pacing, his head down, his perfect posture gone. Behind him, languishing by the reference desk, Jennifer waited.

What was she doing there? Abby stared at Jennifer.

"Don't worry about the trial brief." Delphine patted Abby's back. "Send me anything new that you wrote last night and I'll get Emmett working on it right away."

The trial brief! Where were the laptops and Layla's backpack? In the chaos of the blood and the police and the associate dean's corralling them up, Abby had forgotten about them.

Abby pushed out of Delphine's hold. "I've got to check downstairs and get our laptops and stuff."

"Surely the police—" Delphine started to say, but Abby was already running back to the basement stairs.

If those two detectives thought that Abby and Victor were behind Layla's disappearance and the bloody mess in the basement bathroom, then Abby was going to have to do something to help Layla while the cops chased down the wrong trail. And she was going to need Victor—even if she did have those inappropriate thoughts about him. But first, she had to see what Layla had hidden in her backpack or saved on a hard drive.

CHAPTER EIGHTEEN

$\mathcal{V}$ictor bridled under the strict questioning by Detective Rizzo and finally snapped out, "Look, I was a Master of Arms in the Navy. If you don't know what that is, it means security and law enforcement. I joined while I was still in high school. I'm no crook."

"Yeah, that's what Nixon said too," the detective replied.

Rizzo gave Victor such a hard look that Victor figured Rizzo had already Googled him, or otherwise learned about the accusations that led to his resignation from the Navy. But Victor wasn't going to be the one who brought that up. He matched Rizzo's hard look with one of his own.

"Just tell me again what you were doing in the library basement." Rizzo poised his pen over his notebook, but kept his eyes on Victor.

"I told you. Studying. I fell asleep. It happens." Even Victor could hear how weak that sounded. But, come on, if he'd been the one who had either killed or kidnapped Layla, why would he have called 9-1-1 and still be hanging around when the cops showed up?

"All right. At least you're consistent." Rizzo jotted some-thing down in his notebook before glancing up at Victor again. "But how'd you get in? The assistant dean told me nobody is allowed in the basement after 9 p.m. unless they have an access card."

Victor pondered the best way to answer this. He didn't want to lie to a police officer, but he didn't want to tell the truth exactly either. "I borrowed an access card." There, that was true. He just wouldn't volunteer anything else.

But Rizzo must have sensed something. "Who'd you borrow the access card from?"

Feeling trapped, Victor said, "Law review."

Rizzo scribbled down far more words than just law review, but he didn't ask any more questions about the access card. No doubt the law enforcement officials were already checking the records to see just who had entered the basement that evening after normal hours since every access card was recorded the moment it was swiped through the scanner.

Switching back to an earlier topic, Rizzo asked, "So who besides you knew Layla Freemont would be working in the library basement tonight?"

"I told you ten times already. I didn't know she was going to be here. I had my phone off because I was in a library and I didn't get her messages until this morning. After I called 9-1-1. I showed you my phone already. And I've told you, I don't know who else would know she was here."

Victor heard somebody running and spun around to see Abby skidding to a stop by the study carrel. Her face was pale, but her eyes were red. He wanted to take her in his arms and comfort her, but Rizzo moved between him and Abby as he stepped over to her.

"Don't touch anything, ma'am." A uniformed officer cut her

off before Rizzo reached her.

"I just want to make sure my laptop and Layla's backpack and laptop are all right. That nobody stole them." Abby glared at the officer and pointed. "That's my laptop. And that's Layla's, in the bright cover. And her backpack."

Rizzo stepped up to the backpack. "Layla's stuff was hidden under a pile of books. You want to explain that?"

Abby's pale face pinked up. "I covered them up when I went to the bathroom, so nobody would steal them." Abby reached toward a laptop, but the detective grabbed her hand.

"Don't touch it. That's evidence now. I'll have the evidence tech bag it up. Her laptop and yours." Rizzo dropped Abby's hand but continued to stand in front of the computers and the backpack.

"Mine? Why would you even consider taking my computer?" Abby stepped forward, getting into Rizzo's private space, her hands on her hips and her chin jutting out. When she spoke, she had a sharp edge in her voice. "I'm a lawyer and I have attorney-client privileged materials on that laptop. Layla is our legal intern. As such she is well within the scope and protection of the rule and she has attorney-client privileged materials on hers too. You're not taking custody of those computers and their privileged files without a warrant and an in-chambers review of the materials in front of a judge."

Victor grinned. He didn't know if Abby knew much about criminal law, but she knew how to stand up for herself.

"So you're obstructing justice now, are you?" Rizzo belted out.

Abby didn't budge. Something in her eyes convinced Victor that Rizzo was going to have to jump through several legal hoops before he ever came close to touching either Abby's laptop or Layla's.

Delphine slid in beside Abby, a protective look on her attractive face. "What's the problem?"

The cops and the lawyers all started arguing, talking at once.

Victor stepped back from the gathering of attorneys and police. They hadn't charged him with anything and his attempts at being helpful and honest didn't seem to be paying off so well. He might as well leave and catch up with Abby as soon as he could later. Idly, he wondered if the law school would cancel classes today.

He climbed the stairs to the main floor of the library. As he crossed the floor toward the exit, he passed a well-dressed, good-looking woman who was hovering near the stairwell door to the basement. She looked up and their eyes met. With a start, he recognized her from the photos in *Architectural Digest.* Mrs. Jennifer Draper.

Knowing it would be rude to simply turn away, Victor nodded. "Good morning." He didn't call her by name but somehow her expression suggested she knew him too.

"The plumber." She spoke in soft tones and with a detached calmness that belied the situation.

How would she know? Victor didn't look away, but he also didn't speak.

"Security cameras." Jennifer spoke with an air of aloofness and cut her eyes back to the stairs as if she'd already lost interest.

"Yes, ma'am." Victor stepped away from her, hoping she would say no more. He had no particular interest in explaining anything about his aborted toilet repairs to Detective Rizzo.

When the woman said nothing further, Victor made for the exit as quickly as he could without appearing to be running.

CHAPTER NINETEEN

I'm nearly frantic. Neither Abby nor Layla have returned home and the sun is up already. Where can they be? At least the would-be burglar never returned, but still something is terribly amiss.

I have paced the house, checking every door and every window for a way out so that I might try to find them. But Abby keeps things locked and secure. I cannot escape. When that nice gentleman with the sandy hair, Victor, came to the door earlier in the evening, I did try to communicate to him the urgency of finding Abby and Layla. But the man simply doesn't understand cat language. And people consider us "dumb animals." Even the dullest of cats and stupidest of dogs can understand people language.

Ruminating on the shortcomings of bipeds will do no good, I tell myself, and sniff around the windows one more time. Just as I'm scratching, rather futilely I might add, on the glass pane of a back window, the front door opens. I hear voices and dash to the front, and cry out with relief. Abby is home.

And Victor is with her.

I run to them, demanding to know what is going on. Where is Layla?

What is wrong? It wouldn't take a detective to tell they are both upset. Abby looks as if she's been crying. My head-butting her leg brings only an absent-minded pat and her assuring me she will feed me in a moment.

For once I do not want food—well, maybe some more of that poached cod at some near future date. Now, what I want is information. Turning to Victor, I ask him what is going on in my clear cat voice.

He bends down and rubs the top of my head, but doesn't answer me. I see he hasn't learned a thing about cat language since last night. I turn back to Abby, raising my voice to a querulous level.

"You're not really planning on going to work?" Victor's tone as he addresses Abby has a worried sound. Something has happened, something bad.

"I have to. I'm just going to take a quick shower, grab some coffee and a boiled egg, and go. Delphine and Phillip are expecting me."

I meow at them again, more insistently than ever.

"Okay, I'll feed the cat," he says, giving me another quick pat on the head.

"Should we look through Layla's things?" Abby edges close to Victor and I can see there's a growing bond between them. "I mean, that horrible police detective didn't order me not to..."

At the word police, my ears go back and my tail starts twitching. I meow ferociously and head butt Abby. She bends down and scoops me up in her arms. "You poor thing. You're worried about Layla, aren't you?"

"He's just hungry," Victor says.

But Abby understands me. I rub my face against hers and purr. Then as clear as I can in cat-language, I ask her about Layla.

"She's been hurt. Or...maybe killed. Or kidnapped." Abby starts to cry. I raise my paws to her cheeks, nails carefully retracted, and try to offer comfort. Yet I can't help but think: I told you so. You and Layla

were barmy to go into a basement alone at night when someone was definitely threatening Layla.

Victor moves closer and puts an arm around Abby. He wants to comfort her too. I know he's a good chap even if he's too dense to understand me.

A second or two into our group hug, Victor pulls away. "You shower, I'll look through her belongings, but first, let me feed the cat and put some coffee on." A man of action, I think, and approve.

Abby thanks him and heads to the bathroom.

I trail Victor, meowing in distinctive syllables as if he might still somehow learn to listen to me. What I want him to see is the one posh gold earring I found earlier. I can't say why I know, but now that Layla is missing, I'm thinking this earring is somehow a clue.

Victor prowls through Layla's carryall, taking an interest in the plastic bag of pink flash drives. I edge up between him and the luggage and meow in his face to get his attention. As he shoves the plastic bag with the flash drives into his pocket, I dig out the push-up bra with the hidden silk purse with the earring inside the padding. I pull at the padding until I free the tiny purse. With new urgency, I paw at it until the earring falls out. I tell Victor in plaintive tones that this is not Layla's style but the care with which she has hidden it makes it important.

He turns it over in his hand and reads the inscription. "Love." He squints and studies it closely. "Not Layla's look. She wouldn't be caught dead in anything with a pearl."

Exactly, I meow back. Now he's learning to listen to me.

Victor mutters something about asking somebody about this and slips the earring into the pocket on his plaid button-down shirt. Then he starts flipping through Layla's books. No need to do that, I try to tell him, as the doorbell rings. I race out to the front just as Abby reaches the door.

Abby presses her eye to the peep hole. "Damn." It's not like her to cuss and I press up against her as she says, "Police."

"Let me." Victor doesn't wait for an answer and opens the door. An older man wearing a bad suit and looking as if he's suffering from distemper is standing there with an armed, uniformed officer.

"Ah, Detective Rizzo." Victor doesn't step back or invite him in.

"I have a warrant to look through Layla's things. And to search any and all computers and laptops." He yanks the door open wide and pushes his way in just as Abby shouts out, "Don't let the cat out."

Too late.

I sprint for the freedom of the great outdoors. My job in the house —leading Victor to the earring—is done and I don't fancy being cooped up inside another day when I could be out looking for ways to help Layla.

CHAPTER TWENTY

*a*bby's head ached, almost like a hangover though she hadn't drunk any alcohol in ages. She and Layla never even got to drink that bottle of expensive wine like Layla had wanted to do. Thinking about that made Abby want to cry again.

It was nearly noon, she was stuck at the law office, and she hadn't managed to accomplish anything except dodge questions from curious interns and associates. At least the police and their search warrants were out of her house, taking with them some of Layla's belongings, and, over her loud hand-waving protests, Abby's own PC and laptop. Despite her best efforts, she couldn't defeat their search warrant.

Not only had the detectives taken her computers, they'd let Trouble escape. But Abby knew Trouble would come home. He was a very smart cat. Besides, Victor promised to look for him.

Ah, Victor.

Abby sighed. Nice, smart, handsome, and he also loved cats —and aquariums. For a dreamy moment, she remembered the way his hair hung across his forehead in his eyes like a kid who needed a haircut, and how well muscled his arms were. A little boy's charm and a grown man's body. Abby felt a strange tingling just thinking about Victor, and her face flushed.

Stop it, she told herself. Layla might be dead or dying and here she was, having lustful thoughts about the woman's boyfriend. Do something useful, she ordered herself.

Abby stood up and headed toward the little cubbyhole office Emmett used while he was at the law office. She wanted to question him about what he might have seen or heard at the law school. The police had already grilled him, but they seemed to be so hung up on blaming her or Victor, she frankly didn't trust them and wanted to talk to Emmett herself. She also needed to check on Delphine's brief, which Emmett was now finishing. She knocked at his door and waited. When nobody answered, she cracked open the door and looked in. Nobody. The office looked strangely bare. Abby backed out and headed instead to Layla's old office. Maybe the police missed something when they'd searched it.

Since Abby didn't expect anyone to be in Layla's office, she barged in without knocking. Emmett was sitting at Layla's desk, a laptop opened in front of him and old law books stacked here and there about him.

"Hi," Emmett chirped out, sounding way too chipper. "I was just about to bring this to you." He waved a few sheets of paper at her. "The rest of it should be ready soon." Behind him, a printer rumbled as it pushed sheets of paper out into a tray.

"What are you doing in here?" Abby was angry that Emmett had just taken over Layla's spot in the law firm.

"Working." Emmett gave her a blank look. Then, as he continued to stare at Abby, his eyes narrowed. "More specifically, working on a project that you and Layla failed to finish on time."

Abby jerked back, astonished at the law clerk's boldness. He'd never been rude to her before. Rather, he'd been polite in that ingratiating way he had. She inhaled slow and deep so that she wouldn't give voice to her intensifying anger.

"This is Layla's office." She stopped short of ordering him out of it.

"And Layla is not here, is she?" Emmett's expression briefly shifted into something Abby read as a kind of snide self-satisfaction. But then the nastiness disappeared, replaced so quickly with Emmett's usual eager-to-please half-smile that Abby wondered if she had imagined the whole snide look.

"Layla's office is so much larger than my own and I needed space to spread out the case books while I finished Delphine's trial brief." Emmett swept his hand at the piles of old law books. "Of course, my part of the trial brief is not nearly as excellent as your sections, but I've worked very hard on it, even skipping my classes."

He actually had the nerve to smile. For a brief second, Abby wanted to slap him. But she was also relieved that Emmett was back to just being Emmett. She told herself she had imagined that nasty look on his face.

"How many more pages need to print?"

"About ten."

"Okay." She paused, thinking of the best approach to question him about anything he'd heard or seen last night at the law school.

But before she started her interrogation, Emmett spoke. "I think I should tell you something. It's important."

"About Layla?"

"Yes. I've already told the detectives. They gave me quite

the grilling earlier. Since you told them I was in the library basement, they naturally assume I knew something about Layla's disappearance." Emmett studied Abby as he spoke in a way that made her nervous somehow.

"What?" she asked.

"That man, Victor Rutledge."

"What about him?"

"After you and I spoke in the library basement, I went upstairs to work, and I caught him breaking into Layla's office at the law review suite. He stole a file out of Layla's cabinet. I looked, and what's missing is the folder on oil and gas exploration. We had a number of articles submitted as that's a hot topic with the push toward more offshore drilling." Emmett leaned forward in the desk chair like he was imparting secrets. "He claimed Layla sent him for the file, but I don't think so. After he left, I checked the door carefully and could see where it'd been tinkered with. And I didn't see that he had a key at all."

Stunned, Abby's first reaction was to deny that Victor would break into Layla's office. He probably was picking up something for Layla.

But even as she thought that, conflicting ideas shot through her head. Victor claimed he didn't know Layla was at the law school that night. So why would he be bringing her an article on oil and gas exploration? Plus, if Layla did need the file, she could have gone to her office and gotten it herself.

Abby realized Emmett was staring at her as if trying to analyze her response. She didn't want to give him the satisfaction of knowing he'd upset her, so she put on her best poker face. "All right. Thank you for sharing. Now, tell me what else you saw and heard last night." She tried to make it sound like an order.

Emmett glared at Abby, that snide look back in place. "You sent me away. Remember? How could I see anything if you ordered me to leave even after Layla had called me and specifically requested I meet you both in the basement?" He hesitated as if weighing his next words. "The two detectives thought that was very interesting, too. That you ordered me to leave."

Great, Abby thought. Now he's made Victor and me both more suspicious in the eyes of the police.

Abby decided her best reaction was no reaction to the implied accusation. But she wanted to leave with the upper hand. "Bring me the trial brief as soon as it finishes printing. And out of respect for Layla, please clear out your things and leave her office when you finish." She didn't wait for a reply.

Abby hurried to her own office, her head pounding now as she thought things through, or tried to do so.

Emmett was casting suspicions on her and Victor and he was acting predatory about Layla's office. Everyone knew he desperately wanted to be hired as an associate at the law firm. Yet Delphine had confided that Layla had a lock on that position and the firm would be hiring only one associate this year. Emmett probably knew that or at least suspected it. Also, Emmett had been right there in the law library basement not long before Layla disappeared. Maybe he hadn't left as soon as he'd said he had or maybe he'd returned.

But did ambitious, competitive law students kill other students to get a coveted job?

Surely not.

And Victor? What was he up to if he had broken into Layla's office at the law school?

Abby hated to admit her attraction to Victor because it felt so wrong given the circumstances. But worse than that, what if

Victor were a...a what? A burglar? A killer? A kidnapper? But if
he had killed Layla, wouldn't he have been drenched in blood?
Wouldn't he have run away?

All of which brought her back to thinking about Layla.
Poor Layla. Injured, without her insulin, and no doubt terri-
fied. That is, if she wasn't dead.

As Abby trudged back to her office, her head pounded with
renewed vigor. She fantasized about popping two ibuprofens
and going home. Maybe as soon as she'd reviewed that damn
trial brief Emmett was finishing, she could escape, find Trouble, and start looking for Layla. She made a turn in the hallway
and saw Delphine standing right outside her own office door.

"Have you seen or heard anything from Jennifer?" Without
offering any greeting, Delphine spoke in her husky, yet penetrating voice, the one that was so effective on cross examination that witnesses often blurted out things they never meant
to admit.

"No. Just at the law school this morning."

"Phillip drove her home from the law school, but she's not
answering her cell." Delphine frowned. "Probably taking a
beauty nap or getting a manicure."

As Abby watched, Delphine's frown turned to a grimace,
tension radiating off her. "Phillip wants her to go with me to
the airport to pick up Layla's parents."

Oh, please, Abby thought, don't ask me to go with you.

"I've got enough work—real work—to do around here
without having to play fetch for Phillip, but—" Delphine
suddenly stopped, as if she realized she was talking to an
associate in a way she should not be doing.

"Oh the hell with it. I don't need her anyway." With that,
Delphine stomped off down the hallway in her
three-inch heels.

Abby let out a whoosh of relief. But as she stepped inside the shelter of her office, she flashed back to Jennifer at her door last night, desperate to see Layla. Maybe she'd better call Detective Kelly and tell him about that visit after all—even if it meant breaking her promise to Layla not to tell.

CHAPTER TWENTY-ONE

*T*he view from the back of Detective Rizzo's unmarked car is illustrative as he whips his vehicle in and out of traffic, but not nearly as much as listening to his patter. There's another man riding with him. Judging from their exchanges, this younger biped is Rizzo's partner, someone called Lucas. In contrast to Rizzo, Lucas appears to be a decent chap, while Rizzo is peevish. Still, it was considerate of the grumpy detective to have left his window down when he parked in Abby's driveway so that I could hop in after he let me out her door. What better way to learn what the bobbies are up to in their search for Layla than riding along with them?

"I'm telling you Victor's our man." Rizzo says this with an angry conviction, though it sounds daft to me. "That business of his getting kicked out of the Navy ought to tell us something about his character. And he was in that basement for no good reason with an access card he stole out of Layla's office."

Kicked out of the Navy? I ease forward to hear better, but am careful not to let them see me.

"Navy thing doesn't mean much," Lucas says. "He wasn't convicted of anything. He just resigned."

"Why's a career man resign before his twenty years? Especially when he's been accused of—" Rizzo slams on his brakes and pulls the car into a fire lane and parks. "Do you see what I see?"

I look where Rizzo is pointing. Down the street from where Rizzo has parked is an alley.

Not just any alley, but the one behind Abby's law firm. More precisely, the alley where Layla was mugged.

And, stooped over, nosing around in that very same alley, is Victor.

"Speak of the devil." Rizzo sounds proud of himself. I must concede the man has excellent eyesight, especially for a biped of his age.

"Let me go sneak up on him. See what he's up to." Lucas cracks the car door and waits for Rizzo to answer.

"Yeah, you do that. I'm going inside and have another go at that Emmett fellow. He knows more than he's saying." Rizzo gets out, followed by Lucas.

Once outside the vehicle, Rizzo locks the doors. To my dismay, all of the windows are up. It's easy enough for me to unlock the car with a click of the button, but I cannot physically push the doors open. I need a biped for that.

Putting aside my concern about the heavy doors, I explore inside the vehicle. Too bad each man took his notebook with him, but they might have left something else of interest behind.

I search, sniff, and scratch about, but find nothing that even hints at what they might know about Victor or Layla. And now I'm trapped inside their car. And it's getting hot.

Fine kettle of fish, this is.

VICTOR STEPPED CAUTIOUSLY AROUND in the alley behind the law office building.

He didn't know what he was looking for exactly, but he didn't believe for one half second that Layla's mugging was random coincidence. Somehow he doubted Rizzo and that other fellow, Lucas Kelly, would bother to double check, especially since Rizzo acted convinced that Victor was the guilty party in Layla's disappearance.

Bending down in the dirt and debris in the alley, he poked through the trash with his fingers, thinking as he did that someone should clean the area if law firm employees used the alley.

"They say a crook always returns to the scene of the crime."

Victor's head popped up. How in the world had anyone been able to sneak up on him like that?

Lucas Kelly stood in the shadows, staring right at Victor with the slight trace of a grin.

Ignoring the possibility that Lucas was suggesting Victor was the criminal returning to the spot, Victor nodded. "I had that thought myself."

Lucas took a step closer to Victor on his soft-tread shoes. As if reading Victor's mind, he said, "Hush Puppies and a dad who worked the night shift. I've learned to walk as quiet as a Mohican. I can sneak up on anybody."

"You got me." Victor held up his hands in mock surrender.

"Just so you know, we aren't stupid." Lucas pressed close to Victor, still studying his face. "We've got surveillance in this alley. And we've been questioning the homeless, looking for a man with a hoodie, bad hygiene, and cat scratches on his face."

Victor nodded, assessing Lucas' tone of voice. Neutral, not friendly but not hostile like Rizzo. He decided to push it. "What'd you find out about the mugger? Was anyone able to identify him? Did you check at the homeless shelter or the Lincoln Center to see if they'd treated anyone with cat scratches?"

"You were a Master at Arms in the Navy, I understand, and you've done your own fair share of detective work," Lucas said. "So you know not to mess with another agency's active investigation. Too many cooks spoil the soup, and all that."

"I can't just do nothing. If Layla's still alive, she's wounded. Probably badly from all the blood at the scene. And she needs her insulin. Time is critical."

"Yes, we understand that. Time is always critical in a kidnapping." When Victor didn't reply, Lucas said, "You're a civilian now. Go home. Let us do our job."

Victor stepped away from the back door and headed toward his truck. He didn't need to turn around to know Lucas was watching him. But if Lucas thought he was going home and do nothing, the man wasn't much of a detective.

To my relief, I see Victor trotting down the sidewalk, heading toward the police car. Okay, this is going to be fun. With a quick leap, and a press of the right switch, I turn the siren on. Victor spins around to stare at the vehicle—along with several others. I jump up on the top of the headrest, press my face against the window, and scratch the glass.

For once Victor understands exactly what to do. In a cracking good move, he races to the car, tries the door, finds it's unlocked—thanks to my earlier actions—and opens it. I hop out, give him a very hasty leg rub, and take off at a fast clip. I doubt Rizzo and Kelly will be amused about the siren, so I think it best that Victor and I both be gone in case the detectives become mad as a bag of wet ferrets over the whole escapade.

VICTOR AND TROUBLE raced down the sidewalk, away from the empty patrol car. The siren was still blaring, and no doubt

Rizzo and Lucas would be hot-footing it back to their vehicle. Victor turned a corner and ducked down a narrow side street, Trouble keeping pace beside him. The cat looked supremely proud of himself, and Victor laughed.

"So that's where you've been." Victor didn't pause to pet the cat as he hurried. He didn't want Lucas accusing him of turning on the siren, and no one would believe the cat did it. Victor didn't quite believe that himself.

Once they were out of range of the detectives, Victor bent down and petted Trouble. "You know I looked all over the neighborhood for you. And there you were, cruising with Rizzo and Kelly." He should be fussing at the cat, but instead he found he was glad for Trouble's company. And he was still amazed and amused at Trouble for somehow turning the siren on.

Trouble purred, and looked at Victor with something like a grin.

"All right, buddy, you're with me now, but let me tell Abby I've got you safe and sound. Then into my house for you until Abby can come get you. No more wandering around."

CHAPTER TWENTY-TWO

"*J*ust a quick visit. Nothing important." Abby didn't drop her gaze as Detective Kelly studied her with an intense, cross-examination glare. She had called him about Jennifer's visit, and he had rushed right over to the law firm.

"Did you hear what they said? If not, how do you know it wasn't important?" The detective pushed an inch closer to Abby, invading her personal space to the point she stepped back from him.

"I think you'd have to ask Jennifer. I really don't know." Abby stopped retreating and squared her shoulders, but all she wanted to do was go home and develop a plan for finding Layla —with Victor's help, of course.

"When exactly was this visit?" The man wasn't letting go.

Abby frowned, trying to remember exactly. "Around 8:30 or so."

"The night Layla disappeared?"

"Yes."

Detective Kelly narrowed his eyes as if puzzling through the information or preparing for further cross-examination. "And you didn't tell me about this because...why?"

Abby gave up any pretense of having just forgotten. "I promised Layla I wouldn't tell."

The detective scribbled something in his notebook and stared once more at Abby. "Anything else you forgot...or promised not to tell?"

"No. Really. Detective Kelly, that's all." Abby felt embarrassed and ashamed. She'd broken a promise, and she'd probably made herself look more like a suspect than before.

"Call me Lucas." He tapped his pen against the notebook, a slight frown on his face. "You wouldn't happen to know Layla's password on Facebook? Or her email?"

"Of course not." Abby frowned. Hadn't she mentioned several times that she and Layla were not close friends?

The office door opened a crack. "Abby?"

She recognized the sweet voice of Phillip's administrative assistant, Mary, a lovely older woman with a gentle grandmotherly look and voice, but with a memory just short of Guinness Book of Records.

Before Abby even answered the woman, Mary said—in a tone of voice clearly an order—"Mr. Draper wants to see you. Right now."

Sighing, Abby nodded at Lucas.

"We're done, for now," the detective said.

A moment later, Abby followed Mary down the hallway to Phillip's palatial office with its classic men's club decor. Abby stopped the moment her feet hit the edge of the thick Persian rug. She caught herself just before she gasped at Phillip. His head was bowed, his tie was askew, and his shoulders slumped. When Mary announced Abby—as if Phillip somehow hadn't heard them come in—he looked up. His face was drawn and his eyes raw.

Abby had never seen him look anything but polished and assured.

"What am I going to do?" He looked at Abby as if sincerely seeking an answer, but she didn't understand the question.

Mary pulled a carafe out of the small refrigerator and poured Phillip a glass of something clear. She didn't offer Abby any. Mineral water or vodka, the liquid could have been either.

Phillip sipped.

Mary turned to Abby and explained. "Miss Freemont's parents were scheduled to fly in today, but something came up at his office." She paused, her expression a thinly disguised look of disgust. "They're not coming."

"They're not coming to—" Abby stopped before she said something rude about Layla's parents. Victor had told her that Layla hadn't been close to either her mother or father. But still, this was their daughter and she'd been kidnapped or worse.

"Thank you, Mary." Phillip set his glass down and wiped his mouth with the back of his hand—a gesture Abby couldn't imagine her refined, appearance-conscious employer making.

Taking the hint, Mary left, closing the door gently behind her.

"I need your help." Phillip looked at Abby with desperation in his eyes. "Since you and Layla are such close friends, perhaps she told you something, anything that might help us find her." His voice had a slight quiver in it.

Abby shook her head. "Layla and I weren't that close. It was just that a week or two in a hotel while they fixed her apartment sounded so unpleasant and I had a spare bedroom. It was just a spur of the moment thing that I invited her to—"

"So, she didn't confide in you?"

"No, sir. I'm afraid I don't know anything helpful about Layla. I didn't even know she came from a wealthy family until this morning."

Phillip leaned back in his chair and closed his eyes.

Abby waited.

Just as it seemed Phillip had forgotten she was there, he spoke. "Her father and I were friends growing up and as young men. We're still friends. As boys, both of us were...." He paused, opened his eyes, and sipped again from the clear liquid. "Well, you aren't interested in my boyhood reminiscences."

Actually, Abby was. This was all news to her that Layla's father and Phillip had a strong connection. Perhaps that explained why Layla had—what was Delphine's word?—a "lock" on being hired as an associate. Emmett had never had a chance of being hired if that was the case.

But another thought pushed its way into Abby's head. Victor said Abby's father was in the oil industry in Houston. Phillip and Abby were working with Phillip's oil company client on something about offshore drilling. Even Pam Bondi and the governor had mentioned something about offshore oil drilling.

Had Layla learned something she wasn't supposed to know about oil and gas exploration in Florida? Could it in some way be connected to her father's business?

"I'd like to hear about you and Layla's family," Abby said, trying to sound kind-hearted instead of rabidly curious.

Phillip gave her a feeble smile. She could see he was trying to pull himself together into the polished, controlled man she'd always known.

"Sometime when this ordeal is over, you, Layla, Jennifer,

and I will all go for a quiet dinner and I'll regale you all with stories of her father and me when we were just wild young fellows." He hesitated, as if reluctant to speak further.

"I'd like that, sir."

Phillip murmured, "Layla is my goddaughter. I can't let anything happen to her."

"Your goddaughter?" Abby tried to stifle the surprise in her voice.

"I shouldn't have told you that. I need to keep that a secret. You understand? The others would think there is favoritism involved with her position at the firm." Phillip gave Abby a penetrating look.

"Yes sir, it's our secret."

"Good then. I'll trust you." Once more Phillip sipped from the clear liquid Mary had poured him. "As you know, Jennifer and I were only blessed with our sons. Layla's become like a real daughter to me. And...sadly, her own parents didn't care much about her. They preferred their boys. They found her... defective. Because of the diabetes, and they —" Phillip stopped talking as he surely realized he shouldn't be telling all this to Abby. He folded his arms across his chest and gave her a curt look.

Abby wanted to ask more, but she read his body language and kept quiet.

"Well now, if you don't know anything that will help us find Layla, I guess we better get back to work." Phillip's voice had lost its earlier quiver.

Realizing he was dismissing her, Abby said her goodbyes and left.

As she stood in the hallway outside his door, she wondered what the odds were of finding any of Layla's files. If she only had Layla's laptop, but the police had succeeded in getting a warrant and seizing it.

Ah, but Layla saved everything to her pink flash drives. She'd been compulsive about it. All Abby had to do was find Layla's stash of flash drives.

How hard could that be?

CHAPTER TWENTY-THREE

*V*ictor drove cautiously. It would never do to get caught in a traffic stop reeking of beer and dressed like a homeless man, especially since he'd stuffed his best switchblade in his pocket for protection. He was satisfied with his disguise—dirty yard-work clothes and an old, smelly hoodie, topped off by splashing beer over his undershirt and squishing enough in his mouth that he smelled like he'd been doing some serious drinking. He'd stuffed his other pocket with ten dollar bills.

Of course, the dang cat had escaped while Victor had been perfecting his homeless person disguise, but the animal had proven he was street savvy. No doubt by now, Trouble was back at Abby's lapping up cream. Victor vowed not to worry about Trouble, but to find the man who had mugged Layla.

Once near the homeless shelter in west Tallahassee, Victor parked several blocks away so he could wander among the raggedy men and women who roamed the streets near the shelter. The first man he approached was sitting on a curb, drinking from a soft drink can, and watching Victor approach with slitted, hostile eyes.

"Hey." Victor reminded himself to slur his words. "I'm ... looking for a...my buddy. Got himself scratched up by a cat, real bad. I owe him some money."

"Your buddy got a name?"

"Yeah, but I...we were drinking. I forget."

The man on the curb snorted and waved Victor off.

Victor approached several others, improving his questions as he went. But no one on the street knew anything about a homeless man with cat scratches on his face. Not ready to quit, Victor walked inside the shelter. Trying to blend in, he asked several others residents of the shelter. He even gave away a few of the tens, only to get answers that were useless.

Disappointed, he finally gave up and started back toward where he'd parked. Night was coming on, and the darkness only made Victor feel more desperate. How long could Layla last without her insulin? Had she already bled out from whatever wounds she'd endured? Or, had she simply been murdered there in the library basement and her body removed?

He was almost to his truck when he heard heavy footsteps approaching. Victor turned to the sound and saw a large man jogging toward him. Behind him, a smaller man huffed to keep up. Instinctively Victor reached down into his pocket for the switchblade, closing his fingers around the handle but keeping his hand inside the pocket. He stood still, allowing the two men to reach him.

"What you want with Dogman?" The shorter man's voice was demanding and hostile.

"Praise be to the Lord," the larger man said. "They call me Preacher." His voice was pleasant. "Some of the brethren back at the shelter told me you were looking for an acquaintance of ours. Might we ask the nature of your concern?"

"I owe him some money."

The little man pushed in front of Preacher and advanced on Victor. "You ain't fooling me. You ain't no homeless."

Victor eased his fingers out his pocket. He sensed no danger from either man. For the moment, he wondered if the truth would work best. Often, it did.

"If Dogman is who I'm looking for, he mugged my friend the night before last, and now she's been kidnapped. I want to ask him about the mugging. She's got diabetes and I've got to find her quick or she'll die."

"Dogman ain't no mugger and he damn sure ain't no kidnapper. Man used to be a shoes salesman till the recession and drinking done him in." The smaller man shook his head.

"As my friend here gave witness to, Dogman is not a bad person." Preacher rocked back on his heels and raised his head to the night sky as if in prayer. Then he lowered his head until he stared Victor right in his eyes. "Dogman wouldn't hurt your friend and he most assuredly wouldn't kidnap her. His fondness for drink and street drugs was his undoing."

"I still need to find him." Victor reached into his pocket intending to pull out his last two ten-dollar bills. The gesture set off the shorter of the two men, and he jumped back and pulled out his own switchblade.

"Just wanted to offer you this for your time." Victor pulled the bills free of his pocket with care and thrust the money at the men. "And if you'll tell me more about Dogman. You saw scratches on his face?"

Snatching the money with his left hand, the little man never let down his guard or the knife. "Badass scratches. Said he got 'em fighting with an old alley cat. That was yesterday morning. He ain't been around since then. Stays most nights on the street cause the shelter spooks him. I don't know his real name. Call him Dogman cause he used to own him some fancy kind of big dog and he talked about that dog all the time."

"Do you know where he stays? I mean, on the street?"

Preacher eased closer to Victor as if he did not wish to be overheard. "He prefers to spend his days in the park over by the library. By night, he has a spot under a low-hanging bottle-brush tree by a dumpster in the parking lot by the big Methodist Church near the library. Sometimes the good people at the church buy him food and he reads a lot of magazines at the library. But he doesn't have your girl, I can tell you. Man doesn't have any real meanness in him."

Victor figured this was all the info he was likely to get, and he thanked Preacher. For a moment he was sorry he didn't have more money to offer, but handouts wouldn't cure anything. Whatever had brought this man, with his obvious education, to living on the streets wouldn't be solved by a couple of ten-dollar bills.

Victor drove to the library in downtown Tallahassee and parked. He scrambled out of the truck and hurried uphill to the big Methodist Church, eyeing the benches and ground as he walked. The city street lights kept the area lit, if only in a kind of hazy way.

In no time at all, he found the dumpster behind the church in a parking lot half covered by a thick, low hanging bottle-brush tree. The place smelled rank, probably from the garbage in the dumpster. But even with the offensive odor, it would be a good place for urban camping, shaded in the day with good protective cover and out of the eyesight of casual observers.

"Dogman!" Victor kept his voice low and his fingers on his

switchblade still in his pocket. "I know you're here. I just want to talk to you."

Pausing to give the man a chance to come out—or wake up—Victor kept quiet. When no one spoke and he heard nothing, he stepped into the dark shadow of the bottlebrush branches and looked around. Scattered piles of clothes and a large cardboard box suggested someone was living here. Easing into the spot, squinting now that the tree blocked the street-light, he spotted a pizza box half covered by a towel with a dark stain on it. Victor kicked the towel off and nudged the box open. A whole pizza was inside the box, covered with ants and roaches.

Immediately on red alert, Victor stepped back into better light and wished for his flashlight. He edged closer to the dumpster, his eyes darting around for any danger or any sign of Dogman. Sniffing, Victor picked up the scent of far worse than spoiling garbage. "Damn it," he whispered.

He flung open the dumpster lid.

Even in the shadowy light he could see the body of a man only half covered in trash. As he reached for his cell phone, concentrating on the body in the dumpster and his certainty it was Dogman, he let his caution lapse.

Something hard whacked him on the back of his head and he collapsed to the sidewalk, his cell phone spinning out of his hand.

CHAPTER TWENTY-FOUR

*W*hat a lot of tosh this is. Victor has me shut up in his tiny house. You'd think he would understand my keen detective skills are best utilized when I'm not restrained inside locked rooms, but am left to my own considerable resources.

He's in the other room, dressing up in some kinky outfit, when I decide to make my break. It doesn't take me long to find an opened transom over a side door, and, narrow as it is, out I go. Fortunately, I have a keen sense of direction and personal stamina, and I'm off at a run, heading for Abby's house.

No one tries to bother me as I pad along the sidewalk. For a moment, I put aside my pique at Victor for not offering to take me with him—he's sure to botch whatever he's doing without my help—and I think of those nice china bowls of water and nibbles that Abby keeps in the kitchen for me.

Yet, as soon as I reach her house, my keen cat sense tells me something is amiss. Rather than parade up her walkway, I skulk along in the bushes. Nothing is obviously awry in the front of her house, but something is setting off my internal alarms.

I sneak around the side of the house, keeping to the lush bushes, and *poke my nose out to stare at her back door. It's standing wide open. Part of me wants to think she left it open for me, but the woman is not stupid. She would not leave her back door wide open under the circumstances.*

With great care, I check things out. I sniff and catch a whiff of something faint, but familiar. For the briefest of seconds, I hope Layla has returned here. After I stand and inhale deeply trying to snag a stronger scent, I reluctantly decide this is not Layla's smell that's teasing me. Approaching the opened doorway, I sniff again, but still, this tantalizing trace eludes me.

Eyeing the door, I see no evidence of a break-in and Abby has deadbolt locks. Once more, hope that Layla has returned leaps in my heart and I dash into the living room. Where I stop dead in my tracks and stare.

Obviously the would-be burglar from last night returned—and this time he or she managed to get inside. Someone has completely trashed Abby's living room. Her potted plants, which she clearly cherishes, are knocked down and the dirt is scattered about. Worse, the aquarium has been tilted over and someone has tossed the gravel and rocks on the bottom as if looking for something. Aquatic plants have been uprooted from the fish tank and thrown on the floor. I see a couple of small fish on the tile and edge over and sniff. Dead. Abby will be so upset. However, most of the fish are still swimming around in the tank, though half the water has been sloshed out.

As there is nothing I can do to help the surviving fish or the potted plants, my best move is to make sure no one is still lurking in Abby's house. I pad from room to room, discovering each room has been ransacked. In the back bedroom, a window screen is punched out and the window wide open. Someone wanted something bad enough to break in through a window in daylight, and he or she was savage in the search. Layla's room is a complete, horrible mess—even the sheets have been pulled off the bed and her pillows slashed.

Though I neither see nor hear anything that suggests the burglar yet lurks in the house, somehow I feel that the miscreant is still here. I catch a whiff of that tantalizing scent again. This time, the fragrance is strong enough that I can place it—that same spicy fragrance I smelled my first night here when I chased a person around the corner of Abby's house.

Even if the miscreant is still in the house, I can't just hide till Abby returns. I need to find him—or her—and get a good look at this person. Despite my misgivings, I head back toward the kitchen. The refrigerator door is standing open, and I don't want Abby's supply of cod and salmon to spoil. It takes me a bit of effort, but I finally get the door pushed shut by slamming my body sideways against it. Her canisters of flour, rice, and beans have all been poured out and even her sugar bowl has been dumped on her table.

Whoever searched the house missed one thing. My dish of cat food appears untouched. I poke through the dried kibbles with my paw, making sure Abby or Layla didn't hide something in my food. Nothing but cat food. I much prefer fresh fish, but it's been a long and difficult day so far. I take a brief repose to drink and eat before I hurry to Abby's bedroom.

Abby's jewelry is flung about on top of her dresser, and all the drawers have been rudely yanked open, their contents scattered. Just as I start to sniff around, I hear footsteps coming inside the house from the garage. I freeze. The steps are too heavy for Abby or Layla's tread as both women are light and graceful.

These, I decide at once, are a man's footsteps. I back up under the bed, out of sight. Maybe it's Victor? Or the police?

But I hear a drawn-out cuss word in a voice I do not recognize as the footsteps come closer.

And I smell that spicy scent—this time, strong and clear.

. . .

EXHAUSTED, ABBY PULLED into her garage, so fatigued that
steering took extra concentration. She couldn't believe it was
already night and Layla was still missing. Though she'd called
Lucas Kelly six times, she learned absolutely nothing. He'd
assured her they were doing all that could be done and he
would personally call her with any news. The last time she'd
called him, he'd been downright snippy. Well, it wasn't his
insulin-dependent roommate that was missing. That's what
she'd told him in equally snippy tones.

Earlier Abby had searched anywhere at the law firm that
Layla might have stashed her collection of flash drives. The
police had already been through Layla's office, and so, no
doubt, had Emmett when he moved in. Still, Abby had
managed to find one, tucked away in the cubbyhole in the
kitchen where Layla kept her snacks she used to keep her
blood sugar from crashing too low. There in a box of Glucerna
bars, a bright pink flash drive had caught Abby's eye at once.

A quick run-through of the materials on the flash drive
didn't seem the least bit helpful as they were all law review
related. All Abby had really learned was that despite being
outwardly messy—after all, she'd left a flash drive in a box of
food—Layla was fiercely organized with the law review
materials.

Not surprisingly, Layla had been working on a law review
article on the long history of offshore oil exploration in Florida
and the Gulf of Mexico. Yet nothing in the rough and partial
drafts of Layla's article seemed to suggest a reason she should
be kidnapped—or worse. Between Detective Kelly's dismis-
sive, snippy tone and the fact the drive contained only school
work, Abby hadn't bothered to turn it over to the police.

Still, Abby was bringing the flash drive home with her—
along with a laptop she borrowed from the law office. Since

Rizzo still had her PC and laptop, she felt oddly vulnerable without an Internet connection, and Delphine had given her the okay to use one of the firm's. She planned to take another, closer look at Layla's pink flash drive on the borrowed laptop. If she found anything of interest, then she'd call Lucas Kelly —again.

Abby pulled into her garage with a sense of profound relief, turned off her car's engine, and got out, cradling her purse and the borrowed laptop. When she opened the garage door and stepped inside her house, she was surprised when Trouble rushed up to her.

"How'd you get back in?" Victor had assured her that he would keep Trouble at his house until Abby was home. And Victor did not have a key to her house.

Trouble battered her leg with his head, bellowing a distressed sound.

"What's wrong, sweetie?" Abby tried to soothe Trouble, but the cat spun away from her and stared scratching at the door to the garage. He practically yowled.

He wanted out, that was clear enough.

But when Trouble darted back to her, wrapped his paws around her leg, and pulled—yes, pulled—she realized he was trying to make her leave too.

Warily, Abby looked around. The entrance from the garage led through the laundry room and nothing amiss jumped out at her. With Trouble yowling and pawing at her legs, she stepped into the kitchen, flipped on the light, and cried out. The place was a total wreck.

Pulling away from Trouble's paws, she dropped the laptop and her purse on the kitchen table and ran into the living room. "Oh, no, oh, no," she cried out and fell to her knees in front of the two black mollies on the floor. She picked them up and dashed to the aquarium, tilted as it was on its side and half-emptied of its waters. She dipped the two mollies gently in the remaining waters, but they did not revive.

"My mollies, oh no." She felt a tear, then another roll down her cheeks.

Trouble head butted her with some vengeance. He meowed and pawed her, then ran to the front door. As she watched him, she saw with horror that all of her plants had been dumped too. Dirt and exposed roots were everywhere. Still on her knees, Abby looked around at all the damage, anxiety and anger rising in her simultaneously.

Out of the corner of her eye, she saw Trouble dragging something from the kitchen and turned to see what he was doing. Trouble maneuvered her purse toward her. When he had it near her, he pawed it open and kicked out her cell phone.

As upset as she was, Abby could not help but be amazed. Trouble was telling her in no uncertain terms to call 9-1-1. She picked up the cell phone just as Trouble let out a pronounced yowl.

Before she could hit the nine, someone put a big hand on her shoulder.

CHAPTER TWENTY-FIVE

With his eyes shut tight, Victor rubbed his head and moaned.

"Hangover's the least of your troubles," someone said. The voice seemed to hover high over Victor's head, vaguely threatening and yet diffused somehow.

Somebody nudged him in the side with the point of a shoe. "Open your eyes and get up. Now," another voice said. No mistaking the order and tone of voice.

Victor fluttered opened his eyes despite the fact his lids seemed glued together. Two uniformed police were standing over him. He pulled himself up, conscious of the rollicking pain inside his skull, which was compounded by the flashlight one of the cops pointed at his eyes.

"Been drinking, I see. Got into a fight with your buddy, cut him up and dumped him and passed out. That's how I read it," Cop One said to Cop Two.

In a nauseating rush, it all came back to Victor—the ratty clothes, the beer he'd splashed on himself, and, worst of all, the dead man in the dumpster. "It's not what you think." Victor shifted his right hand toward his pocket to reach for his bill-fold and ID, smelling as he did the robust aroma of beer and the stink of the man in the dumpster. Even over the powerful scent of death, the smell of the extra beer someone had poured over him was strong.

"Get your hands up and away from your pocket and put 'em where I can see them." The police officer without the flashlight rested his hand on his Taser.

"I just want to get my ID."

"We looked already. You don't have any ID. But you did have a real fine switchblade, right there by your hand. Had a bit of blood on it too. Want to tell us how that happened?"

Victor inhaled, forcing himself to focus. He didn't panic. He knew he'd eventually establish his identity and that anyone —especially these street cops—could tell the body in the dumpster was not fresh. He'd been set up. That was easy to see. Maybe harder to explain.

"While we're waiting for the detectives and the coroner, you want to tell us about your buddy in the dumpster?" The cop with the flashlight kept it on Victor's face while he spoke.

"No, sir. I don't want to tell you anything except that my name is Victor Rutledge, I'm a third-year law student, and I was a Master of Arms in the Navy. If you call Joe Rizzo or Lucas Kelly, they'll identify me." Victor rubbed his head, feeling a distinct and painful lump. When he brought his hand forward and looked at it in the glare of the officer's flashlight, he saw blood. "I've been injured, hit on the head from behind." Victor held his hand up so the police officer could see the blood.

"We'll see a paramedic looks you over," one of the cops said, his voice a little less guarded.

"For sure, this body's been dead a while," the other office said to his partner.

Ignoring the golden rule of keeping your mouth shut when facing arrest, Victor couldn't help himself. "I've been set up. Bet you got an anonymous phone call directing you here. Right after someone knocked me out."

"How come you're dressed like that? And smell like beer?"

"I was trying to locate that man in the dumpster and—"

"Looks like you found him," the one cop said.

"So, like, you were what? Pretending to be a cop and working undercover or something?" The other cop's tone of voice was sarcastic and snide.

Victor decided to shut up.

A tense moment later, an unmarked car arrived, followed by a long, dark van which Victor assumed was from the coroner's office. He never thought he'd be hoping to see Joe Rizzo again, but he was. At least the detective knew he wasn't a murderous street drunk.

"Well, well, well." A plain-clothes officer who was not Rizzo looked down at Victor. "What have we got here?"

"The man in the dumpster is implicated in the kidnapping of Layla Freemont. It's Joe Rizzo's case." Victor stood up slowly, conscious of the closeness and the glare of both uniform cops, especially the one who earlier had fingered his Taser. "His street name is Dogman. Two nights ago he mugged Ms. Freemont outside the law office of Kirkus and Draper. The next night, she was kidnapped from the basement of the law school."

After giving Victor a hard look, the detective headed over to the dumpster. He slipped on gloves and began poking around. When he turned back to the uniformed cops, he said, "Get the crime techs out here. Call Rizzo and tell him to meet us back at the station." He jerked a thumb at Victor. "Read him his rights and take him in."

"How'd he die?" Victor stepped toward the detective and the dumpster but the two uniformed cops cut him off. One of them said, "Like you don't know."

"Look," Victor said, "I didn't kill that man. He's been dead for some time. I've got a lump on my head where somebody hit me. My wallet with my ID has been stolen. I've been set up and anybody can see that."

The detective shook his head, his expression impassive. "Might could be, son. But those are a lawyer's arguments, and we're police officers with a dead body and a pretty good suspect with a possible murder weapon and no ID." Turning away from Victor, he repeated, "Read him his rights and take him in."

CHAPTER TWENTY-SIX

A man I do not know has his hand on Abby.

Didn't I try to warn her? But, no, she wouldn't listen. Now here she is, in a trashed-out house alone with some man who probably wrecked her house. I am totally prepared to launch myself at this man's face, only something holds me back. Something in the way I can see Abby is not afraid. She knows this man.

Knowing him doesn't mean he isn't dangerous though and I jump on his feet, closer to his face if I need to attack.

He takes his hand off of Abby's shoulder, glances at me with a puzzled look on his face. "You have a cat now too?"

Somewhat off point, I'd say, and I yowl my most menacing sound.

"Yes, he's the one who saved Layla. The night of the mugging." Abby speaks as if the two of them are sharing tea and crumpets.

The man looks at me through oddly serene and somewhat vague eyes. "Oh, yes, now I remember hearing about him." He reaches down and pets me. "Nice looking fellow, isn't he?"

Hello. This is not a Sunday Social. This is a crime scene. This man has been hovering in Layla's bedroom and Abby is home alone with him—except for me. I meow once more in protest and hop from his foot

to the cell phone Abby dropped on the floor when he touched her. I paw
the phone toward her. In my most plaintive meow, I say 9-1-1.

"I was just about to call the police." Abby glances at the man, then
at the phone, as if waiting to see if he protests or something. Once more
I prepare to attack his face—or something else—if he lifts a finger to
hurt her.

"I'd say that's a very good idea." He pauses, looks around the room,
his eyes lighting for a moment on the fish tank. "Would you like for me
to call?"

No! I meow it as clearly as I can.

Abby shakes her head and punches in 9-1-1. She reports a break-in
with extensive property damage and asks that a detective by the name
of Lucas Kelly be notified as this relates to the kidnapping of Layla
Freemont. The 9-1-1 operator asks if anyone is hurt, and Abby says,
"Just the mollies. They're dead."

This sets the 9-1-1 operator off in a tizzy fit until Abby manages to
explain the mollies are fish. Dead fish, as it were. Told to stay on the
line, Abby holds her phone to her ear but paces around the room.

"Maybe we should step outside. We might be damaging evidence.
Crime scene and all that." The man steps toward Abby, his face weary
and benign.

Nonetheless, I hop between him and Abby. I arch my back and hiss.

"Not so friendly, is he?"

"Just protective." Abby gives me a look that seems to say I should
calm down. "Let me introduce you two." With that she picks me up and
carries me toward the man. "Trouble, this is Phillip Draper, the
managing partner at my law firm. Phillip, this is Trouble."

Phillip pets me. But since I had earlier been hiding under Layla's
bed while the man searched through her books and luggage, I'm not
much inclined toward purring. From the street outside, I hear a siren.
Abby and Phillip turn to the sound, and then head toward the front

door. Abby has her arms around me, and I'm eyeing Phillip with a deep sense of concern.

Within minutes, three uniformed police officers bust into the living room. One of them exclaims "Holy crap, what a mess." Another asks if anyone is hurt.

"No person is harmed." Abby sighs heavily, no doubt thinking of the mollies.

I wiggle to get down out of her arms. When she puts me down, I track Phillip, sniffing at his pants, and listening to every word he says as he explains how, why, and when he let himself into Abby's house. I know it all for a lie, but keep quiet. I've learned police officers rarely care to hear my opinions.

While one officer grills Phillip, another searches through the house, and a third separates Abby and questions her.

I'm getting positively bored by the whole thing by the time the young detective arrives.

In short order, Abby brings Lucas Kelly up to date. He nods a lot and takes a few notes. He asks her for the fourteenth time if anything has been stolen and she says for the fourteenth time she doesn't know because it's all such a mess. He asks if he can wander around through the house and she agrees. After giving Phillip what I construe as a nasty look, the detective suggests that Abby and Phillip wait outside.

Though Abby calls me to her, I prance off after Lucas. He stops to pet me and tell me what a good-looking fellow I am and I return the compliment. This friendliness also tells me he doesn't know I'm the one behind the siren and the unlocked doors in Rizzo's vehicle. Lucas heads to Layla's room, with me at his heel.

Once inside, he looks around at the havoc. Rather than add to the mess with his own plundering, he pulls out his cell phone. He punches a number, and then without even a greeting, says, "You'll never believe who's here with Abby. Phillip Draper."

The voice on the other end yells out, "Well, keep him there. I'll be right over. I've got the warrant."

Lucas puts his phone away, rubs me under my chin, and I reward him with a purr. I start to explain about Phillip hiding in Layla's room and lying, and as I meow the whole story, Lucas nods as if he understands.

But, of course, he doesn't.

CHAPTER TWENTY-SEVEN

"*A*m I under arrest or not, Detective Kelly?" Victor sat on a hard metal chair in a tiny room, where he'd been sitting for what seemed like most of the night.

"Not sure about that myself," the young detective said. "Might be we ought to consider that a possibility." He pulled up another chair and sat down.

"Would you at least verify my identification to the arresting detective?"

"Oh, yeah. I've done that. We even found your wallet. Interesting where we found it." Lucas' face had something almost like a grin on it.

Victor knew he was supposed to ask where they found the wallet. But he figured he already knew. "Can I get a Coke or something? I've got a righteous headache from being hit and knocked out."

Lucas stood up and stepped outside. A few minutes later he came back with a can of Coke and a bottle of Advil. "We'll take you to the ER in a few minutes."

Victor swallowed the Advil with a long, cold gulp of the Coke. "Don't think the ER is necessary."

"Well, can't have you suing us." Lucas gave Victor a crooked grin. "So, okay, you didn't ask, but your wallet was found under the dead man."

"Of course it was," Victor said. "Part of the set-up."

"You want to tell me more about that?"

"Not a very good frame, you ask me." Victor ran his fingers through his hair, feeling the lump on his head. "First, no way I lie there unconscious and unnoticed for the twenty-four hours or so that man was dead. Second, I'd be covered in blood if I'd cut that man's throat with my switchblade."

"Blood splatters." Lucas said the word slowly like he was thinking on something deep.

"Blood splatters," Victor repeated. He'd seen them countless times in the Navy and knew a good bit about the science, but what he was remembering now was the blood splatter in the bathroom at the law school. Victor saw a glint in Lucas' expression which said that Lucas knew something important that he himself didn't.

But suddenly Victor could guess. "It wasn't Layla's blood. I mean, at the law school, in the bathroom. It was the homeless guy's, right? The way his neck was sliced."

Lucas nodded. "We're still running the DNA, but right now we can say this much—the blood in the bathroom was the same type as the dead man's. And not the same as Layla's."

Victor let out a sigh of relief. If Layla hadn't been cut, she might still be alive. He jumped up. "Layla's alive and we have to find her before she dies without her insulin."

"Yep." Lucas nodded. "How 'bout this. I drive you over to the ER and on the way, you tell me what you know and what you think you know since you've been sniffing around."

Victor studied the young detective's face. Was he setting some kind of trap? From the first, Rizzo and Lucas had acted like Victor was their lead suspect, and now the man was being almost friendly.

Curbing his suspicions for the moment, Victor nodded. "Deal. But first, did the dead man in the dumpster have cat scratches on his face?"

"Yes. He did."

"He's the one who mugged Layla by the back of the law firm." Victor said it as an established fact, not a question.

"Way we're figuring it too."

As Victor stood there, he added it up—somebody tried to burn Layla's apartment, hired a homeless man to mug her and steal her backpack, and that someone killed the homeless man, probably in the law library basement bathroom, and then he— or she—kidnapped Layla.

And it had something to do with oil and gas exploration.

"Come on, let's get you checked out at the ER." Lucas put out a hand as if to guide Victor.

As they left the interrogation room, Lucas steered him down a hallway toward an exit door. Before they left the police station, Detective Rizzo crossed in Victor's line of vision, his arm on Phillip Draper's as he led him. Phillip had handcuffs on his wrists and a deer-in-the-headlights look on his face. Victor skidded to a stop as Phillip and Rizzo passed. Phillip looked up at Victor and without missing a step said, "I did not hurt that girl."

"Oh, yeah," Lucas paused, flicking his eyes back and forth between Victor and Philip. "I reckon I should tell you about earlier tonight. Somebody broke into your friend Abby's house and wrecked it. Searching for something. We caught Phillip there, red-handed, with Abby."

"Abby? Is she hurt?" Victor's heart thumped in his chest.

"She's fine. Nobody was hurt except her fish."

"You sure she's all right?" Then, he felt a pang for Abby because he knew she treasured the fish.

"Saw her myself. She's shook up but not harmed."

Victor nodded, his fear for Abby relieved as he walked beside Lucas. He felt terrible about Abby's fish. The whole aquarium, he wondered? He started to ask, but Lucas had his chin thrust out and his lips were a taut, narrow line in his face. Victor figured the young detective was probably not in the mood to discuss tropical fish.

As Victor stepped along toward the fresh, hot outside air, suddenly he wanted to be with Abby more than he wanted his head to stop hurting. He needed to be sure that she was all right and to comfort her, to hold her, to protect her.

And, damn it all, he wanted to kiss her.

He inhaled deeply, making Lucas glance at him with a tired, yet puzzled look. Victor stopped walking as that understanding hit him like a hard-thrown football in the chest—he wanted Abby.

It wasn't just how darn cute she was. He'd seen her character clearly in the last two days and knew she was a strong, loving woman. And smart. And loyal.

He almost laughed out loud at himself. What a hell of time to start falling in love—a dead man, a bloody bathroom, and his best friend kidnapped or murdered. But there you had it, he had to admit. He'd fallen for the pretty redhead.

Fallen hard.

CHAPTER TWENTY-EIGHT

I purr and try to comfort her, but to little avail. Poor Abby. She's trying hard not to cry, but I can see how upset she is. She pets me, wipes her eyes, and stands up from the restored aquarium —minus those little black fish she inexplicably adored.

"What a mess." Abby picks up a few scattered things in the living room, but it doesn't really make any improvement.

I glance over at the clock on the mantel. It's an hour past midnight, and she should go to bed and sleep. It's been hours since that young detective and the old grumpy one arrested Phillip and hauled him out of her house. She'd promptly called somebody called Delphine and told her about Phillip's arrest, and then ran randomly about trying to clean up the disarray in her house. She simply will not try to rest. I meow at her and pad toward the bedroom, but when I turn around, she's still standing in the living room.

"Phillip would never hurt Layla. I don't care what those detectives think." Abby looks right at me when she says that as if seeking my agreement. But I don't know. I can't trust the man. It's not just his aftershave scent that I recognized from the backyard spying my first *day, but the fact he was lurking around inside Abby's house without being invited in.*

Given my own suspicions, I wasn't surprised at all when that rude, older detective came and arrested Phillip—though I first thought it was just for breaking and entering, not for murder or kidnapping.

"Delphine can help Phillip. She'll get him out."

I can only guess she is talking to me, though she is now staring out in space, her voice worried. As she walks, she staggers. Drunk with fatigue is not just a biped expression; it's a very real state of being.

In my most persuasive voice, I tell her she needs to rest and once more try to lead her to her bedroom.

But she heads to the kitchen.

I follow. A midnight nosh—oh, okay, a wee-hours-of-the-morning snack—might be a good idea after all. But Abby digs around in the back of a cabinet and pulls out a bottle of vodka. She pours a stiff drink and gulps a big mouthful, sputtering and spitting most of it out. She tries again, with a smaller, slower sip.

Though I've learned bipeds are not usually eager for me to dance around on cabinet tops in kitchens, I jump up and rub against the bottle and meow a warning at Abby. Getting drunk is not going to clean up her house or find Layla.

We need sleep. Both of us.

Failing that, we need sustenance. A nice piece of cod or salmon would make us both think more clearly.

Abby doesn't fuss at me for hopping on the counter. She puts the glass of vodka down, making a face at it. I leap down and race for the refrigerator. She follows me with her eyes, sighs, and shakes her head, making her red hair fluff about her face.

"I don't know what to do, Trouble. How can I help Layla?"

I rub against the refrigerator door.

Abby pushes herself off the cabinet and opens the refrigerator. I stick my nose in to see if any of her broiled salmon is in there, but I do a double take. Layla's store of insulin, which she kept in a blue plastic container in the cheese drawer of the refrigerator, is not there.

I stare at the spot it used to be. Every time Layla or Abby opened the refrigerator to feed me, with my keen observation I had spotted it. I even watched Layla as she removed the blue plastic box a couple of times.

For a moment, I can't remember if her insulin was there when I pushed the refrigerator door shut after finding it open and the kitchen a mess. A lapse, certainly, in my keen observational skills but I should be forgiven under the circumstances.

The important thing now is to alert Abby, who is pulling out some wrapped leftovers and hasn't noticed Layla's insulin is gone.

Risking rebuke yet again, I rise up on my back legs and stick my nose in the refrigerator and meow in a distinctive "look at this" voice as I claw at the cheese drawer. But Abby doesn't scold me for practically hopping into her refrigerator. She's looking where I'm pawing. She understands me. I can tell from her expression.

"Somebody took Layla's insulin," she says as if I were not the one who pointed this out. "I've got to call Lucas."

To her credit, she plops down a clump of cold salmon in a dish for me before she digs out her cell phone and a little card with Detective Lucas Kelly's private number.

A moment later, she breathlessly speaks into her cell phone. "This is Abby...no, listen, this is important. I'm sorry to call so late...yes, yes. But listen, somebody took Layla's insulin from the fridge. They wouldn't do that, would they, unless she's alive?"

My thought exactly. I meow loud in support of Abby's keen deductive reasoning.

I press up to Abby to hear Lucas's response. He's asking her when she noticed, and she says just now. Then she apologizes again for calling so late.

"Not a bother." This time Lucas's voice comes through the cell phone loud and clear. "I'm about two minutes from your front door. Don't touch anything in the refrigerator and I'll be right there."

Abby ends the call and starts a little dance. "Layla is alive, Layla is alive. I know it."

I dance around with her, tangling in her legs.

Layla is alive. Kidnapped, but alive.

Now we just have to find her.

CHAPTER TWENTY-NINE

*a*bby answered the door the moment Lucas knocked. Once he stepped inside, she was surprised to see Victor trudge in after him.

"What are you doing here?" Abby stared at Victor, taking in his grubby clothes, the bandage on his head, and catching a whiff of beer and something vaguely stinky.

Victor didn't answer. Instead, he swept Abby into his arms and hugged her.

For a moment Abby gave in to the embrace. Victor's arms felt strong and protective, and he stroked her hair with tender touches. She wanted to cry and take comfort from him, but as he continued to hold her, she also felt the strange, unbidden urge to kiss him. She thought of Layla and jerked out of Victor's arms.

"Are you all right?" Victor asked.

"I'm okay." But Abby felt a strange trembling in her legs as she stood next to Victor. So, weak in the knees wasn't just a cliché after all. She couldn't take her eyes off him.

Trouble rubbed up against him and purred.

"The blood isn't Layla's." Victor said it in a rush, as if he were afraid Lucas might order him to be quiet. "In the FSU bathroom, I mean. All that blood wasn't her blood type."

"She's alive. I know it." This time it was Abby who hugged Victor, but she dropped out of the embrace quickly. "Somebody took her insulin from the refrigerator. Whoever has her, wants her alive."

Before Victor could react, Lucas pushed in between them. "I've called an evidence tech to come and fingerprint inside the refrigerator. When they were here earlier, they only fingerprinted the outside of the fridge and around in the kitchen. While we wait, let's have a seat and a long discussion."

"Can I offer you some coffee, or some—" Abby stepped toward the kitchen.

"Stay out of the kitchen, ma'am, please."

She jolted to a stop. "I might have already messed up any fingerprints. I mean, I didn't know...I've taken stuff out of the fridge."

"We'll get your prints for elimination purposes, but don't make it worse. Now, let's sit." Lucas moved toward the living room and glanced around as if looking for a spot to sit.

Abby knocked off some piles of things from the couch. No one sat down, so she did. As soon as she settled into the deep softness of the couch, Victor eased down beside her, his thigh rubbing against hers.

Lucas cleared off a chair in front of them and sat. "We need to talk. You two need to tell me whatever it is you haven't told me. Now."

Abby didn't care for the man's bossy tone. He was acting more like Rizzo. But she also wanted to help Layla. And, she wanted to know whatever it was Lucas and Victor could tell her, including why Victor looked like a drunk and had a bandage on his head. She glanced at Victor, but he sat tight-lipped.

"What's going on?" Abby felt frustrated. The two men knew a good deal more than she did. "And why have you got that bandage on your head?"

"Nope, your turn." Lucas gave Abby a hard look. "Spill it."

"I'm not keeping any secrets." Abby shot a hard look right back at Lucas. "Phillip wouldn't kidnap Layla. He adores her. He's friends with her parents from way back. He told me that today." Abby's tone was emphatic, even though she'd told Lucas and Rizzo that same thing earlier when they arrested Phillip.

"Ma'am, I appreciate that you're loyal to your boss," Lucas said. "But he used his FSU access card to enter the library basement at midnight, and again at 2:35 a.m. the night Layla disappeared. A bottle of Valium with his name on it was found under the study carrel where you were sleeping. We found residual Valium in both of the tea bottles left in your carrel. And we found bits of Layla's busted laptop in his trash can."

Victor shook his head. "Damn. No wonder I conked out. I drank one of those teas."

Abby gasped. Someone had drugged her. That's why she had slept so thoroughly, hearing nothing during the night in the library. But Phillip wouldn't drug her. And if he had, he most assuredly wouldn't leave the empty Valium bottle under her feet, and toss Layla's laptop in his own trash. The man was not stupid.

"It's a frame." Abby spoke with absolute conviction. "Phillip Draper is an acutely intelligent man and he would never be so unwise as to use his own ID—twice—to commit a crime and leave evidence behind."

"Smart people panic and do stupid stuff all the time." Lucas sounded smug and satisfied. "Besides, looks like the others all have pretty good alibis for most of the night. Emmett's roommates agree he came in around eleven and stayed put. The professor's neighbors all claim they saw his car parked right in front of his townhouse from around ten, all night till he left for FSU in the morning. And Delphine—" Lucas paused, a tiny glimmer of a grin on his mouth. "Let's just say somebody vouched for her all night too."

Abby had a fleeting moment of curiosity as to who Delphine's alibi was, but Victor started talking, bringing her back to focus.

"So the laptop in Layla's case in the library wasn't hers?" Victor frowned as if connecting the dots.

"Correct. Wasn't her laptop. Somebody switched them out, and busted Layla's up."

Victor wasn't the only one connecting the dots. Abby couldn't rid herself of the thought: Jennifer would have ready access to Phillip's law school access card, his RX bottle, and his trash can.

And Lucas hadn't mentioned that Jennifer had an alibi.

Had anybody interviewed Jennifer?

Abby started to ask Lucas about Jennifer, but Victor shifted on the couch beside her, making his leg press tighter against hers. This time it didn't excite her. It made her mad. Victor knew plenty more than what he'd told her. That much was clear.

Abby glared at Victor, her irritation plain on her face. "Your bandage? The blood in the bathroom, something about a dumpster. Tell me now."

"I'll do the honors." Lucas actually grinned at Abby, which somehow irritated her more. "Victor decided to dress up like he was homeless and find the mugger who assaulted Layla outside the law office."

Abby glanced at Victor. A man of action. Some of her irritation at him began to soften.

"Long story short, he got hit over the head. I took him to the ER. He's fine. But we found the body of a homeless man with what appeared to be cat scratches on his face in a dumpster near the main library. His throat was cut and his blood matches the blood in the law library bathroom."

Abby swept Victor with her eyes, making sure he really was all right.

Lucas turned and glared at Victor. "Your turn. Everything you know. Now."

There was no mistaking the direct order in the detective's words.

Victor slid back on the couch, ran his fingers through his mussed-up hair, and patted the bandage on the back of his head. But he didn't say anything.

CHAPTER THIRTY

*V*ictor felt as if he were wrestling with himself even though he hadn't moved an inch.

He didn't want to endanger Layla further. Even if her kidnapper had taken the insulin to give to her, she was still in peril. And if her kidnapper was Phillip, and Phillip was in jail, she was in worse jeopardy. He wondered for a moment if Rizzo and Lucas had thought of that.

"Maybe you should release Phillip." He tilted toward Abby, though he was talking to Lucas. "If he really did kidnap Layla, he can't be giving her the insulin she needs."

"Maybe you should let me be the cop and you be the helpful witness." Lucas spoke with apparent frustration.

Victor glowered at Lucas. He didn't want to besmirch Layla. Yet he wanted to help. On the one hand, Lucas and Rizzo seemed to be decent detectives. On the other hand, he couldn't help but feel they had misdirected their energies in the crucial early hours of their investigation when they were pursuing him as a suspect.

Trouble crawled into Victor's lap and started purring.

When Victor's hand drifted down to pet the cat, Trouble rose up and tapped Victor's shirt pocket, and meowed plaintively.

"He's trying to tell you something." Abby sounded sincere, though Lucas made a low rumble in the back of his throat like a man who wanted to laugh but knew better.

Victor wasn't sure if Trouble was really trying to tell him something, unless it was "feed me." Besides, his pocket was empty.

Trouble leapt from Victor's lap into Abby's and began to lick her earlobe.

Despite his despair and weariness, Victor grinned at Trouble. He had to appreciate the cat's innate good taste in ears and women. And Victor couldn't deny that he hoped to nibble Abby's earlobe too, and soon.

Abby brushed Trouble away from her ear, and pulled him into her lap. With her hand ruffling the fur on Trouble's head, she focused on Victor. "Maybe you should tell us what you're holding back. We don't know if Layla is hurt or if her kidnapper knows how to give her the insulin."

The sadness in Abby's voice cut right through to Victor's heart. "All right," he said.

Trouble curled around in Abby's lap to look straight at Victor.

"Layla was...I mean this is what I think. I don't know it for sure." Victor hesitated. He didn't want to accuse Layla. Though, really, he had to admit to himself, who really cared about adultery anymore in a general sense. It wasn't like anyone would make Layla wear a scarlet A around her neck.

But still.

Victor couldn't help but flash back to his own brief, strained marriage. His wife had cheated on him, flagrantly as it turned out, and that had destroyed their relationship. Then she'd pulled that stunt on Facebook by taking advantage of a brewing military scandal and making him look like a vengeful creep and ruining his career in the Navy. Maybe that made him ultra-sensitive and judgmental. Could be that having an affair with a married man was no big deal these days.

No, it was a big deal.

He didn't like to think of Layla as a home wrecker. Did anyone even use that term anymore? But even if nobody cared about that, sleeping with your boss to get hired was a sure way to guarantee professional failure. She'd never live that down if it became widely known.

"Victor?" Abby put her hand on his thigh, and the soft weight of her fingers helped him make up his mind. Layla's life was certainly worth more than her reputation.

"I'm pretty sure Layla was having an affair with Phillip."

Beside him, Abby inhaled sharply. But Lucas leaned forward, so close to him their noses practically touched.

"I have a photograph of them...not, you know, doing anything. But the way they are hugging each other is very close. Very." Victor studied his hands in his lap. There was more than that. "And the way she always spoke about him. Like she was in awe of him—in love with him. Her face would light up when she talked about him. Plus, she spent time in his house with him a lot, especially when his wife was at her Junior League meetings."

"You're wrong. And you're jealous." Abby jerked her hand away from Victor's leg.

"Jealous?" Victor repeated. "Why would I be jealous?"

"Why would he be jealous?" Lucas echoed.

Abby cast her eyes back and forth between the two men, her expression puzzled and unhappy. "Because you were...you are Layla's boyfriend."

If Victor hadn't been so upset, he might have laughed. "Me and Layla?" He shook his head. "Abby, we're just friends. Honest. We've never been anything else but friends."

"I can vouch for that," Lucas said, tilting his head toward Abby. "I've asked everybody who knew either one of them."

Abby flushed red, her discomfort obvious.

For a moment, nobody spoke. Victor didn't know how to soften Abby's embarrassment over her mistake.

"I'm sorry I misunderstood." Abby spoke formally, almost as if she might be addressing a jury. "Nonetheless, you're wrong about Phillip and her being lovers. Phillip was her godfather, as well as her mentor, and he was a father figure. Phillip felt a sense of responsibility for her and he understood her own father was...distant. You told me yourself her dad didn't have much to do with her. See, you're misreading the situation."

Lucas cut his eyes over at Abby and seemed poised to ask her something—probably how Abby knew what she'd just said, but Victor spoke, cutting off whatever Lucas might have asked.

"I hope I'm wrong, but I don't think so." Victor wanted Abby to be right. But a goddaughter wasn't a daughter, and that godchild connection might not have stopped an affair between the two of them. And there was more to his theory that Phillip and Layla were lovers. Victor rubbed his hands on his pants and leaned forward to tell them the rest.

"Layla knew Phillip was trying to lure the governor and the attorney general into hiring the law firm for some kind of deal with offshore oil drilling. I really don't know the specifics. She was very closemouthed about her work with Phillip and the law firm, but I overheard some things when she was on the phone."

Abby nodded. "Yes, the firm—Phillip and Delphine at least —were actively courting the governor and the attorney general. I gave them a tour of the offices while Phillip gave them a sales pitch. He definitely emphasized our expertise in off-shore drilling."

"Was Layla part of that tour and sales pitch?" Lucas asked, perched at the edge of his chair.

"At first." Abby hesitated as if thinking over her next words carefully. "Delphine took Layla away from the governor and the attorney general."

"Why?"

"Delphine doesn't like Layla and I think—just me guessing really—that Delphine thought Layla was being disrespectful to the governor." Abby spit out the words in a hurry, her distaste for what she was admitting evident.

"Okay," Lucas said, dismissively. He turned back to Victor. "I have the feeling you were about to tell me more."

Victor struggled to remember exactly what Layla had said the night Phillip had called her. He'd been working with Layla at her kitchen table, compiling class notes, when her cell phone rang. She'd glanced at the caller ID before asking him to give her some privacy. He'd wandered around in her den, but still heard part of what was said.

"I'm pretty sure Layla said something like she would keep the secret, or maybe that she'd hide their secret. But she also said—and this I heard pretty clearly—that she wouldn't hide 'them' in her apartment." Victor paused, and edited himself. It wouldn't do to admit he'd gone to Phillip and Jennifer's house on false pretenses to look for whatever Layla might have hidden there. He was already in enough trouble.

"Go on," Lucas said, his tone of voice encouraging.

"Layla said something about off-shore oil drilling, but I didn't hear that part too clearly." Victor looked up. Lucas, Abby, and the cat were all staring at him. "Something in her tone made me think Phillip was up to something and she had to help him."

"If you were just listening while she was on the phone, how did you know she was talking to Phillip?" Lucas asked.

"After she was finished, she put the cell phone down, and later, when she was out of the room, I checked. The number was in her contact list as the Drapers' house." Victor felt a jolt of shame after admitting he'd spied on his best friend.

"She could have been calling Jennifer," Abby said.

Victor nodded. "Could be." He cast a conciliatory glance at Abby. But before he could say anything, the doorbell rang.

"Well, it's about time that evidence tech got here to finger-print the refrigerator and the kitchen." Lucas rose and headed toward the door.

CHAPTER THIRTY-ONE

*R*izzo bounds in with the crime technicians, glares at all of us, shoots Victor an especially hard look, then stomps into the kitchen. I pad after him, keeping safely back so he doesn't notice me. For a brief moment, I wonder if he figured out I was behind the siren escapade, but I realize he's not the sort who would think a cat—even one as superior as I am—could do such a thing.

The crime technicians start prowling and dusting and examining, and Rizzo stands guard for a second before peeking back in the living room. I peer around the door facing to see the tableau he is watching—Abby and Victor smash together on the couch, his hand lightly resting on her thigh, her face tilts up at him. Victor is speaking too softly for me to hear. Lucas stands up and moves toward the kitchen. As soon as he is out of sight, Victor's arms go around Abby and he pulls her closer to him. One of her hands strokes the bandage on his head. No doubt they are processing Abby's new understanding that Victor was never Layla's lover and they are giving in to their mutual attraction.

Rizzo rears back as if Abby were his sixteen-year-old daughter and Victor was a well-known predator.

Lucas nods at Rizzo as he steps into the kitchen, but doesn't speak.

Rizzo snarls, as he stares at Victor and Abby, who have obviously forgotten there's a roomful of cops in the next room. I think they look sweet together, but clearly Rizzo doesn't agree.

"Son of a bitch," he says, and stomps toward Abby and Victor.

I follow. Lucas hangs back in the kitchen.

"Can I see you a minute?" Rizzo points at Abby. He doesn't sound chummy.

I can see her reluctance, but she rises and steps toward Rizzo, who immediately takes her arm and shuttles her down the hall. I step along beside Abby, but when Rizzo pulls her into the bedroom, he shuts the door in my face.

I scratch at the door, but Abby doesn't let me in. Frustrated, I press my ear against the thick wooden door. I catch words here and there, mostly Rizzo's. Something about Facebook and a scandal and the Navy.

"I don't believe it." Abby raises her voice as she speaks.

"I have proof." Rizzo practically shouts this.

Lucas comes up behind me in the hallway and makes a move to pick me up. I dart out of reach of his hands and miss the next exchange between Rizzo and Abby.

I'm still playing cat and mouse with Lucas when Abby comes out of the bedroom. Her face is pale, her lips press against each other, and her eyes are narrow slits under her furrowed brow. It doesn't take a skilled detective to read her. She's angry. Very.

She marches in front of Victor, and, with her hands on her hips, tells him, "You better leave now." Her tone of voice is not sweet.

Victor looks surprised and jumps up from the couch. Rizzo grabs him by the arm and pulls him toward the front door. "With your history of abusing women, I think you and I need to have another long chat about your missing friend." Rizzo hits the word "friend" with a sarcastic note.

They are out the door and gone in a flash.

Abby heads into the kitchen, as I trot up beside her.

"*What is going on?*" *I meow.*

She ignores me, glaring at a hapless crime technician.

"*Aren't you people done yet?*" *She's snappish.*

Lucas promises to hurry. Abby retreats to her room, closing her door before I can dash in.

Leaving Abby to sort herself out, I return to the kitchen to watch the crime technicians, with my head whirling over what Rizzo said. Victor has a history of abusing women? I don't think so. The man isn't as quick to catch on to certain clues as I am—but who is, really?—yet I sense no meanness in him.

Undoubtedly this has something to do with his resignation from the Navy.

As I am pondering this, and figuring out how I might learn more, a crime technician empties a shelf from the fridge, and puts a can of cat food on the counter among other items. The cat food catches my eye. The can's been opened, and there is a plastic lid over it, but I don't think anyone has fed me this flavor. Captain's Sea Fairy Banquet. Where do they get these names? I jump up on the counter and sniff the lid, quite sure I've never eaten any of this Sea Fairy food.

So why is the can of Sea Fairy cat chow opened?

With my paw, I guide the can toward the edge of the counter, planning to knock it off and investigate what's inside. Behind me, Lucas says, "Oh, no, you don't," and shoos me off the counter. While I sleuth around, studying everything and everyone, Lucas helps the others put all the items, including the Sea Fairy cat food, back in the refrigerator, and the crime technicians announce they're done.

Abby comes out of the bedroom, locks the door behind the police, and pulls out her cell phone. She punches in a number, waits, and then says, "Jennifer, where are you? This is important. Call me back. Oh, this is Abby."

Abby glares at the phone in her hand like she doesn't quite know what it is. Then she looks at me. "Where the hell is she?"

I meow and shake my head.

Abby gathers up her purse and slips on her shoes.

She's going out! Is she brain-damaged? I try to block her, but she's determined. Since I can't lasso her and tie her to her bed, there's only one sensible thing I can do — I trot along near her, determined to go with her.

Abby doesn't even seem to realize I'm beside her until I hop into the front seat of her Prius. She gives me a baleful look, sighs, and pets me. "You really should stay home."

"Why?" I meow back.

She stares at me for a moment. "That man—he ... and I was falling for him." I meow in a soft tone and rub my head against her leg.

"Oh, Trouble, that man...he's such a...such a...jerk. He put naked photos of his wife—his ex-wife—on Facebook. A whole bunch of the men did the same thing with photos of women in the Navy, all naked, and without their permission. It was a big scandal and he had to resign from the Navy. And now he's blaming Layla for being kidnapped and accusing her of having an affair with her boss, and then he was trying to seduce me. And I thought he was a good guy."

He is a good guy. I'm a superior judge of character, though of course Abby doesn't know that about me. Still, I tell her that we haven't heard his side of the story yet.

She rubs my ears before turning the car on. "Why can't he be more like you?"

Well, yes, I've often wondered why men can't be more like cats, but that's rather beside the immediate point. Where are we going? I meow my question, but Abby doesn't get it and keeps driving.

In no time at all, we drive down an elegant street draped with magnolias, live oaks dripping in Spanish moss, and tall shaggy pines. The houses have acreage for yards and are large, stately, and appear radically expensive.

Abby rounds a curve and another car— it looks like a large, dark

BMW *as I glimpse it—nearly collides with her. She swerves off the pavement into some grass, but regains control, stops her car, and honks. The vehicle keeps going and soon disappears beyond her rearview mirror.*

"That's funny." She says it like she's angry, not amused. "That looked like Emmett's car."

I turn around for another look, but the car is long gone and anyway I don't have a clue what Emmett drives.

"I'm going crazy, Trouble. Imagining things. This town is full of BMWs like Emmett's." She gives me a quick pat and puts the car in drive and soon enough we are pulling into a driveway in front of an impressive home with brick columns and an old-money look to it. The house is dark, and it's around 5 a.m., but none of this stops Abby. As soon as she parks, she puts her cell phone in her pants pocket, shoves her purse out of sight, hops from the car, locks it, and hurries toward the double front doors. I follow, curious and cautious.

Abby rings the doorbell. Nothing happens. She knocks. Nobody comes. I prick my ears up, on edge.

Something is not right. Even Abby appears to know this and takes a step backwards from the door and stares up at the windows on the second floor.

I sniff at the double front doors, catching a faint scent of spice and flowers. The Phillip scent. But I also pick up something else, and it only takes me a split second before I recognize the smell.

Gasoline.

I cry out a warning and press against Abby. Call 9-1-1 I meow, but she is shushing me. I yowl louder.

Frantic to warn Abby, I thump against the double front doors. As I do, one of them opens a crack.

Abby steps forward.

And then to my ever-living horror, she pushes the door open and steps into the house.

CHAPTER THIRTY-TWO

$\mathcal{A}$ bby tiptoed into the front foyer of the Drapers' home. Once inside, she hesitated, wondering exactly what she was doing in the house. Searching for Jennifer, or confronting her, had seemed like such a good idea back at her house, but now she wasn't so sure.

As upset as Abby was with Victor, she knew there was no getting any sleep. She figured she might as well put the time to good use—or that's what she'd been thinking when she rushed to her car. Abby wanted to confront Jennifer and demand answers over her mysterious conversation with Layla the night she disappeared. Those two had a secret that might have something to do with the kidnapping. The detectives were wasting valuable time focused on Phillip. Since Victor was a creep, it was up to her to make Jennifer tell her what was going on between her and Layla.

Abby took a tentative step further inside and looked down at Trouble, who was hissing and spitting at the air in front of him. She wondered what he was seeing. Maybe she should just leave. Jennifer would surely be at Phillip's hearing in the morning and she could confront her then. After all, breaking and entering into her boss's house in the wee hours of the morning was a not a traditionally positive career move.

But the lawyer in her quickly corrected that thought. The door was open. Technically, she wasn't breaking and entering.

Still, this was not nearly as good an idea as it had seemed when she jumped in her car and drove over here, fired up by her new suspicions.

She turned and retreated toward the front door, but Trouble hissed like an inner tube going flat in a hurry and shot forward deeper into the house. Abby wasn't about to leave Trouble inside the house, so she sprinted after him. Running in the dark, she tripped over something in a hallway and tumbled to the floor with a resounding crash. Sprawled out flat, her chin smarting from being smacked on the hardwood floor, Abby lay still, stunned and breathless. Trouble jumped on her, meowing insistently.

If Jennifer was in the house, she was awake by now. Abby pushed herself off the floor and stood, wildly hoping Jennifer didn't own a gun and wouldn't shoot her as an intruder. Cautiously Abby edged forward, running her fingers along the wall, looking for a light switch. No point in pretending she wasn't here anymore. Finally, she found a switch and flipped it on. Light flooded the room, nearly blinding Abby. Trouble kept yowling.

"Jennifer," Abby shouted. "It's me. Abby. We need to talk."

Nobody answered.

Trouble poked Abby hard in the leg and twitched his tail. Unhappy cat, Abby thought, and headed toward the stairs. She'd been in the house for several of the Drapers' soirees and knew her way around. If Jennifer were home, she'd surely be in an upstairs bedroom. But with every step Abby tried to take,

Trouble bumped her and wove between her feet, nearly trip-ping her.

"What?" Abby shouted, and immediately felt ashamed. Trouble was trying to tell her something. Again. She shouldn't take out her anger at Victor on Trouble. "What?" This time when she spoke, it was softer.

Trouble arched his tail and took off toward the kitchen. Abby followed.

As she neared the kitchen, she began to sniff the air. At first she was too tired to recognize the smell. Her normally alert and cautious brain was obviously off kilter with fatigue and worry or she'd never have entered uninvited into an unlocked, dark house before dawn so she could have a chat with the wife of a man in jail on kidnapping charges.

When Abby stepped into the industrial-sized kitchen and switched on the light, she cried out. The scent of gasoline was overpowering, and, on the stove, an iron skillet reeking of burning oil was giving off smoke. She ran forward and snatched the skillet off the hot eye of the stove, burning her fingers as she did. She dropped the skillet on the floor and heard the tell-tale cracking noise as it hit the tile.

A busted tile was nothing, not compared to a burned down house.

Abby switched the stove off, grabbed her cell phone out of her pocket, and hit 9-1-1. "House on fire." Close enough, she thought, and surely that would get a quicker response than "gasoline smell in the kitchen." She gave the address in a rush, but didn't stay on the line despite the operator's insistence she do so.

"I have to find Jennifer if she's here and get her outside in case something explodes." Abby poked at Trouble with her toe. "Find Jennifer. Please."

Trouble twitched his tail, sniffed the air, and started for the hallway. Abby glanced around the kitchen, making sure there were no lit candles or other sources that might ignite the gasoline. Seeing none, she followed after Trouble.

Once in the hallway, she spotted Trouble half way up the wide, circling staircase. From outside, Abby heard what sounded like a vehicle driving up. She wondered how a first responder could get there so quickly.

Trouble took off running and there was nothing for Abby to do but run after him. If it were first responders, they'd find the front door open without her help. If it was the arsonist returning, meeting him at the door wouldn't be any more helpful than running away from him. Meanwhile, Trouble seemed to be on to something.

Abby took the stairs as fast as she could, but Trouble got to the second floor long before her and disappeared into a doorway. His meowing led her into Jennifer's room.

Jennifer Draper was stretched out on her bed, her eyes closed but her lips were parted. Snores in little bursts of noise like engine backfires came out of her mouth. She was wearing black jeans, a long-sleeve black T-shirt, flat black boots, bangle bracelets, earrings, and a gold choker necklace. Dressed like a spy but with sparkle.

Abby leaned over closer, inspecting Jennifer. One of Jennifer's hands was thrown over her chest with the fingers closed over something. The other hand dangled off the bed.

Trouble jumped on Jennifer and started licking her face. Abby shouted her name. The woman didn't stir.

"Jennifer, wake up." Abby shook her, shouting into her face again.

But Jennifer didn't wake up.

Abby shook her again. Trouble meowed. Abby kept waiting for the first responders to call out, but nobody did.

Suddenly the bedroom door slammed shut. Abby spun around and started toward the door to check this out, but Jennifer moaned on the bed. Abby whirled back toward Jennifer.

Trouble meowed and butted Jennifer's stomach.

"Damn it, wake up." Abby wondered if she should slap the woman. That would have worked in a movie, but somehow slapping her boss's wife didn't seem like the right move. Yet Jennifer had to be drunk or drugged or sick to sleep through the racket she and Trouble had just made.

Trouble, persistent in his efforts, rubbed Jennifer's face with his own, purring like a small engine as he did.

This time both of Jennifer's eyes came open. And stayed that way.

"We've got to get out of here. Now." Abby tugged Jennifer's arms, trying to pull her into a sitting position and momentarily ignoring the slammed door. "The kitchen is on fire." Another small exaggeration, but one appropriate to the circumstances in Abby's mind.

"Fire." Jennifer slurred the word.

Trouble arched his back and sniffed the air. Abby was too busy with Jennifer to pay him much mind, but then he squalled like a banshee, leapt off the bed, and knocked the receiver out of the base of the bedside phone. He pawed at the numbers as Abby yanked Jennifer into a sitting position. As Abby pulled Jennifer to her feet, a brown plastic RX bottle rolled out of her hand onto the floor.

Abby stooped over and picked it up.

Valium. The ten milligram dosage.

In a flash, she suspected Phillip's Valium found in the library was something prescribed for him, but actually meant as extras for Jennifer. That explained her eternal and unnatural calmness.

But now wasn't the time to contemplate any addiction issues. Now was the time to get the hell out of the house before some kind of spontaneous combustion set the kitchen on fire for real.

After dragging Jennifer to the bedroom door, Abby paused to strengthen her grip on Jennifer before she reached to open it. Trouble yowled into the phone receiver, jumped down, and ran to the bedroom door.

Abby sniffed, smelling something foul and acrid. Jennifer began to slide to the floor in Abby's arms. Trouble was prancing around, his eyes wide and something like a snarl coming from deep inside him.

Abby wrestled Jennifer up from the floor, swung the door open, and cried out.

The hallway was on fire. The carpet runner danced with flames.

And, strain though Abby might for the sound of sirens, she didn't hear a hint of any fire trucks on the way.

CHAPTER THIRTY-THREE

For the life of him, Victor couldn't understand what had just happened at Abby's. After he and Lucas explained that he and Layla were not lovers, Abby had practically melted against him. One minute she was close to kissing him and running her hand gently over his bandage. Then wham. She was yelling at him to leave.

Was the girl bipolar?

Okay, he told himself, forget the redhead and concentrate on finding Layla—which is what he should have been doing in the first place, not trying to kiss Abby on her couch while the cops plundered her kitchen.

But as he drove his pickup toward his house, he couldn't get the scene at Abby's out of his head. He gripped the steering wheel tightly and went back over it in his mind, step by step.

"Rizzo." Victor shouted it in the empty cab of his pickup. The man had asked to speak to Abby, they went off together, and when they returned, Abby ordered Victor out of her house.

Obviously, Rizzo had done some background digging on Victor and must have reported what he'd found out to Abby.

How much longer was his rash decision to be a gentleman toward his ex-wife going to haunt him? Why hadn't he fought back against her and the accusations?

He glanced at the clock on the dashboard. Nothing to do now except go home, shower, take a nap, and then start looking for Layla.

As Victor drove the pickup into his parking spot and crawled out, he inhaled the damp, warm night air around him. He caught a whiff of some kind of night blooming flowers. Abby probably could have named them. What a beautiful night. Too bad Layla wasn't able to enjoy it.

Once inside his house, Victor showered in a hurry and pulled a frayed robe around him. But he didn't crash in bed like he had first planned to do. Instead, he pulled out the file he had taken from Layla's law review office. He'd glanced through it once before—just as he had looked through all the flash drives he had taken out of her gym bag at Abby's. But nothing had struck him as anything that could possibly be related to her kidnapping. It was just these endless, endless notes, statutes, regulations, and ramblings on off-shore oil drilling, and a rough draft of a law review article with her byline.

Yet, somewhere in all this, there had to be a connection with her kidnapping—and the trashing of Abby's house.

Victor got up to put a pot of coffee on. His head pounded from where he'd been hit, and he decided to indulge in a rare aspirin or two.

While the coffee brewed, he ate a couple of granola bars and swigged down a multivitamin and three aspirin with orange juice. Normally, when he was this confused, he'd go for a run, but tonight he was skipping that. He was also going to skip school later too. The most important thing he could do was find Layla.

With that goal firmly in mind, once he had his mug of black coffee, he sat down at his PC and pulled out the plastic bag of flash drives he had taken from Layla's bag. He intended to go through them again.

The materials on them were repetitious or similar to the items in the law review file he'd taken from Layla's office, although in far greater detail. One flash drive had about ten drafts of a law review article on off-shore drilling in Florida, similar to the one in the paper file, with Layla's name on them all as the author. Yet nothing gave him a hint about where Layla might be.

Could she have uncovered some kind of secret information that one side or the other in the continuing struggle between the environmentalists and the oil companies didn't want her to publicize? Or had she learned something that might jeopardize whatever deal it was that Phillip was working on with the governor and the state attorney?

Unable to come up with any answer that made sense, Phillip put the flash drives back in the plastic bag and tossed them on his desk. He stood, stretched, and headed to the bathroom.

After he brushed his teeth, he pulled on a plaid button-down shirt, and stepped into a clean pair of khaki pants. He wasn't at all sure where he was going, but he had to do something. As he slipped his cell phone in the front pocket of his shirt, he remembered Trouble nudging his shirt pocket as if trying to tell him something.

Running his hands through his hair, he frowned, thinking hard.

Trouble had practically shoved that lone earring at him

from Layla's travel bag when he searched the guest room at Abby's. And the cat had patted the pocket where he'd put the earring.

What the hell could an earring have to do with anything?

How could a cat know much about anything except food and soft laps?

Yet, Abby was convinced the cat was some kind of detective.

Crazy as that seemed, he had to admit at times Trouble did know things the rest of them didn't. Victor stepped over to the wooden box on his chest of drawers where he had dropped the earring and pulled it out. He studied it under the bright bedside lamp. The earring was elegant and expensive if he didn't miss his guess, and appeared to be something an older, conservative woman might wear. The pearl looked luminous and he figured it was real. The gold definitely was. The single word engraved on the back—love—must have been done by an expert as the lettering was a beautiful cursive with a flare.

Who did Layla know who would wear such an earring?

Her mother? Given the way Layla's parents had rebuffed her, he doubted Layla would have kept one of her mother's earrings. Yet, Layla had several photos of her parents displayed in her apartment, so maybe she did treasure an earring of her mom's as a keepsake?

But why hide it?

Thinking about Layla's parents made Victor think about Phillip and Jennifer. Both couples had the same kind of old-money style. Definitely not the Boho, nouveau-hippie look Layla affected, or the casual, comfortable plaid shirt and khakis he wore.

"Like Phillip and Jennifer," he said into the quiet of the early morning.

Though Victor could not begin to imagine why Layla would have any of Jennifer's jewelry, the notion that the lone gold earring with the pearl was Jennifer's took hold in his mind. He pulled up the *Architectural Digest* magazine with the photo spread on the Drapers' house and flipped to the photos. There, in a picture spread across the entire page, Jennifer and Phillip smiled in front of their elaborate fireplace.

Jennifer was wearing small gold earrings with pearls in them.

Victor couldn't make out if they were exactly the same as the one he now held, but if not, they were certainly similar.

Suddenly he wasn't tired anymore.

Shoving the earring into his pocket, Victor rushed toward his pickup. He needed to confront Jennifer and find out why Layla had one of her earrings. No sense in calling first and giving her a heads-up to concoct an answer. No sir, he'd deal with Jennifer now and he didn't care what time it was. Layla needed him.

CHAPTER THIRTY-FOUR

My first instinct is to find a window and leap. Abby could jump too. This is only the second floor after all. But I glance back at Jennifer, conked out on the bed. She's going to be a problem.

Abby whirls around in the bedroom, her eyes big in her face. She doesn't even look at me as she says out loud, "The first thing is not to panic."

A good rule, no doubt, but escape is the urgent matter at hand, not slogans.

I run toward the floor-length draperies on the wall that faces the front yard, looking for a window. Ducking my way behind them, I see the curtains cover two French doors. I press my nose against the window pane in one and discover that there is a small balcony off the bedroom.

Backing out of the drapes, I meow at Abby, trying to tell her what I've found. She gives me a quick, wild-eyed look, and then runs into the bathroom that adjoins the bedroom. In a moment, I hear her running water and dash into the small room with her.

"Wetting towels to put against the door to block smoke." Abby says *it as if reading a script for a documentary. She is definitely not panicking. But I want her to see the French doors and the balcony. If I have judged correctly, we both could jump to the lush green grass. Even a biped should survive without serious injury. Though it would be more problematic, maybe Abby can slide Jennifer off the balcony too. As limp as Jennifer is, I doubt she'd be hurt by a fall.*

But Abby is intent on her own plan. She stuffs the wet towel against the threshold and runs back to check on Jennifer, who is still sprawling on the bed. Abby doesn't bother trying to wake her up again, but runs back to the bathroom, wets another towel and drapes it over Jennifer. The cold wetness wakes Jennifer, and, sputtering, she says "What the hell?" *Her words slur.*

"The house is on fire." *Abby shouts it, some of her calmness breaking.* "We can't get out because the hallway carpet is in flames."

Jennifer blinks and struggles to sit up, but fails and falls back on the bed.

I head butt Abby's leg with all my energy and insistence. Once she is looking at me, I run to the draperies. Grabbing one edge of the heavy drape in my mouth, I pull it back until Abby can see the French doors.

Abby dashes over and opens one of the doors, letting in a burst of fresh night air. She steps out on the balcony with me at her feet.

"We can jump." *She speaks with no hesitation and I am so proud of her. She is as brave as Tammy Lynn, my real biped. I purr to show my approval and rub against her leg.*

In the bedroom, Jennifer collapses on the floor with a thud.

"We can't leave Jennifer." *Abby says it with a determined resoluteness.*

I look at the balcony and think about jumping.

Then I look at Abby and follow her back into the bedroom.

ABBY COCKED HER HEAD to the sound—sirens.

But they were still off in the distance. She ran to the bedroom door and pressed her hand against the flat panel. The door was hot to her touch, and she knew not to open it again. "We can't wait." Abby ran back to Jennifer. She had to get her out on the balcony somehow.

"Come on, Jennifer, we've got to jump." Abby shouted at Jennifer, but she didn't respond. Tugging on Jennifer's arms, Abby tried to pull her up from the floor. But Jennifer did not wake.

Trouble pushed against Jennifer's leg as it to shove her, but failed to move her.

"Damn it," Abby said, under her breath. With renewed vigor, Abby grabbed Jennifer's feet and dragged her toward the heavy drapes, scooting her across the floor, but only inch by inch. Limp dead weight proved harder to move than Abby would have thought.

Dropping Jennifer, Abby ran to the French doors, Trouble by her side. Even if she got Jennifer to the balcony, she wasn't sure shoving the woman off was a good idea.

The sirens were louder now, but Abby didn't see any red flashing lights. Just as she turned to go back inside after Jennifer, she saw headlights. Trouble meowed to alert her as a pickup pulled into the driveway below. A moment later, a man hopped out and started running toward the front of the house.

Victor!

At first Abby's heart thumped hard with fear. Had he come back to finish them off? A man who would do what he did to his wife might well kidnap his friend and then kill to cover up his crime.

Trouble butted her leg. When she looked down, he shook his head and then ran back inside the bedroom.

Abby followed, as her heart rate continued to climb. No, it didn't make sense that Victor had come to kill them.

But it didn't make sense that he'd come to the house at all.

Trouble raised his head, his ears perked up, and his eyes stared at the bedroom door. Abby held her breath and listened. Somebody was shouting. And clamoring up the stairs with something heavy thumping on the steps.

But whether this was Victor bent on saving them or intending to finish them off, Abby didn't know. She wondered if the flaming carpet in the hallway outside the bedroom would protect her, Jennifer, and Trouble after all.

Or merely prevent their rescue.

Either way, Abby needed to move. She grabbed Jennifer's feet and, yanking on them, pulled her toward the French doors. Trouble nipped at Jennifer's feet as if to hurry things along. With Trouble's encouragement, Abby finally dragged the woman toward the balcony. How a thin woman could weigh so much, Abby couldn't figure out.

When Abby got onto the balcony, she let Jennifer slide through her arms and sprawl out on the tiled floor in the cool dawn air. Abby's arms ached from the effort of moving Jennifer, and her hands trembled. Below, a fire truck, followed by a police car, pulled into the driveway beside Victor's pickup. Firemen scattered out of the fire truck. Abby shouted and waved her hand. "Up here. Up here." One of the men heard her, looked up, and waved back. When he shouted something to the others, pointing at her, the firemen broke and ran toward the house.

"Saved, we're saved, Trouble," Abby said.

But Trouble ignored her and paced on the balcony, his head toward the bedroom door, and his nose once more in the air sniffing.

Abby sniffed too. On top of the rancid, acrid smell of the burning carpet, she smelled something chemical, but not gasoline. She could also hear a loud hissing, like someone was using a giant can of hair spray.

The bedroom door burst open, slamming against the wall. Abby jerked back, and hoped that she and Jennifer were hidden by the drapery.

"Jennifer, Abby, where are you?" Victor's voice sounded panicked, something Abby had never heard before from him.

Suddenly Abby understood he was never intending to hurt them in the first place. He must have been using a fire extinguisher on the carpet runner, and that's what Abby had heard and smelled.

"Abby." He cried out the word, his voice anguished. "Where are you?"

"Here." Abby pulled back the drapery and stepped through.

Victor threw a fire extinguisher on the floor and rushed to Abby. He cradled her in his arms, rocking.

Three firemen burst into the room.

Abby broke from Victor's embrace and knelt by Jennifer. "I don't know what's wrong with her, but something is. She won't wake up."

"Smoke inhalation?" A fireman asked.

"No, she was this way when I got here, before the fire." Abby shook her head. "Please, please, call an ambulance."

Victor picked Jennifer up as easily as if she'd been a doll, carried her to the bed, and put her down gently. Then he turned to Abby. "What happened? What's going on?"

Abby dug the empty Valium bottle out of her pocket and held it up to a fireman. "I think she OD'd."

CHAPTER THIRTY-FIVE

The paramedics had Jennifer on a gurney momentarily parked outside the front door of the house while one of the women EMTs re-checked Jennifer's vital signs. Victor and Rizzo were off having some kind of argument. Abby stood by Jennifer, feeling helpless, but holding her hand. Now and then, Jennifer's eyes would briefly flick open, but never for long.

Trouble hopped on top of Jennifer's chest and began licking her face, then her earlobes. Abby went to shoo him off, but the woman paramedic reached over for a quick pet.

"Little buddy, we'll take care of your lady. Promise you." She spoke gently to Trouble, before going back to work on Jennifer.

A moment later, the EMT said, "She's stable, but we're going to transport her to the hospital as soon as we get her loaded into the ambulance. You might want to take her jewelry for safe-keeping."

Trouble put his mouth around one of Jennifer's earrings and tugged as if he were trying to remove it.

"So the cat speaks people?" The EMT grinned.

Abby rubbed Trouble on the neck, and quickly began to gather Jennifer's jewelry, starting with her rings and the bracelet. She put these in her pocket, thinking she'd have to find a container of some kind to keep them together and safe. Trouble meowed, and licked again at the earring.

"Okay, okay." Abby removed both earrings as gently as she could and put them with the rest of the jewelry in her pocket.

When she looked back at Jennifer, she was surprised to see Jennifer staring right at her.

"What...happened?" Jennifer's words slurred.

"Your house was on fire. But don't worry, the firemen have it all under control. Just some damage in the hallway. The house is safe. Now we have to worry about getting you to the hospital and getting you taken care of."

Above Jennifer, the EMT asked, her voice gentle, "Ma'am, can you tell us what you took? What pills? And if you drank any alcohol?"

Jennifer never took her eyes off Abby. "Marshall." It seemed to take some effort for Jennifer to speak the word. After she said it, she closed her eyes.

"I don't understand," Abby said, and pressed her face closer to Jennifer's. As she did, she noticed some slight bruising around Jennifer's mouth and jaw. "Jennifer, wake up."

But Jennifer had passed out again, and the EMTs hurried her into the ambulance. A moment later, the rescue vehicle took off, sirens blaring in the still night.

Victor rushed up beside her and said her name. But Abby was in no mood to listen to him. She turned away from him and hurried toward her car. She wanted to go to the ER and do what she could for Jennifer. And call Delphine. Definitely call Delphine.

But before Abby reached her car, Rizzo cut her off. "Young lady," he said, his tone of voice tired yet still threatening, "I believe you have some serious explaining to do here."

"And you," he turned to Victor. "We have a perfect photo on the Drapers' security camera of a man dressed in a gray hoodie."

"Like the man in the dumpster," Victor said.

"I was thinking it looked more like you the night we found you drunk on the sidewalk by the dumpster." Rizzo moved toward Victor like he was thinking of grabbing him. "Don't either one of you move."

CHAPTER THIRTY-SIX

*V*ictor tensed and lifted his arms, his fingers curling into fists. Enough was enough. He was ready to fight back against the detective. But before either man could strike a blow, Abby angled between Rizzo and Victor, an angry yet alert look on her face.

With one hand shoving Victor back from Rizzo, Abby glared at the detective. "I already told the fire department's investigator everything I saw, smelled, or heard. Ask him."

"No, ma'am, I'm asking you." Rizzo jutted out his jaw, returning Abby's look, scowl for scowl. "And we can do it here or I can take you both to the police department."

"You have no legal right to hold us here, absent an arrest," Abby tossed back at Rizzo. "And you cannot force us to go to the police station unless you arrest us. You have no basis for an arrest, and you certainly don't have a warrant. Given that, I believe I will be on my way." She paused and cast a hard look at Victor. "Mr. Rutledge here can do as he pleases."

Victor wanted to clap his hands at the stunned look on Rizzo's face. Trouble made a hissing noise aimed at the detective that sounded like a warning as Rizzo stood, frozen and angry.

Abby hurried toward her car, but turned back for one last zing at Rizzo. "You should be looking for a person who drives a dark BMW, and I'd suggest you question Emmett, who drives just such a car. And leave Victor Rutledge and me alone. We did not kidnap anyone."

Trouble and Victor sprang into action and raced after the retreating Abby.

THESE TWO, Abby and Victor, really need my help. But Layla needs it more—and quicker. Somehow, I've got to rescue her before I can mend Abby and Victor and get them to realize how much they care for each other.

Right now, while Abby, Victor, and that Detective Rizzo finish their little kerfuffle, what I need to do is sniff around the house, and see what humanoid smell I might pick up. That is, if I can smell anything over the fire extinguisher and the gasoline.

I wish I'd gotten a better look at the driver of the dark BMW. Whoever it was must have recognized Abby and turned around, effectively locking her in the bedroom with Jennifer and trying to burn them with the house.

Whoever this is, he or she is very nasty. Very.

TWENTY MINUTES LATER, Victor sat in his pickup, studying Abby's house. Her car was in the garage and the front living room light was on. He didn't see any sign of danger and he didn't hear any screams. Yet he could not make himself drive away. He was parked in the street in front of her house, and he planned to stay there till the bright morning sun made every-thing safer.

Just because the front looked secure didn't mean the back was. He got out of his truck and, keeping to the shadows, went around to the back. After checking every window and the door, he headed back to his truck.

Rounding the corner, Victor came to a dead halt. Lucas Kelly was standing there, his hand resting on his taser.

"Well, Mr. Rutledge, dang fine thing I'm not one of those quick-to-shoot types." Lucas grinned.

Victor saw nothing in the situation to justify the grin.

"Besides, I recognized your truck. Got your tag number memorized." Lucas dropped the grin. "Believe it or not, I'm keeping an eye out on your lady friend too. Just driving by to be sure she got home safe after that ruckus at the Drapers' house. Now, sir, would you just go home?"

The front door opened, and Abby stepped onto the stoop. Trouble darted out, running toward Victor and rubbing his leg. Abby stood with both hands on her hips, glaring at him and Lucas. "What?"

Lucas hurried toward the front door. "Ma'am, just like I told your fella here, I'm just checking on you. Mind if I come in, look under the beds and things?" His grin reappeared. "Maybe let Victor come in too?"

Victor stepped up beside Lucas on the front porch, with Trouble beside him.

Abby didn't look happy, but she stepped aside and gestured for them to come in.

"Y'all stay here, talk a minute, while I check things out." Lucas hesitated, glancing from Victor to Abby. "Might be I should also tell you something. Rizzo's a fine man, a good detective, but he's frustrated because he can't find Layla. And when he gets that way, he looks for some place to put blame."

Lucas nodded toward Victor. "This young fellow is where Rizzo's putting all his frustration right now. But just because Rizzo says something, doesn't make it true. You hear?"

With that, Lucas stepped down the hallway, leaving Victor with Abby.

CHAPTER THIRTY-SEVEN

Trying to hide her confusion and anxiety, Abby went into the kitchen and put the kettle on. She pulled out some tea bags and took two blue china cups out of the cabinet.

"If you'd rather have coffee, or something stronger, I can fix that instead." She turned to face Victor as she spoke.

"Tea's great." He stood with his hands in his pants pockets, rolling slightly back on his heels.

She felt him watching her as she made the tea, but didn't know how to ease the awkwardness. Rizzo said Victor was a man who had posted nude photos of his wife on Facebook while they were in the middle of a nasty divorce. Was she really falling for a man who would do something like that?

She couldn't deny what she felt for this man. It wasn't just that rush of physical attraction she'd felt when she first saw him. This was something deeper, something real. She wasn't sure if she was in love with him, but she had a definite emotional attachment.

Everything she'd seen about Victor showed her that he was

not the type of man who would do what Rizzo accused him of doing. Yet Abby had represented decent people in divorces and seen them do indecent things.

Still, hadn't Lucas just said Rizzo was wrong? More importantly, shouldn't she trust her own observations and own feelings? There was no meanness in Victor. That's what her heart was telling her.

Could she be wrong?

Frowning as the thoughts tripped about in her head, Abby poured some milk in a saucer for Trouble before she poured the boiling water over their tea bags. "Shall we?" She pulled out a chair at her kitchen table and sat.

Victor did likewise, his face etched with strain and fatigue. Abby couldn't help but worry about him—after all, he'd been knocked out earlier that night and he hadn't slept either.

Quickly, Abby told him about going to confront Jennifer, going inside, smelling the gasoline, and all the rest of the horrid experience. He listened, nodding now and then, but saying nothing while she talked.

Finally, Abby quieted. She sipped her tea. She watched as Victor sat upright in his kitchen chair, with his face a study of concentration.

"We might not have a serial killer on the prowl, but we've sure got a serial arsonist on the loose." He fingered his cup of tea, but didn't drink. "And now we know it isn't Phillip. What better alibi than being in jail?"

"I told you it wasn't him." Abby tried to keep the sharpness out of her voice. But she kept thinking of all the time the police had wasted—first thinking Victor was the kidnapper, then arresting Phillip for the crime. Meanwhile Layla might be dying.

Or already dead.

Abby looked across the table, her eyes meeting Victor's. She could see the compassion, worry, and caring in his expression as clear as if the words had been tattooed on his forehead.

She was as bad as the police, wasting time on some spiteful accusation when they should be working together to save Layla.

"Tell me your side of the story." Abby hesitated, watching as Victor ducked his head. "Please."

"All right." He raised his head and looked at Abby, a hangdog look on his handsome face.

"I want to hear it." Ashamed she hadn't asked him for his version earlier, Abby sat still with her tea steaming in front of her. Trouble finished his milk and hopped into her lap.

"My wife and I met in the Navy. She was a very pretty woman. And she was very proud of that, always showing off her body, wearing provocative clothes when she wasn't in uniform. She was also...promiscuous. I didn't know it at first, and when I found out how many ...affairs...she'd had, I filed for divorce. This made her mad. Apparently I was supposed to overlook her sleeping around."

Abby took a slow sip of her tea. She studied Victor's face and posture for any indications he was lying, but saw none.

"She tried to talk me out of it. But when I asked her to leave our apartment and filed for divorce, she went ballistic and demanded alimony and half of my pension—which I wouldn't even get for another five years—and she wanted the title to my SUV. I hired a lawyer to fight her."

Abby's experiences as an attorney in divorces notwithstanding, she remained amazed at how love could turn to hate.

"Given the circumstances, especially since my wife was a

petty officer in the Navy and didn't need alimony—or my pension—the lawyer was confident we'd win."

Trouble reached out a paw and tapped Victor on the leg, and meowed. Once again, Abby was impressed by Trouble's obvious understanding of human words and emotions.

"Well, she hit on an idea. There was a big scandal breaking with members of the military posting photos—nude ones—of women in the service. My wife had my password to my Facebook account and she posted some photos of herself. Tasteful, studio-quality, but naked. Very naked. I don't even want to know who the photographer was—but it wasn't me."

"And you got blamed for it?"

"Yes. She claimed I'd taken the photos with her permission, but then posted them for revenge without her permission while we were breaking up. She vehemently denied giving me the okay to post them."

"Why didn't you fight back? Surely there was some way to prove you hadn't posted them?"

"How? The photos were posted on my Facebook account from the hard drive of my computer. They were even taken with my camera. I was sloppy, or trusting, leaving all my passwords and my things around for her to get. But I didn't think she'd try anything like that. Hell, I didn't even change the locks on my doors after she moved out."

"But surely you could have explained all that."

"Maybe, but it'd be her word against mine, and I didn't think I stood much of a chance. Or maybe I just didn't have the heart to try. Especially since the offer on the table was to resign with an honorable discharge or be charged with conduct unbecoming an officer. Besides, I didn't really want to call my wife a slut in front of a court martial." Victor dropped his head. "I had loved her, after all."

Abby realized with a huge sense of relief that she believed him. Nothing in Victor's tone or demeanor suggested he was lying. She hadn't been wrong about him, or about how she felt about him. She stood up, and went to where he sat, and, standing behind him, she placed her hands on his shoulders. "I'm sorry I didn't ask you before."

Victor slid back his chair, stood up, and turning around, pulled Abby into his arms. For a long moment, he just held her. Then he tilted his head so he could reach her mouth with his.

When Victor's lips touched her, Abby felt a comforting, yet demanding warmth spread through her body. She arched her back so that her breasts pressed against his chest. Some part of her acknowledged this had been what she'd wanted from the first time she'd seen him. Her lips parted with a will of their own and her hands traveled down his body. Her heart raced.

She had completely forgotten that Lucas was in the house until he cleared his throat. "Reckon the coast is clear. Looks like y'all don't need me."

Abby broke from Victor long enough to say goodnight to the detective. Trouble escorted Lucas to the door, leaving her and Victor alone.

Victor grinned at her. "Much as I want to carry you right into your bedroom and make love to you, what we both need is a quick nap, and to hit the trail again. Rizzo is still too invested in me or Phillip as the kidnapper. We've got to rethink everything. Talk it out. Look at what we know. But first, a catnap, okay?"

Abby nodded, her body registering disappointment that there wasn't going to be anymore kissing—or anything else—at the moment. But her mind knew Victor was right.

Later.

After they found Layla.

CHAPTER THIRTY-EIGHT

*V*ictor yawned and stretched after his nap. He and Abby had collapsed together in her bed, fully dressed because it would have been too tempting otherwise, and miraculously, they'd slept until the alarm woke them. Abby had grabbed a quick shower and now she was dressed in a fuzzy robe with her damp hair twisted up with a clip on top of her head. He rose out of bed, sorely tempted to nibble her ear, kiss the back of her neck, and peel her slowly out that robe.

Standing behind her, he ran a finger lightly up and under the front of the robe, and leaned forward for one slow-traveling kiss along the damp, warm skin of her bared neck. As his lips moved down her neck to below the fuzzy collar of the robe, she dropped a handful of things she'd been holding onto the dresser, and moaned. His fingers began to untie the belt of the robe.

Trouble pounced on top of the dressing table and started pawing and meowing insistently at something.

"Not now, Trouble," Victor said, frustrated by the intrusion.

But Trouble started batting around the pieces of whatever it was Abby had dropped, and his plaintive meows couldn't be ignored.

Reluctantly Victor pulled away from Abby and glanced at what Trouble was so focused upon. Jewelry, several pieces of it, were scattered where Abby had dropped them.

Abby was staring at Trouble now too, the mood broken by the cat's insistent caterwauling.

"It's nothing but Jennifer's jewelry," Abby said, her voice puzzled. "The EMT asked me to take it so it wouldn't get lost at the hospital. I guess I'll put it all in the safe at the law firm."

Victor barely nodded. Two items had caught his eye—just like they had captured Trouble's attention.

"These earrings look like the one that Trouble practically knocked into my hand when I was going through Layla's things in your guest room. Layla had just the one earring, hidden in her padded bra." He looked at Trouble, who sat gloating by the earrings.

Abby leaned closer to study the set of earrings on the dressing table, as Victor stuck his fingers into his shirt pocket and pulled out a single earring. "I know this is going to sound crazy, but I went to Jennifer's to ask if this was hers, and, if so, why Layla had it."

Victor put the one earring from his pocket next to the two that Abby had taken from Jennifer at the EMT's request.

They studied the three earrings on her dresser, while Trouble purred. Upon close examination, Victor saw that the set of earrings Jennifer had been wearing were not identical. One of them had a smaller pearl in it and its gold was duller with a slightly more yellow color.

"They really don't match, do they?" Abby pushed the two

earrings closer together. "But on Jennifer's ears, probably nobody would notice."

"But look at this." Victor moved the one from his pocket next to the better one from Jennifer's ears. "A perfect match."

Abby turned each one over in turn, studying the engraving of the word love. "These two, the engraving is very refined, artistically so." She gestured at the mismatched one with the smaller pearl. "But on that one, the word's rather crudely done."

As Abby spoke, Trouble meowed again and sat on his haunches looking supremely satisfied.

"I've had this one since right after Layla was kidnapped." Victor tapped the earring with his finger. "The police never had it because I took it out of Layla's room before they searched it."

Abby frowned, fingering the earring Victor had taken from Layla's room. "Is that what somebody is looking for? An earring? It can't be that valuable. Could it?"

"I think it's more complicated than that."

"She—I mean Jennifer—must have lost this one." Abby pointed to the one from Victor's pocket. "And tried to get a replacement made."

"But why did Layla have it?"

Abby looked up at Victor, her eyes deep amber ovals in her pale face. "Do you think she stole it?"

"Layla's not a thief."

"Then maybe she found it?"

"Where would she have found it?" Victor wrinkled his forehead. "Unless she took it from the Drapers' house while she was there alone with Phillip."

"You just said she wasn't a thief."

Victor shook his head. "I've been wrong about plenty of things before."

AT LEAST THESE two are finally realizing they are seriously smitten. Beyond having a fancy for each other, they also seem to be learning to trust one another.

Yet neither of them could put the earrings together until I shoved the evidence right in their faces. How will they ever find Layla at this rate?

There is one more task facing me before I let Abby and Victor out the door of this house. That can of cat food in the refrigerator.

No, I'm not talking about mealtime. Though I do recall a piece of left-over salmon in the fridge that I wouldn't object to sampling.

Rather, I am thinking about that can which had been opened and resealed with a plastic top—a can of cat food from which no one had given me any food. Captain's Sea Fairy, to be precise. Why had someone opened it, if not to feed me?

I have my suspicions. Layla is obviously a smart young woman with a flair for hiding things. I'm guessing there is something in that can of cat food that Victor and Abby need to see.

I run into the kitchen while Abby gets dressed. But in the kitchen, I'm confronted once more with the problem of not being able to open the refrigerator door. Despite my attempts, my paws just cannot pull the door open.

I need a biped. And quickly, before they leave.

Zipping back to Abby's bedroom, I find her door is opened just wide enough for me to slip in. Abby is dressing in a pair of slim-legged tan linen pants and a soft white blouse with a touch of lace down the front. I'm not the only one who can see a hint of a peach-colored bra from under her unbuttoned blouse as Victor is sitting on the edge of the bed, watching with a hungry look on his face.

Having discovered long ago it is never too early to try to communi-cate with a biped, I start meowing. In the plainest terms I can imagine, I tell them both what I need. Someone to open the damn refrigerator.

Abby shushes me, something I know she would not do if she were not hopping around on one foot as she slips her other foot into a choco-late-colored ballerina flat.

"Need some help?" Victor asks her.

"Feed Trouble for me, will you please?" Abby steadies herself and slides the second shoe on. I run through the crack in the bedroom door and dash to the kitchen.

Victor hurries after me. I paw at the refrigerator door and he pulls it open for me, casting a curious glance at me. "Looking for chow or another earring?"

He's teasing me, but I don't take time to rebut. Instead, I put my head to the task in front of me and jump into the refrigerator.

"Hey, get down." To his credit, he sounds more amused than angry.

Ignoring him, I push the cat food can with my nose toward the edge of the refrigerator shelf. Victor starts fussing at me, the amusement gone from his tone, as I push the can off the edge and watch with satis-faction as it falls to the tile floor.

Splat. The can hits with a resounding clatter, and I hop out of the refrigerator.

Victor yells and I yell back. He's going to have to learn better manners if he intends to marry Abby.

"What is going on in here?" Abby stands in the entrance way to the kitchen. "I can hear you two in the bedroom."

While Victor starts to explain, I nose the can. The force of the fall knocked the plastic cover on the can loose. With my teeth and paws, I'm able to pull the lid all the way off.

"Meow." I yell as distinctly and loudly as I can—meaning: would you two shut up and look at this?

They do.

Inside the can of cat food, there is no food. Someone—doubtlessly Layla—has scooped out the food and filled the can with a crumpled paper towel.

Victor swoops down and picks the paper towel up. Inside, there is a single gold wedding band.

Sounding like a boastful Mum, Abby says, "I told you he was a better detective than either of us."

"I'm sorry I doubted him." Victor straightens up from petting me and holds the ring toward Abby. "I'm guessing you didn't hide this in the cat food."

Abby shakes her head no. "But this is so weird. I found a flash drive at the law firm, hidden in Layla's diabetic bars in the kitchen. So Layla might hide things in food?"

Victor fingers the ring in his hand. "Not just food. I found a flash drive taped to the toilet at the Drapers' house."

Abby gives him a perplexed look, but doesn't ask what he was doing examining the Drapers' toilet. "All right, then, she's leaving a trail of flash drives, like a trail of crumbs on the forest floor, along with a couple of pieces of jewelry. We just have to figure out what they mean."

Abby kneels on the floor and looks me in the eyes. "Are there any more flash drives, rings or things, or other clues hidden in my house?"

I meow, appreciatively. Then I shake my head. There's a piece—or two—of the puzzle still missing, but it's not here at Abby's.

"Shall we see what this is?" Victor is already heading toward a desk lamp in the living room.

Under the bright light of the lamp, Abby and Victor study the wedding band.

"Look," Victor says, and points. "The word love. The same style of engraving script as in the earrings."

They stare at each other for a moment and rush back into the bedroom, and tumble around among the items on the top of the dresser.

Abby pulls up a wedding ring. I hop on top of the dresser to supervise. The ring Abby took from Jennifer's finger is a decent match for the one in the cat food can, but not exact. As with the replacement earring, the engraving is cruder.

"Why on earth would Layla have two pieces of Jennifer's jewelry, especially jewelry that's so obviously precious to her?" Abby looks at me as if I have an answer.

But I don't.

CHAPTER THIRTY-NINE

*A*bby's cell phone chimed from inside her purse, and she wrestled it out from the clutter. "Delphine," she said, glancing at the caller ID, and her heart kicked painfully in her chest. This would either be about Phillip or Jennifer. Either way, Abby didn't figure it for good news. Not this early.

"I'm working on getting Phillip out of jail so he can go be with Jennifer. But if I can't get him out, you need to get to the hospital and be with her." Delphine hadn't bothered with hello.

Abby swallowed hard. That didn't sound good. "How's she doing?"

"In a coma. Bad." Delphine's voice sounded tired and anxious. "Docs say that she had Valium and antidepressants in her system. A lot."

"I thought I saw some bruising along her jaw," Abby said. "Like somebody had pried her mouth open against her will and maybe forced her to take those pills."

"Yes, that's what the ER doctors said," Delphine replied.

"The bruises became more intense at the hospital, especially after they cleaned her face and removed her make-up."

"Will she be all right?"

"They don't really know yet."

Abby felt tears forming in her eyes and wiped at her face with her sleeve. "I'm so sorry."

"I've got to go. I got a judge waiting to hear an expedited bail hearing."

"Wait, wait, Delphine. Please. Does the name Marshall mean anything to you?

"What's that got to do with Jennifer?"

"It was the last thing she said to me, right before she passed out and the EMTs loaded her in the ambulance."

"Marshall? You mean like the Marshall court?"

"Yes, Marshall. Does she have...I don't know, a brother or somebody named Marshall?"

"No. And I've got to go." With that Delphine ended the phone call.

"Like the Marshall court?" Abby felt like a bell was going off in her head.

"Victor, we need to get to the law school. Right now. I'll explain on the way." Abby didn't pause to see if he agreed, but grabbed her purse and her keys. "You too, Trouble. We might need you."

A moment later, they were all crowded into Victor's pickup, and he was driving.

"Okay, now, you want to explain this to me."

"The Marshall court," Abby said.

"You mean, like *Marbury vs. Madison* and all that?"

"Yes."

"Follow me on this, okay." Abby paused, once again trying to gather her own thoughts into a coherent pattern. "We both know that Marshall was the Supreme Court justice in 1803, and that he authored *Marbury v. Madison*, the case that established beyond doubt the independence of the U. S. Supreme Court."

"Yeah, I remember all that. We spent a whole week studying the case in my constitutional law class. It's a famous case. And it changed the way our government and our country have functioned ever since then because it established the Supreme Court's right to knock down laws of Congress if the Court found them unconstitutional."

"Bravo. You get an A." Abby grinned at Victor for a second before worry creased her forehead again. "But there's a connection between that and ...well, Layla. Maybe."

Victor ran a red light, but in the early morning traffic, no one was about. Still Abby cut her eyes at him and frowned.

"A connection? I don't see how. You're not saying Layla was researching or writing something on the Marshall court? I mean hasn't everything that could ever be written about that been written?"

"Yes." Abby paused, waiting to see if Victor connected the dots on his own. Trouble let out an insistent yowl, but she ignored him.

"Professor Miguel." Victor pounded the steering wheel. "He wrote that book on the Marshall court and how it changed American history. We all had to buy the damn book and read it in Con Law. He must make a fortune off the sales since practically every law student in the country has to buy the book." Victor drove, one hand on the steering wheel, and the other pushing back the hair drooping over his eye.

"The night Layla disappeared, she and Miguel were talking about her doing some research for a sequel to his book." Abby tried to remember exactly who had said what, but she'd been distracted as they'd talked.

"So Miguel and Layla were working together on something? And that something might have to do with the Marshall court?" Victor sounded dubious.

"Maybe." Abby closed her eyes as if to remember better.

"But how could a book that man wrote about the Marshall court have anything to do with kidnapping Layla, killing that poor homeless man, and trying to burn down Layla's and Jennifer's places?"

"I don't know." Abby knew it sounded far-fetched, but she had a feeling she was on to something. "I think we might be able to find out in the law review offices and maybe in the law library. And I want to find out what kind of car Miguel drives. If he drives a dark BMW, it could have been him rushing away from Jennifer's after he tried to kill her."

Perched over her shoulder and looking out the back window of the pickup, Trouble let out a resounding yowl.

CHAPTER FORTY

*V*ictor parked the pickup in the student lot at the law school. He hopped out quickly so he could open the door for Abby, but before he rounded the back of the truck, she was already heading toward the school, holding Trouble in her arms.

Victor hurried after her. "How are you going to find out what kind of car the professor drives?"

Abby didn't slow up. "Ask."

Victor felt a little stung at the tartness of her reply, but he knew Abby was exhausted and stressed. And he understood too: Miguel was a heartthrob. Most of the women at the law school—student, teacher, or administrative—had crushes on the man. Probably any female inside the law school would know what he drove and, no doubt, his shirt size, his birthday, and his favorite liquor.

"Let's go to the law review offices first. I want to see if I can find any research Layla might have been doing for Miguel that might tell us something about what's going on. Then we'll find out if he drives a dark BMW and then we confront him, or stalk him, or torture him, or whatever it takes to find Layla." In Abby's arms, Trouble meowed as if agreeing.

"It's a plan." Victor spoke as they raced inside the building. He worried somebody might object to the cat, but they hurried into the law review offices without anyone even speaking to them.

In his billfold, he still had the law review key card he had taken from Layla's office the night she was kidnapped. He pulled his billfold out, yanked out the key card, and a moment later the door sprang opened. On a hunch, he tried the key card on Layla's office door, and it sprang open too.

At once, Victor saw Layla's PC was gone from her desk, and he figured Rizzo and Lucas had taken custody of it. Abby put Trouble down and looked around the office. Surely anything of any real interest was in police custody, like the computer. But it didn't hurt to search again.

Or maybe they were just wasting time while Layla died.

As glad as I am to see Victor and Abby getting along so well, they need to stop chatting it up and get a move on.

To get them back on track, I jump up on the credenza and start sniffing along the edge of the book shelves, with my nose on red alert.

From the moment I entered this office, I could catch the faint whiff of that same spicy aftershave I'd smelled in Abby's backyard, in Layla's room, and on Phillip. Of course, Layla might have brought the scent into her office on herself, or she might have had a visit from Phillip. But somehow, I think the smell itself is more tangible than something lingering from a past visit.

Abby and Victor stop what they're doing and watch me.

On the top shelf, I pick up a stronger scent trail, definitely the aftershave or cologne that Phillip was wearing at Abby's, and I shove my nose between the books. I find what I'm looking for and meow loudly to alert the bipeds, as I start digging at the source.

Victor jumps over to me and pulls the book I'm focusing on from the shelf. Abby joins us as Victor flips open the book.

"Look at this," he says and pulls out a set of papers about the length and width of an average paperback, though much thinner, and stapled in one corner.

"Page proofs." Abby takes them from Victor's hand and looks through them. "Final page proofs for an article analyzing the national implications of Florida's determined stand against offshore oil drilling on its tourist coastline. By Professor Miguel Angel Castillo"

"But that's Layla's article." Victor sounds mad and also quite sure of what he said as Abby turns pages. "I read several drafts of it on those flash drives from her gym bag and the one taped to the back of the toilet."

"Me too." Abby sounds indignant. "I read some revisions on the flash drive I found in her diabetic snack bars at the law firm."

"Plagiarism?"

"Hell, yes, plagiarism. It's got Miguel's byline and is set for publication in the Texas Law Review. That lousy, thieving son of a bitch." Abby slaps at the page proofs as if it were the papers' fault. "All that publish or perish. I guess it got to him, and he stole her article."

"But would he kidnap her to hide that? I mean how does that help him? And to kill that homeless man, and try to burn Layla's apartment and the Drapers' house? That seems a bit too much."

I meow some encouragement at the two of them, and tangle around their legs trying to hurry them up. We need to be confronting Miguel if you ask me, not having a chat.

But chat they do. Humanoids!

"You're right," Abby says. "I don't see him killing or kidnapping over this. I mean, he'd just say he wrote it and Layla was making it up that she did, or exaggerating. Or that she helped some with the

research, but he did the actual analysis and writing. This kind of thing goes on a lot in grad schools. You know, it's a he said-she said kind of thing. The professor denies it and the student looks bad. The professor gives the student poor recommendations or blackballs them if the student objects. It's a no-win situation."

"But Layla wouldn't have taken that." Victor practically tramples my tail as he stomps around the office.

"Exactly," Abby says, her voice a rising sound of comprehension. "All those drafts, and the research notes, that proves she wrote the law review article and not him. Don't you see that?"

Even I comprehend the stratagem, but Victor still has a small frown on his face. Nobody but the author of the law review would have all those drafts showing the progression of the article from research notes to rough outline to final version. Miguel couldn't just dismiss Layla as a liar because she had the proof he was the cheat, not her. The only way out of that for Miguel was to find and destroy all the flash drives with Layla's work in progress.

"So is that it?" Victor stares at Abby, the puzzled look fading. "That's what he's looking for then? Right? The flash drives with Layla's various drafts. If he destroys them, then he can just deny Layla wrote the article, and she wouldn't have any proof."

Victor and Abby stare at each other. "That's why the fires—he was trying to destroy any flash drives he couldn't find," Abby exclaims.

Bravo, bipeds! Now on with the chase.

CHAPTER FORTY-ONE

I hop down from the credenza and run to the closed door. I paw at it and bellow a clear command. Let me out.

Abby scrambles to open the door for me and I take off running.

I don't bother to look behind me, as I know Abby has enough sense to follow me. And surely Victor will follow Abby if only to protect her.

Once more, I trust my nose. The scent of the aftershave is strong enough that it's easy for me to follow it down the hallway toward an office. A few students, and even a dean-type person, look at me, mostly friendly, as I zip down the hallway.

I turn down one hallway into another one, and finally arrive at a door where the scent is quite strong. Almost unpleasantly so. At least that Phillip person had the good taste not to drench himself in the stuff.

Stopping in front of the office, I see a brass name plate on the door that reads Miguel Angel Castillo. The door is slightly cracked, and I see no reason to wait for Abby and Victor to catch up with me. Shoving my weight against the door, I push it open. Miguel is sitting behind his desk, his PC on, and a frown on his face.

I meow and he jumps, startled no doubt by my invasion of his office.

He grimaces, and I sense that in a moment he will throw something at me, or at least shout at me. But Abby knocks on the door and pokes her head in at the same time.

"Oh, my goodness. Look where my kitty ran off to," she says, her voice in an unnatural tone I know at once is her fake perky voice. Hopefully Miguel doesn't register the bogus chirping quality.

"My cat, Trouble," Abby points at me. "I'm sorry, but he got away from me. May I come in and get him?"

Miguel's former scowl suddenly transforms into a smile. "Hello, Abby. I was just thinking about you. What a wonderful surprise."

He's lying. I can hear it in the strained inflections of his voice, and I glance at Abby. Satisfied that she knows too, I slink forward toward him. I want a close-up sniff to be sure the smell is actually his after-shave or cologne.

Abby lunges for me, but I evade her and jump on Miguel's desk. He jerks back as if he is afraid of me and I hiss at him, thinking how much fun it would be to actually bite him.

Instead, once more, I follow my nose. Jumping about, ever just out of reach of his hands, I locate the drawer in the desk where a strong scent of the aftershave radiates out of the space. Unless I miss my guess, he has a bottle of the stuff in that drawer.

I meow and swat at the drawer. Miguel swats at me. Abby grabs for me, and this time I let her catch me, but not before I make one last determined and conspicuous swipe at the drawer with the aftershave.

"I'm so sorry." Abby says it breathlessly but smiles at Miguel as if she is trying to flirt. "He's usually so well behaved."

I swat at the drawer again, and meow.

"Well, he certainly is misbehaving today, isn't he?" Miguel smiles back at Abby, before turning to give me one of those if-looks-could-kill glares. I wiggle half out of Abby's arms and claw at the desk drawer.

"He must think you have catnip or salmon in that drawer." Abby *grins and tilts her head so that her hair flips over her face, Veronica Lake style.*

Okay, a bit of overkill on the play-act flirting. I meow at her to tone it down. But Miguel seems to buy her act and leans toward her. "Shall we see?" With that, he opens the drawer, and I lunge out of Abby's hands and land inside the open space.

There, among a few odds and ends of personal toiletry items— including a comb, brush, and handheld mirror, each with matching tooled silver handles in a kind of Spanish style—is a bottle of after-shave. It looks expensive. I paw at it, knocking it over.

The top is not on it tightly, and a wave of spicy, yet flowery, smell floods the room as the aftershave spills. Amber and iris, with notes of geranium, and definitely patchouli.

Miguel grabs for the bottle, smacking me on the head as he does.

"I'm so sorry." Abby snares me as she gets a very good look at the bottle. "He must really like your aftershave. Maybe they put catnip in it?"

"This is expensive cologne, not aftershave," Miguel says, sounding petulant and no longer pretending to flirt. "It's L'Homme Prada cologne."

"I'm so, so sorry. I'd be glad to replace it." Abby has stopped smiling and flirting too. Miguel stares at Abby, and then at me, now lying in Abby's arms like a peaceful lap cat. I grin at Miguel and purr.

"No, no, that's quite all right." Miguel regains his composure, smooths his hair, and tries another smile at Abby. "Not that much spilled."

"I bet a lady friend gave that to you?" Abby flips her hair back and licks her lower lip.

Once more I suspect she is overdoing it. But Miguel gives her a sheepish grin and nods. "But it's over now. The relationship, I mean. Perhaps I should stop using it."

"*I like Spicebomb.*" *Abby's voice is suddenly husky, as she runs her fingers through my fur with her eyes focused on Miguel's. "I'll bring you a bottle of that to make up for what my kitty spilled.*"

I don't like being called a kitty, and start to protest, but then remember Abby is acting. Thank goodness Victor has the good sense to stay outside the room and leave this to Abby and me.

"*I'd like that. Very much.*" *Miguel is puffing out with ego, and yet again I stifle the urge to bite the man. "But it's not at all necessary. Not just yet, anyway." He positively twinkles as he looks at Abby.*

Abby gives him a broad smile, touches her hair again, and rocks me in her arms.

"*Forget the spilled cologne. Why don't I take you to supper, and we can catch up with each other? It's been a long time since you were the prettiest redhead in my class.*"

Abby nods, still smiling. "That would be lovely. Say around six? You can pick me up at the law firm. Oh, and what kind of car do you drive?"

If Miguel thinks Abby's question is odd, he doesn't show it. Probably too busy hatching whatever plans he has for Abby.

"*A red Audi TTS. You'll love riding in it. Drives like a dream.*"

I can feel Abby's hold on me tighten. She was no doubt hoping he was going to say he drove a black BMW.

"*Till then." Abby smiles as she glides out of Miguel's office, but her face goes flat and hard the moment she shuts his door.*

CHAPTER FORTY-TWO

$\mathcal{A}$bby dashed down the hallway and collided with Victor. "Come on." She grabbed Victor's arm and they sped around the corner, Trouble racing along between them with his head up as if on alert.

By the time she pulled Victor into an empty conference room, Abby was slightly out of breath.

"What?" Victor asked, too loudly.

Trouble and Abby both shushed him.

"What?" This time Victor's voice was lower, but no less demanding. "What happened in that office?"

"Jennifer." Abby said it with finality, as if that explained the whole thing.

Victor backed up, eyeing Abby, his face a study in puzzlement. "What do you mean?"

"I mean Jennifer and Miguel were having an affair." Abby inhaled deeply as Trouble looked up at both of them and nodded his head. "See, even Trouble figured that out."

"I'm sorry I'm not clairvoyant like your cat. Maybe you could explain this to me." Victor put his hands gently on

Abby's arms and pulled her closer to him. "What did you learn that makes you think that?"

"The cologne. He had a very expensive bottle of cologne."

"So?"

"It's the same kind of cologne Jennifer buys for Phillip." Abby had smelled delightful whiffs of L'Homme Prada from time to time on Phillip. "Jennifer gave him a bottle at our office birthday party for him this past winter. We all passed it around and admired it."

"Okay, so they both wear the same kind of expensive men's cologne. A little pretentious of both, but how does that equate to an affair between Jennifer and Miguel?"

"Don't you see?" Abby sounded exasperated. "How better to hide any...well, lingering scents...if you give your husband and your lover the same cologne. Phillip's not going to think he's smelling someone else's cologne on her, or her things— he'd just figure he was smelling his own."

Victor dropped his hands from Abby's arms and took a small step backwards. His face became a mask. "And you know this trick because you've used it?"

Abby glared at him. He was accusing her—well, insinuating anyway—that she was practiced in the art of cheating. Without thinking, she blurted out. "I've hardly had any boyfriends, let alone two at the same time." She paused, trying to control her rising anger. They didn't have time for this. They had to figure out how they could trick or force Miguel into revealing where Layla was.

But staring into Victor's hard face just made her angrier. "I'm not a cheater!"

Abby flung herself away from Victor and dashed out of the conference room. Once in the hallway, she started running, passing by students and staff without looking at them. Trouble kept pace beside her. She ran down the hallway toward the library, where she could find a quiet study carrel to fume in solitude.

And not just fume, but figure this out. She needed to have a coherent story when she went to Rizzo and Lucas or a fool-proof plan if she confronted Miguel herself.

If Victor was going to be such an ass, she'd just have to save Layla by herself—that is, she and Trouble.

Damn Victor anyway. His first wife cheated, so naturally he assumed she would too.

And he hadn't even let her finish explaining.

It wasn't just the same cologne. It was the tooled silver vanity set she'd seen in Miguel's drawer. She'd seen the same set on a table in a spare room at the Drapers' house with a host of other, unwrapped presents during a Christmas party.

Abby pushed through the library doors and headed imme-diately downstairs to the basement where the quietest spots in the whole law school were. Trouble kept pace beside her, but he didn't meow or rub against her. He seemed preoccupied. That, Abby could understand.

Once in the basement, she found the same carrel she'd been in the night Layla disappeared. Though it was draped in yellow crime tape, Abby sat down. Trouble leapt for her lap. But he didn't curl up or purr; instead he licked her earlobe, where she wore a simple silver hoop earring.

"Okay, Trouble. The earring. I get it. And the wedding ring. But...I don't get it."

Trouble meowed and licked her ear again. Then he lowered his head and pressed his head against her chest. Where her heart was.

Abby thought as hard as she could. The earring was a matter of the heart. That's what Trouble had just told her. And of course, obviously, the wedding ring would be a matter of the heart too.

A missing wedding ring and a missing earring from a set. And Jennifer had been concerned enough to get duplicates made, even if the copies were not as finely crafted as the originals.

The earrings must have been a gift from Phillip and probably a cherished present. The wedding ring should have been priceless to Jennifer.

No doubt Jennifer didn't want Phillip to know her ring and one of the earrings were missing—or more likely, why they were missing. Though Abby had no way to know for sure, she concluded that Jennifer had copies made in the hopes that Phillip would never notice the lost originals.

Maybe she lost her wedding band and the missing earring at Miguel's house? She could imagine Jennifer taking off her ring before she fell into bed with Miguel. And the earring might have fallen out while they had sex.

But wouldn't Jennifer have noticed and reclaimed them?

Trouble head butted Abby again, with a persistent meow. He turned his head back toward the elevator that led to the hallway to the professors' offices and let out a hiss.

Of course. Miguel stole the ring and earring. That's what Trouble was trying to tell her.

"Okay, Trouble, I get it. Miguel took Jennifer's jewelry. But how did Layla get it?

Trouble rubbed his head against Abby's cheek, and she looked into his green eyes. As she stared, she remembered what Victor had told her and that police detective about the phone conversation he'd overheard between Layla and someone at the Drapers' house. Something about Layla agreeing that she would keep the secret, or hide the secret, but only if the other person promised to help her do something about all that off-shore oil drilling stuff.

Victor was so sure Layla had been talking to Phillip.

But what if she'd been talking to Jennifer?

"Trouble," she said, not feeling silly at all for talking to him. "See if this makes sense." Abby's head felt as if it were twirling.

"Okay, here goes. Jennifer and Miguel were having an affair. He stole her ring and earring. And he was using them against her as a kind of blackmail. Since Layla and Miguel were working together on that law review article, Jennifer thought Layla would have access to his stuff, and she asked Layla to get the jewelry back."

Abby paused, scrunching up her forehead. She thought about the wariness between Layla and Jennifer. They weren't great friends, but they were allies of some kind.

She thought about that weird scene between Miguel and Layla the night Layla disappeared. There'd been a lot of sexual tension between the two of them, enough that it'd made Abby uncomfortable.

What if Miguel and Layla had also been having an affair? That might even explain why Miguel was so sure he could get away with stealing Layla's article. As vain as he was, he probably figured he could seduce her into silence.

It wouldn't be unusual for a student and a professor to hook up and certainly Miguel was handsome and charming. The man was well aware of his sexual appeal to women. That had been obvious back when Abby was his student. She'd seen him act seductive with students and faculty members alike. As smart as Layla was, she was still a young woman, very young really. She might not have been able to resist Miguel's allure and his looks. Abby wouldn't have been able to had he ever tried to seduce her when she was as young as Layla.

Abby remembered Phillip had told her Layla's father had spurned her as defective because of the diabetes. Such a rejection could make Layla eager for a man's attention, especially a somewhat older and successful man like Miguel.

And Jennifer might have been more vulnerable to Miguel's obvious charms given her age. She had grown sons, and no matter how beautiful she was, she had to be keenly aware she was an older woman in a culture that favored the young. Having a desirable man like Miguel, with his striking looks, fall for her could have assured Jennifer she was still attractive. It also could have trapped Jennifer into a sordid mess.

But that still didn't explain why Miguel was blackmailing Jennifer.

Still thinking, Abby heard the sound of the elevator coming down into the basement. She stared at the elevator doors, waiting for them to open. As she did, her eyes dropped to the umbrella stand by the elevator.

Like a scene from a movie, Abby saw Layla heading to the bathroom and tossing something in the umbrella stand. Abby had assumed at the time it was just some of Layla's endless supply of chewing gum. She'd even joked with herself that at least Layla hadn't tossed the gum into a potted plant.

But what if it wasn't her gum?

Abby jumped up and ran toward the umbrella stand, but she heard the elevator jerk to a noisy stop. Students took the stairs, professors took the elevator—it was a strange unwritten rule. Suddenly afraid that Miguel would step from the elevator doors and kidnap her, Abby scurried behind a bookshelf, out of sight.

At least she hoped she was out of sight as the elevator doors ground open.

CHAPTER FORTY-THREE

*V*ictor inhaled, furious with himself. Trust. He had to have trust. In Abby and in his own instincts.

After all, she had trusted him and accepted his story about the nude photos on Facebook.

But then what had he just thought of her? When she'd explained the trick of a woman buying the same cologne for her lover and her husband so neither would detect the scent of the other, he had jumped to the conclusion Abby had used that deception herself.

What a mess between them. It was his fault and he had to fix it. He was in love with Abby, and there was no point denying it. She was the woman he wanted to marry. But first he had to work on himself, maybe get some kind of counseling, so he'd stop projecting his ex-wife's infidelities on other women.

Suddenly Victor realized that it wasn't just Abby he'd done that to. When he'd seen that photo of Layla and Phillip, he'd jumped to the wrong conclusion and accused Layla of sleeping with a married man, and one who was her boss. When he'd accused her of that and tried to talk her out of it, she'd become angry with him. He'd tried to convince her that, even aside from the adultery, she would ruin her career if word went out that she was the kind of woman who slept with her boss as a way of promoting her career.

That had made Layla furious with him, and she'd slammed the door on the way out of his house.

And that's where they were—estranged and angry with each other—when someone tried to burn Layla's apartment and she'd gone to stay with Abby.

He had to face it. His suspicions had potentially ruined a valued friendship and maybe torpedoed a developing love relationship. Yep, he needed therapy. But not right now. No, now was the time for doing something.

He had to find Abby. And they had to confront Miguel and force him to tell them where he had stashed Layla.

Victor stood in the hallway, looking left and right, wondering where Abby might have gone. At once he knew. The library. She'd been a librarian after all, and no doubt she would find solace in the stacks. As he hurried down to the next floor level, classes let out and the corridors crowded with students.

Victor glanced back down the hallway and spotted Delphine and Emmett rushing toward him. He paused to greet them, but they had their heads together and didn't even see him as they hurried past. Delphine was dressed in a red tailor-made suit that fit her curves. Emmett wore a suit, the classic law student gray with white shirt and maroon tie. Victor wondered why he appeared dressed for court while at school, but he didn't wonder why Emmett was at the law school. He was, after all, a third-year student. But Delphine's presence raised a red flag.

Victor huddled in behind them in the milling crowd of

students, ducking his head a bit to hide his face, as he struggled to hear them.

"You were brilliant." Emmett spoke with enthusiasm, his voice carrying. "You handled that hearing so smoothly the judge had to rule your way."

What a brown-nosing toad. Victor wondered if Delphine would fall for the praise.

Delphine said something he couldn't hear over the jostling and buzz of the hallway, but her expression was carefully neutral.

"Well, maybe so, but Phillip is out of jail now. Thank you for letting me assist you. It's good for me to learn from such a masterful mentor." Emmett pressed in close to Delphine. "And thank you for letting me help you here today."

Once more Victor couldn't hear Delphine's reply and stepped up closer behind them. If they turned around, all he had to say was "Hello" and act as if he'd been hurrying behind them to speak with them.

Delphine stopped in front of the elevator and hit the down button. "All right. But we better find that file you say Layla took."

"She must have hidden it in the law library." Emmett pounded on the elevator down button with some force.

Victor stopped in his tracks.

Why would Layla have taken Delphine's file? And why would Emmett say it "must" be in the library basement unless he'd already searched Abby's house and Layla's apartment?

CHAPTER FORTY-FOUR

*A*bby huddled behind the bookshelf with Trouble crouched at her feet, ready to leap out to defend her. After the elevator door opened, Delphine and Emmett stepped out. Abby exhaled with relief, only then aware she'd been holding her breath.

She started to step out from behind the books, but Emmett's voice stopped her.

"Well, I know you think the world of Abby and she was certainly distracted, but that trial brief she and Layla were preparing for you was not up to par. If I hadn't put in all those extra hours on it, you wouldn't have won that motion." Emmett all but preened as he finished speaking. "Of course, Layla was sabotaging the brief too, so maybe that excuses some of Abby's poor work."

Abby stifled the urge to rush out and defend herself and Layla. Instead, she waited to see if Delphine would speak up for her.

Delphine cut her eyes at Emmett for a half second before she strode into the basement of the library like a woman on a mission, with Emmett scurrying behind her to catch up. Over her shoulder, Delphine snapped out, "We better find that file you say Layla took. I'll start in the back of the stacks, you start here."

What file? Abby eased out closer to watch Emmett. Trouble rubbed against her leg, staying both close and quiet.

Emmett looked around, but he didn't spot Abby behind the stacks. He pulled a folded manila legal-sized envelope from his jacket and smoothed out the fold. Once more he glanced around. Then he tucked the file between two books on a shelf right in front of him and hurried off in the same direction Delphine had gone.

Abby waited until he was out of sight before she rushed over to the envelope and yanked it out from between the books. If there was anything inside that would help her find Layla, and Emmett had been hiding it, so help her, she was going to slash his tires, paint his windshield black, and petition the dean to expel him.

Once she had the envelope in hand, she rushed to the umbrella stand and looked down. She wanted to find whatever it was Layla had dropped there right before she disappeared. Random pieces of trash and dust were collected in the container, but no umbrella. Abby stuck her hand inside and felt around, hoping she didn't touch anything too gross. In short order, she found candy wrappers, a cigarette butt, scraps of paper and gum. Lots of gum. Abby was disgusted and started to pull her hands out. But as she did, her fingers found what she was looking for—yet another flash drive. Unlike Layla's trademark bright pink flash drives, this one was standard issue black.

While Abby doubted this was Layla's, nonetheless, she grabbed the flash drive and ran for the book stacks. There wasn't anything she could do about reading the flash drive right at the moment, but she could damn sure see what was in the envelope Emmett had hidden.

Beside her, Trouble meowed and jumped up on a shelf until he was level with Abby's hands as she tore open the envelope. He wanted to see too. Abby smiled at Trouble but didn't speak for fear of alerting Emmett.

She pulled out a set of documents pertaining to a will—affidavits and notarized codicils and such. Then, to her surprise, she found an original will. It was yellowed a bit but looked intact. She inhaled so sharply that Trouble rubbed against her and uttered a very soft meow of apparent concern.

These were materials—vital documents—from Delphine's upcoming contested will trial that Abby had been working on when all of the troubles started. Delphine would need these original documents to win her case once the trial actually began. It was fundamental in a contested case that the party relying on the will actually had to produce the original will. So losing the will was the same as losing the case.

Why on earth did Emmett have that original will and other documents?

It didn't take a second for Abby to conjure up a satisfactory explanation. Emmett had worked on that case too. He had access to all the documents, and he knew he needed to sabotage Layla if he were to get hired as an associate at the law firm. He must have stolen the documents and cast the blame on Layla. Now he would become the hero of the moment when he found them where everyone would assume Layla had hidden them the night she disappeared.

Was this why Layla had been kidnapped? To keep her from protesting that she hadn't taken or lost these critical documents?

Abby thought back to the dark-colored BMW that had nearly run her off the road. The driver's face had been a blur in the night, but Emmett drove a black, late-model BMW.

Abby began to connect the dots.

Professor Miguel drove a red sports car, so he wasn't the person who had run her off the road fleeing from Jennifer's house. He might be a plagiarist and promiscuous, but he wasn't an arsonist or a kidnapper.

Emmett was.

Just as she came to this realization, the doors to the stairs opened and Victor rushed into the basement. He called out her name, not once, but twice.

She ran up and put a finger to her lips in the age-old silent gesture for shut up.

From around the corner, Emmett's voice grew in intensity. "I'm sure that's what I saw. Stuffed between two books. But I didn't touch the envelope. That's for you to do."

"Don't be so melodramatic," Delphine snapped.

"But Layla took it and hid it. You can see for yourself. She was trying to sabotage your case." Emmett's voice had the sound of somebody in a losing argument.

Victor cocked his head at Abby, a look of puzzlement on his face. Trouble jumped down from the book shelf and rubbed against Victor. Abby held the documents in one hand and gestured for Victor to duck behind a book shelf. She wanted emergency back-up if her confrontation went badly.

Delphine and Emmett came around the book stack. Emmett came to an abrupt stop and glared at her.

"How long have you been here?" Emmett asked, stepping close enough to her to get a look at what she held in her hands.

"Long enough to see what you—not Layla, but you—hid in the book case." Abby didn't wait for a denial. She handed the documents to Delphine. "I was behind the bookshelves when you two came in. After you left, I saw Emmett pull this envelope from inside his jacket and hide it there." Abby pointed. "Between those two books. Then he ran off to find you."

"That is so not true." Emmett's face turned a deep coral shade. "You're lying to protect your girlfriend. Layla's the thief."

Delphine pushed between Emmett and Abby and took the documents. She glanced at them before turning toward Emmett. "You're fired. I'll be filing a complete report with the Florida Board of Law Examiners and if I have anything to do with it, you'll never practice law a single day in your sniveling little life."

"Layla." Abby spoke too loudly in the library basement and the name seemed to echo. "You just couldn't stop hurting her, could you? Even now!"

"Oh, yes," Delphine added after a quick glance at Abby, "I suspect the police would like a word with you over Layla's disappearance."

CHAPTER FORTY-FIVE

*V*ictor stood near Abby while Detectives Rizzo and Kelly handcuffed a stricken-looking Emmett. As Rizzo and Kelly began to escort him away, Emmett paused by Abby.

"Layla beat me out for editor of law review, she beat me out for moot court, and she beat me out for best paper in estate and gift tax. I couldn't let her beat me again by getting hired at the firm—not when I needed that job."

"Why this stunt? Why now?" Abby asked.

"Don't you see?" Emmett stood his ground, looking at Abby as if she were the judge hearing his plea. "When she gets rescued, she'll be this big hero, with everybody sympathetic towards her, and I'll never have a chance against her again. What I did was...stupid... and desperate, trying to blame her for tampering with a file. But that's all I did."

Rizzo tugged at Emmett. "Save it for the jury."

Emmett gave Abby one last quick look. "Honest, I didn't hurt her."

Abby looked away from Emmett as Rizzo pushed him

toward the elevator. Trouble sat quietly, yet protectively, at Abby's feet. Victor studied Abby a moment to be sure she was all right.

Lucas stopped long enough in front of Abby and Victor to say, "Y'all don't worry, we'll get him to admit where he's got Layla hidden. If he won't tell, we'll retrace his tracks and find her. We'll have her back before you know it."

"Over a damn job." Delphine muttered as she tucked herself between Abby and Victor. "Destroying all those lives to discredit Layla so he could get her job. I know law students are competitive, but that's just sick."

"Lucas—that is Detective Kelly— says they figured out how Emmett got the dead homeless man out of the bathroom." Victor leaned toward Delphine to explain in a soft voice, not wanting the gathering crowd to overhear. "They found traces of the dead man's blood in the freight elevator and on a dolly that the librarians use to move books. They'll be examining Emmett's car for other evidence."

"I gather from all I've heard that Emmett's plan was to have the homeless man kidnap Layla and leave that ransom note in the bathroom, no doubt while Emmett created an alibi. But something went wrong." Delphine shook her head. "That poor man. Killed over such pettiness."

What about Layla, Victor thought, but didn't ask Delphine. Instead, he watched Abby as the elevator doors closed on Rizzo, Lucas, and Emmett.

Once the detectives and Emmett were gone, Abby turned to Delphine. "How's Jennifer?"

"Phillip is with her. She's still in a coma, but her vital signs are good. I think the doctors are optimistic." Delphine smiled at Abby. "Thank you for saving her in the house fire. No one will forget what a trouper you've been during all of this."

Abby ignored the comment as her frown deepened. "But why hurt Jennifer? And why try to burn their house down? I mean I get it that Emmett would have access at the office to Phillip's things. His law school library access card and his prescriptions were in his desk. I get the frame-up. And," Abby glanced back at Victor, "we can all see the trap he set for Victor, though it certainly wasn't well done." She paused, looking from Delphine to Victor. "But why hurt Jennifer?"

"She must have known something or figured something out. Maybe she remembered Emmett borrowing Phillip's library key card." Victor spoke, keeping his worried gaze on Abby. She was tough, but how much more could she take? But he also wondered why Emmett would want to hurt Jennifer.

"Well, it's not over until they get Layla back. What if...I mean he killed that homeless man, didn't he? Why wouldn't he just kill Layla too?" Abby wobbled on her feet and spoke with a catch in her voice.

Victor could tell Abby was trying hard not to cry. Trouble rubbed against her leg and hummed an encouraging purr.

"Let me take you home, tuck you into bed. I'll keep company with Trouble, maybe feed him some salmon while you sleep." Victor figured Rizzo and Lucas would break Emmett quickly and they'd have Layla back before Abby's nap was over.

And after that, Victor had some definite and slightly wicked ideas of how to wake up Abby.

The elevator doors opened and Miguel and another professor stepped off and into the crowd. A campus police officer approached the two, probably warning them off. Victor only glanced at them before his eyes focused back on Abby. But Miguel moved to Abby's side.

"I'm so glad that this is over," Miguel said. You'll have your friend back very soon now. I'm sure she'll be just fine when the police locate her." He sounded sincere as he rested his hand lightly on Abby's arm, rather possessively Victor thought, as he glared at the professor. Abby dusted Miguel off with a quick swipe of her free hand, and barely whispered a "thank you."

Miguel continued to stand by Abby, his expression calmly neutral. "Given all the excitement, why don't we postpone our date tonight? When Layla is back with us and has recovered, I'd like to take you and her both out to eat in my new car and we'll celebrate her rescue." He glanced over at Victor. "You'll be most welcome to join us, of course."

Victor wanted to punch the man even though Miguel was being perfectly polite. Obviously, Miguel didn't know they'd figured out he was a plagiarist.

"We're all very tired. Let's just wait and see how it goes." Abby stepped away from Miguel and hurried toward the elevator, motioning for Victor to follow her. Trouble, who'd been plastered against Abby's legs, moved along beside her.

Once they were in the elevator, Abby spoke. "Everybody'll know soon enough about Miguel's plagiarism. But let's wait until we get Layla back. That way, she can have the pleasure of turning him in." Abby ran her hand across her face as if to wipe it clean. "And to think I used to have a crush on him."

"You did?" Victor stared at Abby. But no sense of jealousy or mistrust rose in him. He realized with a rush of love and peace that he trusted Abby. His ex-wife's behavior had left him distrustful, and maybe a tad paranoid. Now that he understood his earlier suspicions arose from his own past, and not from Abby's behavior, he could heal from the fallout of his first marriage. His newfound trust flowed through his whole body as he put his arms around Abby, hugging her close to him.

A moment later, Victor opened the outside door of the

law school and they stepped into the clean, warm air of a Tallahassee September. The magnolia tree by the law school's side entrance was glossy and green in the intense light. With Abby and Trouble beside him, Victor felt a new life opening for him. With a new faith in Rizzo and Lucas, he believed they'd have Layla safely home in short order.

They walked in silence toward the parking lot. Even Trouble kept quiet. Once they were all sitting in Victor's pickup, he reached over and took Abby's hand and held it between his own two.

"I'm sorry I insinuated that you were experienced in the ways of cheating."

"That's all right." Abby sighed. "I thought some pretty bad things about you too."

"I'll get some counseling. Something I probably should have done after all my ex-wife did to me. I don't ever want to mistrust you again." Victor leaned forward and kissed Abby on the cheek. "I promise."

Abby squeezed his hand and gave him a tiny, tired smile. "Maybe I'll go with you to counseling. I don't ever want to doubt you again either."

"Let me get you home." He started the pickup.

"You know, there're some loose ends and I don't get the ring and earring—" Abby stated.

"Maybe Emmett planted them—like he did the documents Layla supposedly stole, and the Valium. If Jennifer thought Layla had stolen her ring and earring, that would have done her in for good with Phillip and the law firm." Victor's hands tensed on the steering wheel. "Don't forget how Emmett set me up. And tried to insinuate you were involved by sending him away that night."

"And I saw him driving away from Jennifer's when he ran me off the road." Abby hesitated. "That is, I saw a car like his."

Trouble meowed, but it was a pensive sound. Victor cut his eyes toward the cat and Trouble looked right back at Victor and held his gaze.

Victor could swear the cat was telling him it wasn't over.

CHAPTER FORTY-SIX

$\mathcal{A}$bby threw down her purse and eyed the inside of her house. It was still a mess. She needed to finish repotting the plants, but a quick look at her aquarium told her the fish were adjusting well to the unscheduled changes in the tank.

Victor stood beside her, an arm loosely around her waist. "I'll help you finish cleaning up and we can repot the plants. Together."

She liked the way he said "together."

Abby turned to him, catching the look in his eyes. With her own, she signaled yes. In case he missed her answer, Abby pulled him to her. She kissed him, tentatively at first, but with increasing fervor as his hands stroked her back, and then dropped lower.

One of her hands inched to his chest, and her fingers found their way inside the exposed triangle at the top of his shirt. She traced a path across his skin before she pulled her hand free and started unbuttoning his shirt. As she began to undress him, his hands cupped her buttocks and his thumb rubbed up and down across the fabric of her pants.

Abby wanted to rip her shirt and pants off. But she made herself slow down. Pulling her lips away from his, she pressed her mouth to his bare chest, making a slow, deliberate path downward and then up again. His chest was covered with sandy blond hair that felt silky under her lips and tongue.

Though she was not usually so brazen, she also wasn't usually so hungry for touch.

His touch.

Her fingers slipped down to the zipper on his jeans and lingered for a moment. His hand pressed down on top of hers and she felt him rise, hard and long, beneath her fingers.

With his other hand, Victor began to unbutton her blouse. In a moment, they broke apart so that she could slip it off entirely. His shirt hung unbuttoned off his shoulders. As soon as she threw her blouse toward the couch, she pulled his shirt off him. For a moment, she just stood there, appreciating the ripple of his muscles, the flatness of his stomach, and the brush of the sandy chest hair.

She looked into his eyes and saw that he was giving her much the same appreciative gaze.

"May I?" he asked as he reached for her bra.

She nodded. He unsnapped it and flung it toward her blouse. "Perfect," he said, and ran his hands over the soft mounds, with his thumbs flicking the nipples ever so lightly. Abby arched her back, pushing herself closer to him and increasing their skin-to-skin friction.

His hands traced patterns up and down her bare back, sending ripples of sensation everywhere he touched, as his teeth nibbled gently on her bottom lip. She opened her mouth and his tongue slipped in.

Abby once more reached for the front of his pants. But even as she struggled to undress him further, his fingers tugged down her zipper with exquisite slowness. Once he had her pants unfastened, she stepped back and kicked them off, glad as she did that something had told her earlier to wear a lovely peach-colored matching set of bra and panties.

Before she could work his pants free, Victor had his fingers under the lace edge of her panties, trailing along their bikini lines. Her breath was coming fast as she yanked harder at his pants while he bent his head to her breasts and began to suck on first one nipple, then the other.

LATER, ABBY STOOD in front of her dresser with her back to Victor, who sat on the edge of her bed. Her whole body still tingled from their lovemaking and she wore only a loose cotton shirt. Her robe would have felt too heavy against her bare skin with her body's newly heightened sense of touch. Earlier, they had barely made it to her bedroom, leaving a trail of her panties and his pants and boxers along the hallway. She could feel Victor's eyes on her and it made her skin flush.

As Abby swept her hair into a loose ponytail, Victor rose off the bed. He moved behind Abby, wrapping his arms around her and the thin shirt she wore. He wore nothing and the strength in his bare arms as he held her tempted her to toss her shirt on the floor.

Victor nibbled at her ear as he put one of his hands over the front of her shirt and rubbed the soft fabric against the skin on her stomach.

She pressed back against him, arching her body, as delightful shivers shot through her. Throwing that damn blouse to the floor was feeling like a better idea all the time.

Their love making—and the nap afterwards—had refreshed her, but not nearly as much as her acceptance that this was the man she loved. Her body had never before responded to another's in quite the way she had just a couple of hours before. A small smile flirted about her lips as she realized her body had known she was in love, even if her emotions had still held out some doubt.

But that doubt was gone now.

Her shirt began to slip a bit under Victor's hands. Abby felt the warmth of his breath on her neck. His fingers continued to rub the fabric against her bare skin, creating a pleasurable sensation of heat and tension.

Trouble, who had had the common decency to make himself scarce the last two hours, ran into the room. After a decisive jump to the top of the dresser, he looked at her with piercing eyes. Trouble meowed in a distinct pattern of sounds, like he was explaining a matter of some importance to them.

Abby sighed. Trouble was right, she needed to check on Layla. The romantic moment was over. For now.

"I'll call Lucas and see if they've found Layla." Abby expected Victor to protest, but he agreed.

She hurried to the living room and dug her cell phone out of her purse. Victor followed. Expecting to hear only good news, she called Lucas—she had his number memorized by now. Without bothering to say hello or identify herself, she asked breathlessly, "Have you found Layla?"

"No." Lucas paused. "We're tracking Emmett's where-abouts and his haunts, and we have a team at his apartment and going over his car. But he keeps denying he took her."

Abby said goodbye and ended the call. As she gave Victor a worried look, Trouble knocked her purse over, spilling its contents about the couch and floor.

"Somebody's jealous," Victor said.

"No, he's trying to tell me something." Abby looked at the mess scattered about. "What, Trouble? What do I need to see?"

With his nose, Trouble butted a black flash drive out of the pile of items on the couch.

Abby picked it up. "I found this in the umbrella stand by the elevator. I really don't think it's Layla's because she always used pink flash drives. I was going to check anyway. But," she paused, looking embarrassed, "I just forgot about it, with...you know." Her face burned with a blush.

"Even if it is Layla's, it's probably just more drafts of her law review."

"Probably. But, you know, it doesn't all make sense." Abby held the flash drive up to the sunlight streaming through the sheer curtains on the front window as if some how she could see what it contained. As she did, Trouble reached up and touched the flash drive with his paw.

"Even Trouble knows something is missing." Abby dropped her hand with the flash drive. "I brought a law firm laptop home to use while those detectives have mine. Let's see what's on this."

Victor nodded.

"Oh, and maybe you better get dressed." She gave him an admiring look. "I like the view just fine, but I wouldn't want to give my neighbors a shock."

CHAPTER FORTY-SEVEN

*V*ictor, fully dressed once more, plugged the flash drive into the USB port on Abby's borrowed laptop. Trouble butted his leg, meowed, and looked up at Victor as if to say "get to work."

"Okay, okay," he muttered at the cat.

Abby was in the kitchen, brewing coffee and scrambling eggs. He could smell the coffee and his mouth watered. He studied the screen on the laptop as the flash drive opened with two folders, one labeled "microfilm" and the other labeled "the book."

More research, Victor thought. He was tempted to turn off the laptop and get some coffee. But once more Trouble butted his leg and meowed.

"You'd have made a good drill sergeant." Victor glared at Trouble, but opened the microfilm folder, and squinted at the scanned microfilm. Barely readable. He opened the other folder on the flash drive.

Trouble jumped from the floor to Victor's shoulder and peered at the screen before nudging Victor and issuing a series of distinctively patterned meows. Not for the first time, Victor wished he spoke Cat.

He went back to reading the folder on the flash drive.

A moment later, he shouted out to Abby in the kitchen, "Damn, it was more than the law review."

HERE I AM, once more trying to communicate with bipeds and having them miss my point.

New car. I meow this phrase as clearly as I can to Victor.

He's too busy shouting for Abby to listen to what he found on the flash drive.

I try again, this time with my face in front of his and my paw on his leg. Miguel said he has a new car. If the red car is brand new, might his old car be a dark BMW? Might he still have had the BMW the night someone in such a vehicle nearly ran Abby off the road as that person fled the Drapers' house after forcing pills down Jennifer's throat and trying to set a fire?

Victor brushes me aside as Abby rushes in from the kitchen to stand over Victor. They peer down at the computer screen.

"That book, the one on the Marshall court that Miguel is famous for writing." Victor pauses, watching Abby's face. "This is what Layla has on this flash drive. There're scans from some really old microfilm from the Library of Congress."

"The Library of Congress," Abby repeats. "Miguel mentioned something about that the night Layla disappeared."

"Yeah, well, so he knew she knew then."

"Knew what?"

"He *didn't* write that book." Victor taps the screen for emphasis, and once more I try to communicate with him.

"*Quiet, Trouble,*" he says to me before turning to Abby again. "Miguel stole it from a law professor in Miami. And that professor had taken most of it from a rare, ancient manuscript written by Marshall's faithful law clerk, who had access to Marshall's papers and very thoughts."

"He plagiarized a plagiarism?" Abby looks puzzled, her hands now resting on Victor's shoulders.

"Looks that way." Victor's eyes flick over the screen. "I'm still reading."

"If Layla knew, why didn't she—?" Abby says. "I mean, once she knew this, why didn't Layla report him? She had proof, didn't she? Plus the law review article."

"Look, she explains it. She was protecting Jennifer." Victor reads another line off the computer. "Here's what she says. 'If I turn Miguel in for plagiarizing my article and stealing his book, then he'll ruin Jennifer and Phillip's marriage by telling Phillip about their affair. That's why Miguel stole her wedding ring and that earring, the one Phillip gave her as an anniversary present. He intends to use them to prove the affair.'"

Abby shakes her head and mutters, "So that's what Miguel was blackmailing Jennifer about—to make her help him keep Layla quiet." But she frowns, her face a study in confusion. "Why would Layla want to protect Jennifer? I don't think they were that close."

Abby is missing the point. I meow and rub against her. Once again, I press my head against her chest where her heart beats.

Victor throws me a curious look before he answers. "She wasn't protecting Jennifer. She was protecting Phillip."

"So, a stand-off." Abby lowers her face until she is looking into Trouble's eyes. "What changed? Why the fires and the murder and the kidnapping?"

I lick at Abby's ear and nibble at the small silver hoop she wears in her earlobe. Haven't they figured it out yet?

"The earring." Abby and Victor shout it out at once. "And the wedding ring."

"Miguel stole the most personal of Jennifer's jewelry so he could prove the affair and blackmail Jennifer so she'd have to control Layla. But Layla stole the jewelry back from him. He must have known she'd put all these flash drives all over the place and that's why he was trying to burn her apartment and the Drapers' house—to destroy the evidence." Abby is practically shouting and I rub her cheek and meow a word of caution.

"Absolutely, if you can't find the evidence against you, destroy it. Burn it."

"But how did Layla figure out about his stealing the book?"

Victor turns once more to the computer monitor and scrolls down. "She might have been blinded by love—that's her phrase—but eventually she realized Miguel wasn't a good enough writer—or thinker—to have written the book that made him semi-famous among constitutional law scholars. When he stole her law review article, she realized he was a plagiarist."

Abby takes up reading over Victor's shoulders. "Once Layla sank her teeth into it, it was only a matter of time before she found out what he'd done. She is, after all, an excellent researcher."

"When Miguel was a lawyer, he represented a professor from the University of Miami School of Law and found a copy of an old manuscript the professor was using in writing his own book on the Marshall Court and how it changed the history of this country. Only that professor died before he finished." Victor paused in his reading. "I bet if we Google that professor we'll find out he died under suspicious circumstances."

"So, with that professor out of the way, Miguel took the manuscript and passed it off as his own." Abby rubs my head, but as nice as it feels, I can't purr. Instead, I jump down, run to the door and yowl.

They both look at me, but then Victor turns back to the computer. I yowl again. We need to be finding Layla. Now. Miguel believes this *whole ordeal is over with Emmett's arrest. He has little reason to keep Layla alive any longer.*

But Abby and Victor keep chatting on, as if time didn't matter at all. I head butt Victor's arm, but he ignores me as he keeps reading the computer screen.

"Layla found the only other existing copy of the old manuscript that the Miami professor was using, a surviving copy in the Library of Congress. An archivist there emailed her scans of the microfilm made from the original." Victor points at the screen as if Abby would doubt him. "For Layla to put the whole story together like this, you know she knew she was in danger from Miguel. The mugging probably tipped her off that the stalemate was over, but I'm guessing she didn't really know what to do—other than leave a new flash drive with all this info."

"She wasn't at home the night of the fire." Abby looked at Victor as if for confirmation. "And the mugger had a plastic knife, for heaven's sake. So, Layla probably thought Miguel was just warning her. Since they'd been lovers, she probably thought that he wouldn't really hurt her."

"Yeah, she misread him for sure."

"That night in the library, he said something about Layla doing research in the Library of Congress, and she acted weird, and then she ran outside in the hallway. And called Emmett. And later you." Abby scrunched her fingers through her hair. "That's when she realized he knew she'd found out about the book. So, she was calling reinforcements —she thought you and Emmett could protect us in the library."

Abby shook her head, her expression distressed. "What I thought was this weird sexual vibe between them was just plain old-fashioned fear. How could I have misread it so?"

"Don't blame yourself. Too much was going on." Victor fingers the flash drive in the USB port. "But after Miguel tipped his hand, Layla hid this flash drive with the whole story on it in the umbrella stand."

"Why hide it? Why didn't she just give it to me?" Abby sounds hurt. "Didn't she trust me?"

"I figure she was trying to protect you—and she was still mad at me, so she couldn't give it to me. Who else did she have? She couldn't give it to Phillip or Delphine. So, she hid it. I bet there's another one somewhere we haven't found yet."

"No—" Abby says. "She sent the info on this one to Jennifer. She told Jennifer the whole story. She had to have. That night at the library, as soon as we got to the basement, she typed like crazy on her laptop. I bet she was emailing Jennifer."

"But..." Victor hesitates. "Why Jennifer?"

"Who else? After Miguel's crack about the Library of Congress, Layla must have been scared of Miguel, especially since he knew we were in the basement. So, she probably emailed him that she'd hidden the flash drive with all the info and told someone that if anything happened to her, they should send it to the cops. And that somebody was Jennifer, though of course she wouldn't tell Miguel that. Why else would Jennifer say the word 'Marshall' to me?"

I yowl another warning at Abby and Victor, but Abby's thoughts must be spinning so wildly in her head she ignores me.

"That's why Miguel had to kill Jennifer and burn the house." Victor's voice is loud with excitement and he hops out of the chair and takes giant strides about the room. "He knew Layla told Jennifer and also told her about the evidence about the damn book."

"Let's email Layla's info to Delphine and those detectives. And to the Texas Law Review and the whole world. Then we'll call Lucas." Abby curls into the chair in front of the laptop and starts typing as Victor reaches deep into his pocket.

"Here," he says, offering Abby a business card. "I knew I had Lucas's email."

Abby types something. "There, I've got the document attached. Let's send it, then call those detectives." Abby's finger hovers over the mouse.

"Wait, no." Victor suddenly puts his hand on top of Abby's to stop her from hitting send. "This is our ransom. We might need to trade this flash drive for Layla." Victor runs his hand through his unruly hair. "Miguel knows Layla had something like this flash drive that he hasn't found or he would have just killed her. He's holding her, I'd guess, until she tells him where she hid the last of the flash drives."

"But where would he be holding her? And where is he anyway?"

CHAPTER FORTY-EIGHT

*a*bby's finger hovered over the send button. She wanted the world to know what Miguel had done and the sooner the better.

"Why don't we call Rizzo and Lucas?" Abby thought maybe this was the time to pull in the detectives.

"Because they won't try to negotiate with him. They'll just arrest him and we might not find Layla in time. If he's got her tied up somewhere without her insulin and the cops lock him up, she could die before anyone found her. If we can't find her on our own, we have to contact Miguel and offer to trade the flash drive for Layla and we have to mean it. He'd know the cops wouldn't make a trade like that and let him go."

Abby nodded. She didn't like it, but maybe it made sense.

Victor glanced at the wall clock. "He'll be teaching his American Jurisprudence class in just a few minutes. So he's at FSU now and he'll be there at least an hour, probably more. We need to check his house while he's at the law school."

Abby didn't know where the professor lived, but she knew

how to find out. She pulled up the Leon County Property Appraiser's official website and typed in Miguel's name.

"Here's his address," she said. "One of those new townhouses at the edge of downtown Tallahassee, near the law school. But he couldn't have taken Layla there—somebody would have seen them." Abby frowned, thinking hard. "He said something to Phillip about a place by the lake, but there's nothing listed here about another property."

"There's that big lake in Grady County, lots of cabins and get-away places. Maybe it's there?" Victor suggested.

Abby pulled up the Grady County property appraiser's office and typed Miguel's name. "Yes. Grady County, right across the state line, only thirty miles from here." Abby kept reading. "A lakeside cabin, small from the description. Sounds isolated."

"That's where he'd take her," Victor pounded on the back on the couch. Trouble meowed as if agreeing.

Abby scribbled something down on a piece of paper, forgetting for the briefest moment that Miguel was a dangerous man who had already killed. "I've got the address. We can sneak in and find Layla and get her out of there while he's still teaching." Abby spoke without hesitancy, but her heart raced. "And if he's there, we negotiate with the flash drive."

"Let's go." Victor paced, jangling his pickup keys.

"Wait a minute, let me Google-map the address."

MAYBE I HAVE MORE faith in Lucas than they do. Maybe I'm not currently love-addled. But it seems to me that the email to Lucas needs to be sent. Now. While Miguel is teaching and Abby and Victor are spinning around the living room getting ready to rescue Layla.

I prance over to the opened laptop and I hit send.

CHAPTER FORTY-NINE

*A*bby read out the directions as Victor sped through a series of narrow roads in Grady County as they rushed toward Miguel's lake cabin. Trouble sat tensely in Abby's lap.

The drive took them thirty-five minutes before they found the long, dirt road that Google-map promised them led to the lake cabin's front door. "Let's walk it from here. Element of surprise and all that just in case he's there." As he spoke, Victor pulled the pickup off the paved road into a thicket. He pulled an extra switchblade from his locked glove compartment. He put the knife in his pants pocket.

Abby wished he had a gun, but between the knife and Trouble, they'd surely be safe enough.

"Let's just pray he's teaching at FSU and not here." Abby shut her eyes for a second and said a quick prayer. Beside her, Trouble issued a quiet meow.

They crept silently up the edge of the heavily treed dirt road, with Trouble keeping his nose in the air, sniffing. Abby marveled at what a beautiful place Miguel had, though the distance from any civilization was a bit disconcerting. No doubt this was where he took his lovers. She wondered how many students he had seduced in the place.

Even hurrying, it took them ten minutes to find the actual cabin. The building came into view when they rounded a sharp curve in the road. Abby paused, drawing a sharp intake of breath. Trouble halted briefly, before easing a few steps ahead of her.

The curtains were drawn, bushes were overgrown, and the place had an air of abandonment, yet it was undeniably a beautiful, lush spot on a small lake. But best of all, there was no little red sports car or any other vehicle in the driveway. Abby started toward the house.

They hurried, keeping to the heavy bushes as they approached the front window. Abby pushed past Victor and looked inside. She didn't see Layla, but she saw the plastic container with the blue lid where Layla kept her insulin. Scattered vials of insulin littered the table. "It needs to be refrigerated," she said, a new burst of fear for Layla rising in her.

"I'm calling Lucas. Since Miguel's not here, we won't need to negotiate with him and we might need some help." Victor said it in a tone of voice that didn't invite discussion. He pulled out his cell and started punching in numbers.

Abby tiptoed away from him to look in another set of windows. This time she spotted Layla, tied to a chair, her head slumped to one side. Abby called out to Victor, forgetting the need to be quiet. "I see her, I see Layla." Trouble let out a resounding meow as if to second Abby.

"Damn it to hell and back," Victor said. "I can't get a signal. We're too far in the woods."

But Abby barely heard him. She was racing toward the door and to Layla, Trouble moving ahead of her, running full out.

CHAPTER FIFTY

*V*ictor cursed his dead phone. So much for that "can you hear me now" ad.

Maybe it didn't really matter. Surely they could just scoop Layla up and get back to his pickup long before Miguel's class ended.

He ran after Abby and the cat, catching them both in only seconds. Together, they sprinted to the front door. It was locked, and Victor saw at once it was a deadbolt. "I can't pick it without some tools," he said.

"Try the back," Abby said, but she was already eyeing the wide, low-slung window by the door.

Victor sprinted around the house. As he ran, he heard the shattering of glass and spun back to the front. Abby hadn't waited. She'd busted through the glass with a large rock.

Once he reached the front, he scooped up Trouble, not wanting the cat to cut his feet, as Abby kicked the shards of glass out of the frame.

"Careful," he said, as she crawled through the opening.

A moment later, Abby opened the front door and Victor

hurried inside. Once past the busted glass, he dropped Trouble on the floor as he ran toward Layla. Abby was already there.

"She's unconscious." Abby patted Layla's cheek and then checked her pulse. "Her heart rate is slow."

Victor scanned the litter on the table for any blood sugar monitoring device but saw none. If Layla was suffering from low blood sugar and they gave her insulin, they could kill her. But if her blood sugar was spiking high enough to make her unconscious, and they didn't give her insulin, she might die.

They had to call 9-1-1.

"Abby, try your phone. Call for an ambulance. And for Rizzo and Lucas. I'll cut her loose." Victor pulled out his switchblade and in no time had the ropes cut away from Layla. Dropping the knife to the wood floor, he lifted her from the chair and carried her over to a couch near the front door. As he rested Layla on the couch, she slid sideways, still unconscious.

Abby snatched her cell from her pocket and started punching numbers. "No way," she said as she looked up in shock at Victor. "I can't get a signal."

"Damn it!" Victor shouted. "Stay here, I'll bring the truck to the cabin so we can take her straight to a hospital."

"Look for a landline," she said.

"You look. I'll run back to the truck." Victor glanced down at Trouble. "You stay here and watch out for Abby."

Victor started for the front, but before his hand reached the knob, the door flung open.

In the entrance way, Miguel stood, holding a large gun in one hand and a rope in the other. Trouble swiped at Miguel's leg, but Miguel aimed a vicious kick at him, knocking him a few feet away.

When Trouble rolled to a stop, Miguel lunged forward and

kicked him again, once more knocking him a few feet in front of him.

"Leave him alone." Abby cried out and stepped toward Trouble, but Victor jumped in front of her and blocked her. He shoved his hand in his pocket and felt for reassuring coldness of his switchblade—but he'd dropped it on the floor after he cut Layla loose.

"Be still." Victor whispered as he hovered in front of Abby. He wanted to keep his body between Abby and the man's gun, but he also wanted to block Miguel's view of the knife.

"You people just couldn't leave well enough alone, could you?" Miguel pointed the gun at Victor's gut. "Here I was, coming back to get rid of Layla once and for all, and I see your pickup half-hidden in the bushes." He grinned. "Not a good judgment call on your part."

Neither Abby nor Victor moved. But Trouble rolled over, and, limping, crept toward them. Victor glanced down at him, wondering how badly Miguel's kicks had hurt the cat. Trouble rubbed against Abby's leg as if to reassure them he was all right, but kept going away from them. Victor cocked his head, just far enough to see that Trouble headed straight to the switchblade.

Acting quickly to distract Miguel, Victor made a lunge toward him. Miguel side-stepped and pressed the gun against Abby's stomach. "Try that again, and I gut-shoot her."

Victor stood still, but glanced out of the corner of his eyes to see what Trouble was doing. The cat was sprawled out on top of the knife. While he looked like an injured cat, Trouble also effectively hid the knife from Miguel's view.

Trouble meowed, with the sound low and plaintive. As Victor once more glanced at him, Trouble looked up toward the bookshelf and meowed again. But this time his cry had a distinctive, clear tone. Trouble was trying to tell Victor something.

Victor followed Trouble's gaze and saw a large clock in a heavy-looking marble stand sitting on a bookshelf. Below it, on a desk sat a laptop with the lid opened. The laptop appeared to be attached to a series of cables, with a black modem by it.

"Here's what we're going to do," Miguel said.

Victor focused back on Miguel, momentarily ignoring Trouble.

"You're going to tie Abby to that chair." Miguel pointed the gun toward a ladder-back chair by the kitchen table.

"Abby, sit." Miguel held up the rope.

Abby didn't move.

"Do it unless you'd rather see your boyfriend get shot."

Abby gave Victor a look that said she was sorry, and she sat.

Miguel tossed the rope to Victor, who caught it handily. "Tie her up, and make it tight. I'll be checking."

Victor stretched the rope out in his hands, wondering how he could tie her up and yet leave some leeway.

No, Victor knew he couldn't risk it. He had to wait for a better chance to fight back.

"What are you going to do?" Abby leaned forward in the kitchen chair as if she might stand up.

Miguel stepped closer to her, his back now to Trouble. "After your friend here finishes tying you up, I'm going to tie him up. Then I'm going to set the kitchen on fire. I've learned a good deal about accelerants and arson since my first attempts —and how to plant clues. At this point, not much reason to make it look accidental as I've set another, better trap for Phillip."

"Shoot us first. Don't let us burn." Victor's voice was steady, but out of the corner of his eye, he saw Abby shivered.

"Trouble." Abby almost cried. "Let the cat outside. Please."
Miguel snorted.

"The cat," Victor said. "Let him out. I'll cooperate if you
promise to let Trouble out."

Miguel appeared to be considering Victor's offer. "If you do
exactly as I tell you—no resistance—I'll put a bullet in both of
your brains. You won't be alive while you burn." Miguel spoke
as if he were assigning a classroom to read a chapter in a book,
his voice so rote and unconcerned that Victor realized he was
some kind of sociopath. "And I'll let the cat out."

Miguel walked over to Layla, sprawled out on the couch,
and poked her shoulder with the barrel of the gun. "I had to
keep her alive until she told me where all the flash drives were.
I had to dangle her insulin in front of her a few times before
she talked." Miguel grinned. "Better than torture and not
nearly so messy."

Victor sensed movement and glanced toward Trouble, who
was standing up. Moving quietly so as not to attract Miguel's
attention, Trouble bent down toward the switchblade.

Wanting to distract Miguel from what Trouble was up to,
Victor asked, "Why kill that homeless man?"

Miguel pointed the gun at Victor's stomach. "Start tying
her. Tight."

"I mean, really, why kill him?" Victor looped a strand of
rope around Abby's waist, but kept his eyes on Miguel.

"He was supposed to have killed Layla that night at the law
firm and stolen her backpack, then I was going to burn down
her apartment and Abby's house to get rid of any flash drives.
And take out Jennifer too. But the man was too drunk."

Victor pretended to tug on the rope as he felt Abby slowly
sucking in her breath and pushing out her chest and stomach.
Good girl, he thought, realizing she was trying to make herself

as large as possible. When she exhaled, the ropes should go slack.

"But then I found out that damn bitch had copies of microfilm from the original manuscript of my book. I had to get that back. He was supposed to kidnap her and bring her to me, so I could make her talk. But he called me on a burner phone, drunk, hiding in the bathroom, with Layla knocked out. That's all he'd manage to do—knock her out."

As Victor maneuvered the ropes around Abby's wrists, he left the strands as slack as he dared. He could feel her pulling her crossed hands slightly apart to make the bonds even looser.

"I had to kill him and take that stupid bitch out of the library myself. I was going to get Jennifer and then come back and take care of you," he pointed at Abby, "but you wouldn't believe how long it took to get that dead man in the dumpster. But that Valium I snuck into the tea bottles did the trick. You two slept through it all."

Victor twisted a knot and stepped back from Abby. "All done." He kept his eyes fastened on Miguel, not daring to look at Trouble for fear that Miguel would follow his glance.

"Sit," Miguel said, pointing to a chair beside Abby's. "Try messing with me, then I shoot her in the knees and leave you both to burn alive."

Victor cast a sad look at Abby before he sat in the chair. She closed her eyes tightly. He didn't blame her.

Suddenly Abby's eyes popped open. "Jennifer knows, doesn't she? That's why you tried to kill her with pills and burn the house down."

Miguel grunted and jerked on the rope around Victor. "Those two stupid bitches. Yeah, Jennifer knows. Layla emailed her the whole damn story that night in the library as some kind of guarantee I wouldn't hurt you two while you were in the basement. Worked out well, didn't it?" Miguel snickered. "As long as I had the wedding ring and earring, they weren't going to rat on me because they couldn't stand to see their precious Phillip get his feelings hurt."

"But after Layla stole the jewelry back, Jennifer could just deny the affair. Phillip wouldn't believe you." Abby twisted on the ropes around her wrists as she talked. "He'd believe Jennifer and Layla over you. That's why the ring and earring were important."

"Yeah. It was a pretty interesting game of cat and mouse for a bit, especially with that little co-teaching gambit with Phillip, which gave me ready access to Phillip's stash of pills and key cards. But I'd say it's over now."

"But what if Jennifer recovers?"

Miguel glared at Abby. "You don't think I can charm my way through the nurses and kill her if she even looks like she'll wake up?"

With that, Miguel kicked at Victor's chair and went into the kitchen. As soon as Miguel was out of the room, Trouble leapt toward Abby, the switchblade in his mouth. But Abby was already working the loosened ropes from around her hands. "Take it to Victor," she whispered.

Victor heard a match strike at the same time Trouble pushed the switchblade—still opened from where he had cut Layla free—into his hands. As he started sawing awkwardly at the ropes around his wrists, he smelled smoke.

Miguel came out and grinned at them. "Ah, shucks, boys and girls, good thing my insurance is paid up what with that nasty, crazed wife-killer Phillip burning down my cabin for revenge." He reached into his pocket and pulled out some lighter fluid. "This should speed it all up." He squirted the stuff around the kitchen table, putting his back to Victor as he did. Victor hacked at the ropes with renewed vigor.

As Victor sawed his ropes, he glanced at Trouble, who was inching along the bookshelf. Miguel gave an extra squirt around the couch where Layla slumped.

"Oh, and, yes, that was my old black BMW you saw speeding away from Jennifer's house." Miguel turned back to Abby. "When I saw you, I came back and set the carpet on fire and squirted lighter fluid around the bedroom door, figuring I'd take you both out at once. I'd already purchased my new car, but I wasn't foolish enough to drive a distinctive red car to a crime scene."

Miguel waved the gun at Abby's face. "That's why my new red beauty is parked in my driveway at home right now, where my neighbors will see it and testify I was home while you two burned, but the BMW is parked right beside your pickup, hidden by the trees."

Victor turned around as far as he could in the chair. He couldn't see for sure, but he thought Abby had her hands free. But she was still tied about her chest to the chair. To Victor's horror, he saw flames in the kitchen.

"Oh, and that promise about shooting you in the head?" Miguel shrugged. "What's one more little lie?"

Miguel backed away from Abby and Victor, grinning.

The man was definitely some kind of sociopath. How had he managed to succeed so long without getting caught in his own evilness?

But what did that matter now?

CHAPTER FIFTY-ONE

*V*ictor wasn't going to die like this, not burned to death by a madman. And he wasn't going to let Abby die that way either.

He leaned forward in the chair, his feet firmly on the ground, and he twisted his hands, working the knife until his hands were free. Gripping the switchblade behind his back, he managed to cut loose one loop of rope around his chest. But he was running out of time to saw through the rest of the rope. "Come look me in the face, you psycho."

"Or what? You'll huff and puff and blow my house down?" But even as he jeered, Miguel stepped closer to Victor.

Beside Victor, Abby wiggled until the loops of rope around her chest began to slide down. Victor rolled his eyes at her, trying to signal her to be ready.

Even though Miguel pointed the gun at his stomach, Victor had to be able to plunge the knife into Miguel while still partially tied to the chair. Victor didn't believe for one moment he would survive the attempt, but he was hoping to create enough disturbance and damage to Miguel that Abby at least had a chance to escape the flames. And maybe if he could wound Miguel enough, Abby could get Layla out before the cabin burned.

As Victor tensed his legs to lunge, he heard Trouble meow, a low sound but with an edge to it. Victor swung his head around to look. Trouble was standing behind the heavy marble clock on the bookshelf. As Victor watched, Trouble pressed his head against the back of the clock. Then he raised his head, stared right into Victor's eyes, meowed a single, clipped cry, and pointed at Miguel with his paw.

Trouble wanted Victor to lure the man in front of the bookcase so he could push the clock off onto the man's head. That had to be the message, Victor thought, as he marveled at Trouble before turning back to Miguel.

Victor had to admit it was a much better plan than his idea of plunging a knife, while he was tied to a chair, into a man armed with a gun.

But he had to get Miguel over by the bookcase and in range of the heavy clock.

"This is all for nothing." Victor fastened his hand around the knife's handle just in case this gambit didn't work. "I've already sent the info on Layla's flash drive about you stealing the book to Detective Kelly and to Phillip and Delphine. I even used your laptop over there." Victor held his breath for a moment, hoping he hadn't misread the cable and modem.

Miguel glanced at the laptop, his eyes narrowing. But he didn't move.

"Layla's flash drive is still in the port." Victor nodded toward the computer. "Go ahead, take a look yourself."

Miguel made a sound like a growl deep in his throat, but he stepped to the desk and looked at laptop. Above his head, Trouble pushed the brass clock off the edge of the bookcase.

The clock hit the back of Miguel's neck, smashing the man down on top of the keyboard, and his gun skittered out of his hand and across the floor.

Abby winched and yanked on the ropes around her chest as Victor struggled against those still binding him. In the kitchen, something hissed and popped and flames leapt into the living room, ever closer to Abby and Victor.

From the bookcase, Trouble knocked a couple of heavy textbooks down on top of Miguel.

Abby flung herself free of the ropes and dove for the gun on the floor just as Miguel rolled off the desk and struggled to stand up.

Miguel staggered toward her, but Trouble pounced, ripping into the man's face with teeth and claw. As he howled and Trouble tore into him like an angry tiger, Abby picked up the handgun Miguel had dropped. She raised it as high as she could and brought it down with a resounding thunk on the man's head. He collapsed with an oomph onto the floor.

Victor strained and bucked in the chair, still caught by one last loop of rope. The flames would soon catch on the throw rug near where he sat. Already he could feel the heat flare up around him.

A smoke detector went off, emitting a loud, sharp screaming noise. The fire was only a few feet from him, and he couldn't get the last rope cut. "Abby, run, go!" No sense in all of them dying like this.

"I'm not leaving you and Layla," Abby shouted over the roar of the flames. She dropped the gun and started yanking at the ropes that still held Victor, tearing them loose where he had already half-sawed through the strands.

Victor broke free of the rope. "Go, run. Get out. I'll get Layla." He stood up and raced for Layla. He lifted Layla from the couch and headed for the front door as Abby scooped down and picked up Trouble. They sprinted for the exit.

Once they were all outside, Victor laid Layla on the ground as gently as he could. Inside the cabin, the flames were crackling. Victor heard sirens in the distance and relief flooded through him. Fire truck or police, whoever was coming could get Layla to the hospital.

Layla would be all right.

They were all going to be all right.

Then he thought about Miguel. The man deserved to die.

But it wasn't in Victor to let that happen. "Damn it," he yelled out as he raced for door.

"No! Don't go back in," Abby shouted.

But Victor dashed back inside. The flames licked at the fringe of the throw rug only a few inches from Miguel, who was a limp mass on the floor.

Victor grabbed the man's arms and unceremoniously yanked him across the floor and out into the fresh morning air.

The sirens were closer.

Victor collapsed on the ground and cradled Layla in his arms. Beside him, he could hear Abby begin to cry. As he held her, Layla shivered.

Trouble licked first Abby's face, then Layla's.

DAMN FINE CHOICE on my part to send that email back at Abby's house. Lucas no doubt had the good sense to look up this cabin's address when he got the message. I see an ambulance and a Grady County Sheriff's car, and Rizzo and Lucas' car speeding up the dirt driveway.

I rub against Abby and lick her face. Then I curl against Layla, giving her my warmth.

CHAPTER FIFTY-TWO

*A*bby kept jumping up to hug Layla as she packed her belongings from Abby's guest room. Layla's apartment was ready and she was eager to go back to it, though Abby had insisted Layla stay with her longer.

"No, you've been greater than I can ever say or thank you, but you need your life back." Layla grinned and flung a pack of sugar-free gum at Abby, who reached up and caught it.

"No, really. Stay. Help me figure things out." Abby studied Layla, thinking she was still too pale and edgy to be alone.

"Figure what out? You told me you were quitting the law firm and had snared that great job as a law librarian at FSU. Go for it."

Abby still wasn't sure she was making the right decision, especially since working as a law librarian put her right back in the building where Layla had been kidnapped. But the position combined both her librarian experience and her legal training, and it paid well enough that she could still make her loan and mortgage payments—and buy plenty of primo salmon for Trouble.

Phillip and Delphine had promised her a partnership at the law firm next year, but Abby had seen too much damage done by ambition in the last week. She wanted off that train; she wanted her quiet life back, one where she had the time to spend with her plants, her garden, her fish tank—and with Trouble and Victor.

Despite some misgivings, Victor planned to finish law school. Then he'd be looking for a career in law enforcement. That's what he'd always wanted, though side-tracked by his bitter resignation from the Navy. Rizzo and Lucas had promised to help him.

Abby pushed the thoughts of her and Victor's career changes out of her head, focusing once more on Layla. She jumped over to her and gave her another hug.

"Chill, babe," Layla said, but she laughed.

"It's over, really over." Abby wanted to hug Layla yet again, but held back.

Once Layla recovered from her diabetic coma, she'd told her side of the story. She and Miguel had been lovers for a semester, and she had never believed he would really harm her. When she found out he'd submitted her article to the law review with his name, she'd broken it off with him and threatened to expose him. She'd hidden all the pink flash drives with the various drafts of her article to prove she had written it, not him.

Trying to protect himself from scandal, Miguel had stolen Jennifer's wedding ring and earring during a tryst at the lake cabin. He made Jennifer promise to control Layla and keep her from turning him in for plagiarism—or he'd wreck Jennifer and Phillip's marriage and Jennifer's reputation.

But Layla had begun to suspect he had also plagiarized his book, and set out to prove her theory. When she discovered the rare manuscript at the Library of Congress, she tracked it to the dead professor in Miami, and the rest of the puzzle fell into place.

Layla gathered her evidence and planned to expose Miguel, but Jennifer begged her not to do so in the phone conversation Victor overheard. Knowing the stakes were high, Layla had managed to lure Miguel into one more night at his cabin. While he slept, she found Jennifer's ring and earring and stole them back.

After the accidental meeting with Miguel in the law school the night she disappeared, Layla realized he knew she'd figured everything out, no doubt alerted by her theft of the ring and earring. Desperate that night at the library, Layla feared Miguel would try to kill her and Abby. That's why she'd told Miguel that Emmett and Victor were going to join them, and she'd invited both men for safety and backup. But Abby sent Emmett away and Victor had his cell phone turned off.

When Layla couldn't get Victor on the phone, she knew if she and Abby left the library, even with Emmett in tow, Miguel might be waiting and might kill them all. Frightened, and perhaps not thinking clearly, Layla dropped the flash drive in the umbrella stand after she'd emailed the whole story to Jennifer.

Layla told Jennifer where the flash drive was, and to contact the police if anything happened to her. Then Layla had emailed Miguel and told him she'd put the information that would destroy him on a flash drive and had hidden it in the law school, but he'd never find it. She also told him she'd sent an email with instructions that if anything happened to her, the receiver of the email was to deliver the flash drive to the police.

Soon after Layla had recovered and told her story, Jennifer

came out of her coma. She and Phillip would have to have a long talk soon, but no doubt they could work out her infidelity and her addiction issues.

In the meantime, Jennifer managed to tell them that she'd tried to get the flash drive out of the umbrella stand so she could trade it for Layla, but the library basement remained full of police and detectives. Wanting to save both Layla and her marriage, rather than go to the police as Layla had instructed, Jennifer had confronted Miguel the morning after Layla disappeared, but without the flash drive Layla had told her about. Miguel admitted to Jennifer that he had Layla, but threatened to kill her if Jennifer said anything about him or his plagiarized book. Jennifer bargained to trade all the incriminating information—including the location of the flash drive—for Layla's safe return. But she lied and told him the key flash drive was in her house. After that, Miguel had overcome her and forced her to swallow the pills. When Phillip was arrested, Miguel had taken a semi-comatose Jennifer back to her house in the wee hours of the morning, set up the kitchen to catch fire, and left her upstairs to die.

Jennifer admitted she'd come to Abby's house the night Layla was kidnapped to ask for her jewelry back. But Layla had refused to return the items as she was afraid Jennifer—under the influence of Valium and not clear-headed—might try something foolish, which, of course, later Jennifer did in trying to negotiate with Miguel instead of following Layla's instructions to contact the police.

Now, as Layla packed, and Abby tried to help—between hugging Layla—Trouble scouted the room, meowing his approval and watching over the two women.

The doorbell rang and Abby ran to answer it, hoping it was

Victor. She knew without doubt that her attraction was far more than physical—she was in love with him. Now she saw him for the genuinely kind, brave, and loyal friend to Layla that he had been. And she knew he would be as kind, brave, and loyal to her.

Just as she reached for the door knob, Trouble meowed and tapped at Abby's ankle. She laughed and looked out the peephole. "It's Victor," she told Trouble, stooping down to give him a big pat before opening the door.

Victor step inside, one hand holding a plastic bag of water with two black mollies swimming around, the other a potted hydrangea. He set the plant down on the floor and placed the bag with the tropical fish near the aquarium. Then he grabbed and hugged Abby, finishing off the embrace by twirling her around the room in his arms. He laughed and stroked her hair.

"I love you." Victor grinned, his face more handsome and relaxed than Abby had ever seen it be before.

"I love you back." She leaned against him and felt like she had finally found her place in the world as he pulled her face to his and kissed her.

ABBY AND VICTOR'S embrace deepens, as if they've forgotten Layla is in the other room. These two will be fine now. So will Layla.

My job is done here, though I might stick around for the wedding. After that, I want to find my way home to Tammy's house in Alabama.

As I'm imagining ways to get back home, the doorbell rings again.

Victor and Abby don't even break their embrace.

After the third time the bell rings, Layla comes out of the guest room, glances at Victor and Abby, and tosses out, "Get a room." But she's laughing as she glances out the peep hole.

"*Now what?*"

Layla opens the door and Lucas Kelly steps in. "Um, I've got kind of a problem and need a good detective. I wonder if I can borrow Trouble?"

I guess I'm not going home just yet, and I rub against Lucas and purr.

ACKNOWLEDGMENTS

I thank Carolyn Haines, Rebecca Barrett, Janet Kerley, Barbara Nicolazzo, and Sally McDonald for their excellent input, their skills and talents, and their most generous editorial assistance on *Trouble in Tallahassee*. In the midst of their busy lives, they gave me their time and made *Trouble in Tallahassee* a far better book.

ABOUT THE AUTHOR

Claire Matturro admits she used to be a dog person. But then she rescued a black kitten and there was no going back. She's been a journalist in Alabama, a lawyer in Florida, an organic blueberry farmer in Georgia, and taught at Florida State University College of Law and as a visiting professor of legal writing one long, snowy winter at the University of Oregon. She now lives with her husband and two rescued cats in Florida, where it doesn't snow. Her books are: *Skinny-Dipping* (a BookSense pick, *Romantic Times'* Best First Mystery, and nominated for a Barry Award); *Wildcat Wine* (nominated for a Georgia Writer of the Year Award); *Bone Valley* and *Sweetheart Deal* (winner of *Romantic Times'* Award for Most Humorous Mystery), all published by William Morrow. She remains active in writers' groups and contributes regularly to *Southern Literary Review.*

www.clairematturro.com

facebook.com/authorclairematturro

twitter.com/ClaireMatturro

bookbub.com/authors/claire-matturro

amazon.com/author/clairematturro

goodreads.com/clairematturro

TROUBLE IN SUMMER VALLEY

Familiar Legacy #4

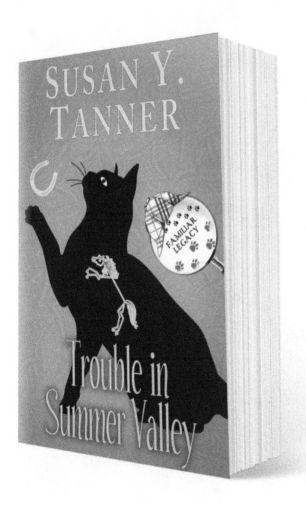

TROUBLE IN SUMMER VALLEY

Chapter 1

*J*uly is – by far – not the most congenial of months in central Alabama. Invariably, a thunderstorm, brewed by climbing afternoon temperatures and typically quite fierce, will mar the washed out blue of the summer sky. And, as a matter of interest, I do believe that is thunder I hear rumbling in the distance. A soaking is not my preferred method of hygiene by any means, but the late afternoon breeze carries the faint but unmistakable scent of a fast-approaching storm. What I wouldn't give for a dark and brooding English day.

Nevertheless, here I am at the base of the courthouse steps, sweltering in the heat rising from the sidewalk, and here I'll remain until I enter the next phase of my assignment.

I've had company for quite some time, though the broad shouldered man has not shifted his position since he stepped from the silver embellished, dark pickup truck, sliding equally dark sunglasses into place all in one smooth move. The only interest I've seen him exhibit was *toward the motorcycle rider who sat rather conspicuously upon his bike across the street for some time. And even that interest waned when the gentleman – and little though I like to judge by appearances, I use the term gentleman sparingly – donned his helmet and went on his way.*

There is something about his demeanor that refutes idleness and I've given him more than a fair share of side looks in the hour or so since his arrival. I do so again, in time to see him push away from his seemingly somnolent position against the hood of the truck. Forewarned, I turn and am rewarded for my patience at last. There, looking far less fresh than when I watched her arrive at nine on the dot this morning, is my target. At some point, those rich tresses escaped their smooth upsweep and now tumble into dark curls. Earlier, I'd judged her hair to be ebony but the strands hold the late afternoon sun just enough to prove them dark brown instead.

She looks more like her photographs now than when I first laid eyes upon her. That could be due to the diminished strain upon her face, a lessening which mayhap signals a favorable change in her circumstances. I certainly hope so. The differences are subtle and likely difficult for human eyes to discern, though quite evident to a feline as observant as myself. There is a distinct decline of trepidation in those wide, expressive eyes, a slight easing of the tension along her jawline. And, I must say, it is a remarkably firm jawline for, if my research is as impeccable as usual, a woman of forty-nine years maturity.

I see no evidence, now, of this morning's dread and anger when she was confronted on these very steps by her 'significant other' as I believe the ridiculous phrase to be in current vernacular. They had a somewhat heated exchange as he insisted she would lose the battle ahead and suggested vehemently that she 'cut her losses' and sign the papers he waved in her face. If I'm any judge of circumstances and people – and I believe myself to be quite astute – he was wrong.

It was apparent to me that the man was already near desperation.

If I surmise her victory correctly, he will be even more desperate and very likely dangerous as well. My role could turn – as it so often does – to protector as much as investigator.

So now I must find my way to this 'working' horse ranch she is purported to own and manage with a certain flair for the unusual. I must say that such an outdoor and very physical lifestyle could contribute to the supple lines hinted at by the slim fitting skirt she wears with a tucked-in blouse. Her lightly tanned arms as well as the calves of her legs are nicely shaped so that would fit as well. Yet, there is also a certain elegance about her light movements on black stiletto heels as she descends toward me, an elegance that could well suit a board-room career. I should know, as I've breached that world in the line of my profession as well. A definite contradiction, so we shall see. She may, perhaps, be merely the owner with an entourage at her beck and call in the stables and paddocks and a well-fitted home gym where she spends her days in air conditioned comfort while others labor on her behalf. But I think not.

And, there now, she is close enough for me to bring into play my Sherlockian skills in order to catch her attention. If I have misjudged her, the proverbial goose – mine! – may well be cooked.

AVERY STARTED IN surprise as a solid black feline leapt lightly onto the step just below her feet. Her inclination to give a moment of attention to the striking creature was outweighed by the knowledge that Craig would soon be emerging from the courthouse behind her. A Craig wrapped in the fury of his defeat.

With that knowledge pressing in on her, Avery sidestepped rather than stopping as she normally would have to let her fingers glide through the gleaming onyx fur. The cat surprised her, yet again, with a move that placed him firmly in her path. The movement was so precise it seemed almost intentional. Despite her haste and the remnants of dread that gripped her still, Avery allowed herself to smile and stooped to stroke the animal. "What a beauty you are," she murmured, as the cat arched in appreciation against her caress. The expensive leather collar and sleek condition of the cat's coat told her plainly that this was someone's beloved pet. If that had not been the case, she would gladly have taken him home with her.

Green eyes looked calmly into hers but the sound of voices – angry male voices – had Avery quickly straightening her back. The thud of heavy footsteps warned her it was too late to turn her back and exit gracefully. She would look cowardly if she did so now and Avery was not a coward. Knowing how fiercely Craig hated cats, she ignored all precautions about handling unknown animals, particularly a breed known for its disdain and intolerance of clumsy humans. Without a second thought, she scooped the cat up in her arms. She had a quick vision of Craig booting the innocent creature out of his path, if for no other reason than having seen Avery pet the animal.

Avery shifted to one side of the broad steps, giving plenty of room and silently willing Craig to take his venom elsewhere. Her ex came down the stairs, his attorney following close at his heels. Andrew Morgan looked as irritated as Craig looked irate.

Craig came to an abrupt halt just inches away and Avery resigned herself to enduring one last ugly scene. Ugly was the best word she could give to anything to do with Craig these days. She marveled at the change the last five years had wrought in the man she'd once believed in and trusted completely. The handsome, energetic man at the height of a successful career had been replaced by this gaunt caricature of a person with poorly cut hair and ill-fitting clothes. She recognized the expensive gray suit. She'd selected it for him as she once had all of his clothing and, at the time, it had fit his muscular shoulders to a tee.

"You won't win," he snarled at her.

Avery said nothing, knowing nothing she said would make any difference. Reminding him of the fact that she *had* won would do no good and serve only to fuel his resentment.

Andrew Morgan, once his closest friend and advisor and still his attorney, laid a hand on Craig's shoulder. "Don't do this, Craig. Let's get that coffee now."

Craig ignored him, thrusting his face closer to Avery. She stood her ground, despite a tremor of alarm at the lack of control in his expression. She couldn't let him see that it affected her. Her silence seemed to infuriate him even further. She watched as his pale face darkened with red blotches.

"Don't think this ends here."

"It has ended," she said finally, quietly. "It's done, Craig."

His harsh laugh had the cat tensing in her arms and she instinctively snuggled him more closely to her chest.

"You stupid bitch! You would've been a hell of a lot smarter to take what I offered and gotten the hell out of Alabama. Summer Valley is mine, every acre, every horse."

She could see the hatred in his eyes where once she'd imagined she'd seen love. And she supposed Craig could see with equal clarity the emptiness she felt when she looked at him.

"Over my dead body." She kept her voice steady by sheer strength of will. Her exhaustion was bone-deep. "The judge gave you twenty-four hours to remove the rest of your belongings from the ranch. Carlee is welcome to continue on with me."

"Carlee is my daughter, just like that ranch is my property!

Over your dead body, you said," he reminded her of her own words. His lips curled. "I hope you meant it ... because that's just what I'm going to step over to take back what you've stolen from me."

"Craig, what the hell ..." Andrew Morgan scrubbed a hand over his face in disgust.

Shock and fury hit Avery in a tidal wave of heat. "I can and will defend what's mine." Her voice was hard with the reminder of all she'd been through, all he'd put her through. "You should listen to your attorney, Craig. He might just keep you out of jail."

"Don't threaten me, you emasculating bitch."

Even more shocking than his threats, Craig grabbed her shoulders, his fingers digging in so hard she sucked in her breath. As bad, as nasty, as things had gotten between them, Craig had never laid hands on her – until now.

In one, blurred moment, she felt rather than saw the cat swipe unsheathed claws at the hand on her shoulder.

Craig howled and jerked away with a string of curses more vulgar than she'd ever heard from him. He flung drops of blood from his hand, staring at the gash in disbelief before lunging forward. Avery could not tell if she or the cat was his target.

Andrew tried to restrain Craig but his ineffectual attempt proved unnecessary. Before Avery had time for real fear, she watched in amazement as a complete stranger stepped past her, effortlessly pulling Craig's arm behind his back so hard that Craig's features contorted with pain rather than anger.

The man leaned in close and spoke with quiet effect. Avery wished she could hear the words that drained all resistance from Craig's taut body. Craig stared in disbelief then jerked backward as the other man loosened his grip.

The stranger turned his back on Craig in dismissal. A cool, assessing gaze skimmed Avery and the cat. "Mrs. Danson."

Avery was vaguely aware of Craig stumbling past them, his attorney trailing behind.

"Ms. Wilson," she corrected automatically. She'd taken her own name back as soon as she'd filed for divorce more than two years earlier. For a moment, she stared at him. His eyes were hidden by dark, aviator style glasses but she could almost feel his gaze, a gaze that seemed as feline as the animal in her arms, only far more predatory and dangerous, more in line with a panther than someone's pet.

"Ms. Wilson," he returned, without a hint of a smile. "I've been waiting for you. We need to talk."

Instinctively, Avery took a step backward and shook her head. "No."

The man who had just come to her rescue lifted one dark brow and she flushed at her own rudeness but she was exhausted, stretched to the limit.

"No," she said again, but less forcefully. "But thank you for your help."

"I understand your caution but I've traveled a significant distance to meet with you."

"Who are you?" She felt completely bewildered by this turn of events. She was drained by hours of courtroom drama and knew she wasn't at her best mentally. Even so, she knew she wasn't expecting a visitor of any kind, particularly not one with the authoritative air of the man standing in front of her. "What do you want with me?"

"This is not a sidewalk conversation." His tone brooked no argument. "Look, it's late. You've got to eat. I need to talk with you and it may as well be over food."

Whoever he was, Avery, realized, whatever he wanted to talk with her about, he wasn't going away until that happened.

End of excerpt from *Trouble in Summer Valley*
by Susan Y. Tanner
Familiar Legacy #4

TROUBLE CAT MYSTERIES

Please join our Trouble Cat Mysteries page on Facebook:
fb.me/TroubleCatMysteries

www.troublecatmysteries.com

Familiar Trouble | Carolyn Haines
Trouble in Dixie | Rebecca Barrett
Trouble in Tallahassee | Claire Matturro
Trouble in Summer Valley | Susan Y. Tanner
Small Town Trouble | Laura Benedict
Trouble in Paradise | Rebecca Barrett
Turning for Trouble | Susan Y. Tanner
Trouble's Wedding Caper | Jen Talty

Bone-a-fied Trouble | Carolyn Haines
Trouble in Action | Susan Y. Tanner
Trouble Most Faire | Jaden Terrell
The Trouble with Cupid: 10 Short Mysteries Spiced with Romance |
Multiple Authors
Trouble Under the Mistletoe | e-novella | Rebecca Barrett
A Trouble'd Christmas | e-novella | Susan Y. Tanner
Year-Round Trouble: 14 Original Cozy Holiday Mysteries | Multiple
Authors

TROUBLE'S DOUBLE CONTEST WINNER
Sebastian

Hi there. My name is Sebastian, and I would like to tell you a little bit about myself. My mom Jo Ann Hunter adopted me when I was 5 weeks old. I was so small I fit in the palm of her hand. I grew up to be a big boy weighing in at 19 lbs. I love climbing up to the kitchen cabinets, and surveying the household from the basket of one of mom's plants. (shhh, don't tell her I told you).

I also have a cat cave bed, but refuse to sleep in it. Instead I lay on top of it, and cave it in. I have always been an indoor cat, but once I snuck out behind mom. I took one step on that stuff you call grass, and couldn't get back inside quick enough. I do like looking out the windows at squirrels and birds. Mom says it's not nice when I tap the window with both front feet just when the birds get in the bird bath and scare them away. But I think it's fun.

I share my home with 2 dogs, Cocoa and Lady. I ignore them. I also have a new cat friend who came to live with us when her owners moved away leaving her behind. Her name is Little Cat, and she's very shy, but we get along. I've never had to experience the life of an outdoor cat as she has. I am now 12 years old, and am living a wonderful, happy, spoiled life with my family, and I plan on continuing to look after them all.

— JOANN LOWE HUNTER